EISENHOWER PUBLIC LIBRARY

3 1134 00405 2320

W9-AIV-817

5/14

8/5
5 c/o

Eisenhower Public Library

4613 N. Oketo Avenue

Harwood Heights, IL. 60706

708-867-7828

FIRST EDITION NOVEMBER 2013

DARK ALLEYS. Copyright © 2013 by Richard Polad. All rights reserved. Printed in the United States of America.

This is a work of fiction. Names, characters, places and incidents either are the product of the author's imagination or are used fictitiously.

ISBN – 978-1-939548-07-8

10 9 8 7 6 5 4 3 2 1

Cover art and book design by Gary Lindberg

Follow the author at:
www.facebook.com/spencermanningmysteries
www.rickpolad.com
@rickpolad

To my Uncle John

One of the finest people I know

Other Spencer Manning Mysteries

About the Author

Rick Polad teaches Earth Science and volunteers with the Coast Guard Auxiliary on Lake Michigan. For over a decade, Rick has given editorial assistance to award-winning photographer Bruce Roberts and historian/author Cheryl Shelton-Roberts on several of their maritime-themed publications including *North Carolina Lighthouses: Stories of History and Hope,* and the third edition of *American Lighthouses: A Comprehensive Guide to Exploring Our National Coastal Treasures.* Rick also edited the English version of *Living With Nuclei,* the memoirs of Japanese physicist, Motoharu Kimura. This is the second Spencer Manning mystery. The third is underway.

Acknowledgements

This book would not exist without the help and support of several special people. To my readers and friends, Mike Polad, Tom Tallman, Carol Deleskiewicz, Gary Lindberg, Katie Tomlinson, and Ellen Tullar Purviance, thanks for your edits and input. Any remaining errors are the property of the author.

Thanks also to Theo Darden for technical consulting. Theodore Darden is a Professor and past Coordinator of Criminal Justice at the College of DuPage. He worked as a law enforcement officer and investigator for 17 years in the State of Wisconsin and has received numerous law enforcement awards including the Law Enforcement Officer of the Year Award and six Meritorious Service Awards.

Special thanks to my publisher, Gary Lindberg (best-selling author of *The Shekinah Legacy*) and Carol Deleskiewicz for pushing me beyond my comfort level with "You can do better than that!" This is a much better story because of those pushes.

And, as before, to all my friends and readers who have asked for more Spencer, my undying thanks.

Dark Alleys

Chapter 1

He slowly opened the eye that wasn't buried in the pillow and squinted toward the clock on the table next to the bed. Eleven—something. Couldn't quite make out the minute hand. But it didn't matter—he had no intention of staying awake. The hum of Saturday morning car traffic drifted up to the second-floor bedroom.

He'd go out and get the late edition of the papers and see what they had to say this time. Two weeks ago, they had just referred to him as a "deranged killer". Maybe after two bodies they would have more respect. The papers hadn't said anything about the coins. That had made him angry. He had put a lot of thought into that—his planning deserved recognition. And they should be thanking him, not calling him deranged.

Everybody treated him like he was stupid. He didn't have a college degree, something his wife kept throwing in his face. But he didn't know anyone who knew as much about history. He'd show them.

He had forgotten to pull down the shade when he went to bed, and the sunlight sent a stabbing pain to the back of his head. Shaking his head vigorously, he tried to get rid of the ache. As usual, it didn't work. He always woke up with a headache. Enough alcohol and anyone would. He considered pulling down the shade, but found he couldn't move anything but his eyelid, which had already closed.

Chapter 2

Why do you watch these dumb game shows?"

"Hey, you're sitting in my chair, eating my corned beef, extra lean by the way, drinking my beer, and you got the nerve to criticize?" Lieutenant Stanley Powolski, one of Chicago's finest, brought the bottle of Schlitz to his lips and took a long drink followed by a good-sized bite of a sandwich.

Spencer shook his head. "Stosh, this is American mediocrity at its worst."

"Aw, wadda *you* know. It ain't mediocre. I learn somethin' new all the time."

"Stosh, there has to be something better on." The show went to a commercial for hemorrhoid relief. "See, I was right, this *is* better."

"Sometimes you're a real pain in the ass."

"Thanks. I try. You want another beer?"

"Sure, thanks."

Spencer Manning got two beers from the kitchen, popped off the caps, set one down on Stosh's tray, and sat back down.

"Anything new on the hooker killings?" Spencer asked.

Stosh shook his head and wiped his mouth on his sleeve. He set the bottle down on the tray. "Nope. Hard to get anywhere on what we got. Tough to solve random killings."

Spencer nodded. "Both on a Friday. Could that be a pattern?"

"Can't call two things a pattern. Probably just coincidence."

"Don't believe in coincidence," said Spencer. "You know, all this could be solved by legalizing prostitution and letting the government run it."

"Yeah, I know. I've heard your bleeding heart nonsense. It's the law, Spencer."

"Yeah, well maybe the law is shortsighted. We spend millions of dollars trying to stop it, not to mention the thousands of man hours you could be using for real crime."

"It *is* a real crime."

"Who does it hurt?" asked Spencer.

"It hurts people who pick up disease, and it hurts the average citizen trying to live a good life. How would you like *your* neighborhood overrun with ladies of the evening and their clientele?"

"I agree, Stosh. You're making my point for me." He took a drink of beer. "If it were legalized, it could be run where it's controlled. The women and their clients could be checked for disease, the right precautions could be used, and the government could collect taxes on income that's now swept under the table."

Stosh gave him a disgusted look and shook his head. "You done?"

"No. Look at alcohol. All prohibition did was make a very good living for fellows like Capone and turn the streets of Chicago into a bloodbath. Look at the taxes now on a bottle of whiskey."

Stosh said nothing.

"And you wouldn't have two murders to solve."

Stosh resettled himself in the chair and took a deep breath. "I'm not saying you're right, and I'm not saying you're wrong. I'm saying it's the law. I enforce the law. You change the law and I'll enforce that."

Spencer settled back into the chair and pulled up the footrest, knowing that was as much agreement as he would get out of Lieutenant Powolski. "Think there will be more?"

Stosh shrugged. "I hope not." He paused. "Probably."

"Any ideas about the coins?"

Stosh swallowed, wiped his mouth with the napkin, and put his empty plate on the tray. "And where would you have heard about coins, as if I need to ask?"

"Nothing I couldn't get from the paper." Spencer was guessing—he hadn't read the paper.

"Sure you did. I'd rather you get it from the paper instead of one of my detectives, but we haven't released information on the coins. I'll have to have a talk with Rosie."

Spencer laughed. "Stosh, you know if there was something I wanted to know, anybody there would help, including you, so don't pick on Rosie. It's not her fault she can't resist my charming personality."

Rosie Lonnigan was a red-headed Irish girl Spencer had known since he was a kid. They had gone through the police academy together. Rosie had joined the force and Spencer, feeling frustrated by a system that seemingly gave criminals more rights than victims, had become a private detective.

"I could make a comment about your charming personality. Don't be bothering Rosie about this case."

Spencer's eyes narrowed. "Is there something more to tell?"

Stosh waved his hand in the air. "Now what kind of a detective would you be if you got all your information from the cops? Why don't you go out and do some detecting?"

"Okay. Just trying to help. You decide you want this thing solved, give me a call."

"I wish your dad was here. He'd whoop your butt down to size," said Stosh with a smile.

"I wish my dad was here too, Stosh."

Stosh sighed and frowned. "Sorry, kid. That was the wrong thing to say."

"That's okay, Stosh. I know what you meant."

Spencer Manning's father was a captain on the Chicago police force, well-liked by all. Stosh had become like an uncle to Spencer. A year ago, Spencer's parents had been killed in a car accident that was a warning gone wrong.

"Seriously, Stosh, don't you feel frustrated because you can't do anything till after the guy strikes?"

"Yes, of course. But as long as the working girls won't stay off the streets, we're going to have a problem."

"Everybody's gotta make a living." Spencer stretched his legs, yawned, and rolled his head around, stretching the neck muscles. "I'd better hit the road."

"At eight o'clock? I was hoping for a game of gin. I need a chance to make back some of that money you cheated me out of."

"Not tonight. I'll take a rain check."

"Hot date?"

"No. I was out last night doing surveillance. I'm beat."

They both got out of their chairs.

"Good luck this weekend," said Spencer. "Maybe he'll stay home."

"I hope so. It's been Friday night both times, with two weeks in between."

"Anything else the same?"

Stosh rubbed the chair arm with two fingers. "Both just off Broadway. Five blocks apart. Both stabbed and left in an alley; carved up pretty bad. We'll have extra men out, but you can't be everywhere."

"And then there's the coins," Spencer added with a slight smile.

Stosh buzzed his lips. "Memory like an elephant."

Spencer shrugged. "Just trying to help."

"Join the force. Then you can help all you want. Till then, I get to know something you don't. And hopefully all the wackos out there won't know either."

"You'll get him, Stosh."

"Sooner or later. Let's hope it's sooner."

They met in the center of the room and shared a bear hug. "Stay safe, Spencer. Your daddy left me in charge of you. I might've declined if I'd known what a chore that'd be."

Spencer winked. "Got to keep you on your toes. See you Saturday."

"Good. We'll watch some baseball."

"Yes sir!" replied Spencer with enthusiasm.

Spencer had spent Saturday afternoons and a weeknight with Stosh almost every week since his parents died. It was time both of them enjoyed. Time to relax, share some thoughts, and hold onto the past.

Stosh got Spencer's jacket, tossed it to him, and saw him to the door. "I won't tell that harem of yours that you spend two days a week with your Polish babysitter."

Spencer laughed and waved as he headed to the car.

Stosh didn't close the door until the car started. As he was cleaning up the living room, he let his thoughts wander to Spencer's folks and how they had made him a member of their family. He knew Spencer was capable of taking care of himself, but he also worried because this wasn't a safe business. You never knew what you were getting into. And Spencer sometimes let his emotions run ahead of his common sense.

Spencer let the Mustang idle for a minute and then backed out of the drive and headed home. When he had first hung up his P.I. sign, he was living and working out of the same rooms on the south side. Last fall he had moved into his parents' house on the north side and confronted the ghosts shimmering in his dreams. They were visiting less often.

His folks had left him the house and enough money to be very comfortable for the rest of his life. But he'd give it all up just for the chance to have said goodbye.

Spencer knew that the killer had left a stack of coins next to the victims. And he also knew that those coins had been stacked in what looked like a pattern. But his source hadn't said what the pattern was. He didn't want Stosh to know that he knew even that much. There would have been hell to pay at the station—probably for Rosie, and it wasn't Rosie who had told him.

Chapter 3

The bailiff picked a file off the desk next to the bench where Judge McCalister was trying to stay awake through the Tuesday afternoon call. There was little dissension, and they were making good progress, and might even make it through all the cases on the docket.

"The State of Illinois versus Laura Douglas," called the bailiff.

Benjamin rose from the wooden bench in the third row of the courtroom. "Yes, your Honor. Benjamin Tucker of the Public Defender's Office representing Miss Douglas." He took Miss Douglas' arm and almost pulled her up off the bench. He had told her to dress conservatively. She wore a red miniskirt and a white blouse. He hadn't expected much better; she was young and scared. He led her to the bar to the left of the bench. The bailiff handed the file to the judge, who took a minute to look it over.

Judge McCalister, peering over the top rim of his glasses, looked down at Benjamin and his client. He gazed down at the red miniskirt. Benjamin wondered what his reaction was, but knew it really didn't matter. This was just another case, and the words coming out of the judge's mouth would be the same as they had always been.

"Young lady, you are charged with prostitution," he said sternly, adding a scowl and a shake of his head. "Are you aware of the charge?"

She didn't answer. Benjamin leaned over and whispered in her ear.

"Yes, your Honor," she said meekly.

"Um hmm." He looked back at the folder. "How old are you?"

"Nineteen," she whispered.

"You can speak up, Miss Douglas. No one here is going to bite your head off."

She nodded.

The judge knew exactly how old she was. He could read. But he always asked. Benjamin didn't see the point.

"You are charged with one count of prostitution. How do you plead?"

Laura Douglas looked down at the floor and didn't answer. Again Benjamin prodded her.

"Not guilty, your Honor." Her voice was a bit louder, but not much.

The judge put down the file and shifted in his chair.

"Counselor, you are supposed to counsel your client before your appearance in my court, not during."

"Yes, your Honor. I apologize."

This girl should have been in school somewhere, not in a courtroom. And no matter how much Ben counseled her, she would still have been afraid to answer.

"Next time, please be prepared."

"Yes, your Honor. I certainly will be."

"Are you aware that the charge of prostitution carries a maximum sentence of six months and a maximum fine of $2,500?"

"Yes, your Honor," answered Benjamin. "However, we respectfully dispute the charges."

Judge McCalister looked bored and held his hand out, palm up.

"Your Honor, we contend that Miss Douglas was only talking to someone in a car through an open window. What she was doing had nothing to do with prostitution."

The judge looked skeptical. "She was talking about the weather, I presume?"

"I don't know what, exactly. I didn't hear it and neither did the officer. The police car pulled up and she was arrested after the car pulled away."

The judge sighed. "Officer..." He looked down at the file. "Williams. Please approach the bench."

"Officer Williams, did you hear the conversation between Miss Douglas and the person in the car?"

Williams took a deep breath. "No, your Honor, but..."

"So what is your basis for this charge?"

Williams shuffled from one foot to the other. "It was obvious what was going on, your Honor. And with the recent..."

The judge held up his hand and peered over his glasses. "Last I checked, there is no law against talking to someone in a car. Next time, please bring me something that is actually against the law. Case dismissed." He turned to Miss Douglas. "Young lady, I have no doubt about the obviousness of what you were doing. And women doing that sort of thing have been dying, as Officer Williams was about to point out. I would rather not see your name in the paper."

Ben led Laura out of the courtroom as the bailiff called the next case. He held the door open and glanced at the judge. He knew the judge had already forgotten about Laura Douglas and was only trying to get through the afternoon cases and get home to a martini.

Chapter 4

Spencer Manning's phone rang at a quarter to seven Wednesday morning. He wasn't up and had no plans to be, despite the ringing telephone. The machine would get it. He expected it to be a salesman, in which case the line would go dead as the message started. But it didn't. The entire message ran: "You have reached Spencer Manning, Private Investigator. Please leave a message and I will call you back as soon as possible. If this is an emergency, you can page me at 733-555-5555." Spencer listened with half an ear and tried to stay awake till the caller came on.

"Spencer, it's Ben. There's something I could use your help with. It's a personal..."

Spencer untangled his legs from the sheet and reached the phone on the table next to the bed. "Hang on Ben, I'm here." He waited for the machine to stop. "Okay Ben, sorry about that."

"No. I'm sorry to wake you."

Spencer switched ears and sat down on the edge of the bed. "You didn't wake me. I just came in from my run."

When Ben had stopped laughing he said, "That's the biggest load of bull I've ever heard. Maybe staggering back from the bathroom, but certainly not running at this hour."

"Now, Ben. Is that any way to talk to someone you need a favor from?"

"Who said I needed a favor?"

"I heard *personal*. Personal means *favor*. Favor means *free*. You should be building me up, not cutting me down."

"Sorry. I forgot you were so sensitive. But I do need a favor."

"Can you hang on a second?" Spencer asked.

"Sure."

Spencer put down the phone and pulled on a sweatshirt that was laying at the foot of the bed. "Okay, shoot."

"This may sound a bit strange. I had a client the other day. Prostitution. Same old thing. Nothing out of the ordinary except that she's younger than the average."

"How young?"

"Not sure. Driver's license says nineteen."

"Okay, probably not uncommon. What's the problem?"

"Problem is she got to me." Ben was silent, trying to decide how to explain. Spencer waited patiently and yawned.

Ben continued. "I'm pretty used to the people that come my way, but this girl should be in college somewhere. She's a nice kid who sure as hell doesn't belong on the streets of Chicago."

Spencer took a deep breath and yawned again. "Yet here she is on the streets of Chicago." When Ben didn't respond, Spencer added, "People end up where they don't belong for any number of reasons. And there's nothing you can do about it no matter how much you'd like to." Spencer had seen more than his share of sad stories.

"Thanks for the lecture. I know all that. I've been thinking about it and feeling pretty damned helpless. This morning I decided I had to do something."

"And that something involves me?" Spencer asked.

"I hope so. I'd like you to see what you can find out about her. I have a name and address. See if you can get some history. Where is she from? Any family? Anything that might help."

Spencer's eyebrows went up. "Help with what?"

Ben sighed. "I don't know. Maybe keeping her alive."

They were both quiet for a minute. Spencer thought about working for nothing, again, and decided he owed it to his friend. Ben had called after Spencer had solved his first case and had sent several clients his way. It was also a good cause.

"Okay, Ben. I'll see what I can do."

"Great." He gave Spencer the name and address. "When can you start?"

"Well, if you'll give me time to pull on some pants, I'll get right on it."

They both laughed.

"Actually, I could use a couple more hours of sleep. I've been on an all-night surveillance case that ended a couple nights ago." Spencer looked at the clock which showed a few minutes past seven. "How about I make some calls this afternoon?"

Ben smiled and felt his shoulders loosen a bit. "Thanks, Spence. I really appreciate it. You've got my numbers."

"Yup. I'll let you know what I come up with."

"Great."

"Ben." Spencer mustered his best serious tone. "Don't get your hopes up. She's not where she is because she has a lot of rosy options."

"I know, Spence. But I can't just sit and hope I don't read about her in the paper."

"Okay. You're a good man, Charlie Brown."

"Not that good. Probably just some flaw in my childhood."

"Yeah. But if you want analysis I'm going to have to charge you. We'll discuss my fee over a beer—on you. We'll see how many it takes to work off your debt."

"Deal."

They hung up. Spencer sat and thought for a minute. He could get history on almost anybody. That was the easy part. Doing something about it would be the trick. But maybe she was young enough to be salvageable. Yawning again, Spencer pulled the twisted sheet over him as much as a twisted sheet can be pulled, and went back to sleep.

Chapter 5

Charles Lamb checked his watch and then glanced at the gas gauge. It was 9:15 and the tank was almost empty. Making his way to the inside lane, he drove for two more blocks and pulled his old Chevy into a Shell station. The daytime temperature had reached 78 degrees as spring threatened to turn into summer. Street lights reflected in puddles left by the afternoon rain.

The hinges creaked as Charles swung open the door and, ducking his head, stepped out of the car. On the other side of the pump island was a black stretch limo. Tinted windows hid whoever was inside. A black-suited chauffeur stood by the pump, minding his own business.

Charles inserted the nozzle into the tank and started the pump. "Bitch," he muttered under his breath. "Just once, I'd like to see her fill up the damn tank." Sarah had her own car but would sometimes take his. He had no idea why. He never put in more than ten dollars of gas, but tonight he was distracted by the limo as he tried to make out shapes in the light playing through the windows. The heavy click of the pump shutting off brought him back to reality.

"Damn." He yanked the handle out of the tank and angrily banged it back into the cradle. Eighteen dollars and twenty cents. That left him less than four dollars to make it until Friday, and this was only Wednesday. He could try asking his wife for extra money, but she never gave him any, no matter the reason. All he ever got was a lecture.

As he screwed the cap back onto the tank, the rear door of the limo opened and a woman started to get out. She had on black high heels and black nylons that ran up to the edge of a very short skirt. Charles fumbled with the cap as he stared at her leg.

Whoever the leg was attached to was arguing with someone in the car. Charles was close enough to hear clearly.

"Take your hand off of me," said a controlled female voice filled with disgust.

"Fine. But don't expect any more business from me," said a deep, gravelly male voice.

"I don't expect anything from you except money. Everything you have you've had to pay for."

"I suppose that's some kind of slap in the face."

She swung her leg back in the limo but left the door open. "You owe me five hundred dollars."

He laughed rudely and yelled out the door, "Hey, Rocky. You hear that? She wants five hundred dollars!" He laughed again.

Charles glanced at the chauffeur, whom he assumed was Rocky. But the chauffeur didn't respond. He didn't move or even blink.

"You pay me, or I send a few love letters."

"Is that a threat?"

"Pay me."

Charles could just make out the side of her right leg. He was slightly behind the limo and couldn't see the man. But he would always remember the deep, gravelly voice.

"Here's your money, you damned whore. I hope you choke on it."

Several bills fluttered out the open door, followed by both legs this time as the lady slowly got out of the car. She leaned back in, picked up bills off the floor, and then started picking up the ones that had floated down to the ground. One had landed a few feet from Charles. It was a fifty. He picked it up, looked at it with wide eyes, and waited.

Rocky gently closed the door and, after finishing pumping the gas, paid and got back in the limo. The limo then slowly pulled away from the pumps and out into traffic. Charles watched the red tail lights disappear around the corner.

As the woman picked up the bills, Charles got a good look at her. She was the most beautiful woman he had ever seen. He pretended he was screwing on the cap, which was already tight, as he tried to watch out of the corner of his eye. As she picked up the last bill, he closed the cover of the gas fill and walked around the pump to where she was standing staring out into the street.

He wasn't sure what to say to her. He startled her when he cleared his throat. She jumped slightly and turned quickly, starting to raise her arm.

Keeping his arms close to his body, Charles raised his hands in front of his chest. "I'm sorry to startle you, ma'am. I wanted to give this to you." He held out the fifty.

She quickly looked him over. He was much larger than she and looked very intimidating, but her face immediately changed from fear and anger to a look of calm and relief. She looked at the bill he was holding out to her.

"Thank you," she said slowly.

Charles thought her voice sounded like what an angel must sound like.

"It is a pleasure to meet a gentleman." She took his hand and curled his fingers around the bill. "You keep it."

Charles stared at her hand touching his and felt electricity running through his large body. "No, no, I can't," he stuttered. "It's your money."

She laughed and sighed. "I have plenty." She eyed his car covered with dents and rust. "You need it more than I do."

He looked at her questioningly.

She squeezed his hand tighter. "Please, keep it. It means a lot to me. Good night."

She glanced at the street again and then turned and walked into the station.

Charles opened his fist. His hand was shaking and he almost dropped the bill. He took a deep breath and went to pay for the gas. Waiting in line, he saw the lady standing at the pay phone on the wall next to the newspaper rack.

He started to pull the twenty out of his pocket and then realized he had better break the fifty. Sarah would wonder where he got it and would never believe the truth. Sometimes people were just in the right place at the right time. But it was never him—until now. Charles gave the kid behind the counter the fifty.

"That the smallest you got, mister?"

"Uh, yeah," Charles lied.

"Christ." The kid gave him a disgusted look and called his supervisor. It took two calls before a grizzled old man stuck his head out of the office.

"What?" the old man growled.

"This guy's got a fifty."

"That the smallest he's got?"

"I wouldn't wake you up if it wasn't, now would I?"

"I got no idea what the hell you'd do."

Scratching his back, the old man shuffled over to the register, looked at the crisp new bill, and then squinted at Charles. He held the bill up to the light. Looking at Charles again, he threw the bill onto the counter and shuffled back to the office, still scratching.

The kid rang the register and handed Charles the change. Charles stuffed it into his pocket and turned to go, stealing a glance at the lady. She was talking on the phone. He couldn't help but stare at her legs. As he walked toward the door he overheard her conversation. She was calling a cab company.

"I really don't want to wait here for an hour. Don't you have someone in the neighborhood?" She listened for a few seconds, then closed her eyes and rolled her head back and around to the side. "No, thank you. I'll call another company... well, I'll just take my chances."

She hung up and searched in her purse for more change. Charles walked over to her. Standing behind her again, he admired the shape that Sarah never had.

"Excuse me, ma'am."

She turned, again startled. But her look softened when she saw who it was.

"I'm sorry to bother you again, but I overheard your conversation and I, uh, I'd be glad to give you a ride if you need one."

She smiled and politely refused, saying it would probably be quite a bit out of his way.

Charles shook his head. "It's no trouble. And besides, I should really do something to earn this fifty."

"You already have, mister—"

"Lamb. Charles."

"You already have, Mr. Lamb, Charles. Just by being kind. Not too much of that going around these days."

"No, I mean something real, like giving you a ride home."

She tilted her head to the left and looked into his eyes. Charles felt his heart jump. "Sure. Okay. Thank you, Charles Lamb, my knight in shining armor. Have you paid?"

"Yes."

She reached into her bag, pulled out another fifty, and held it out to him. He looked at it and asked what it was for.

"For the ride home."

"Oh, I couldn't take more, ma'am. I already have fifty dollars."

She tried to push it into his hand. He pulled his hand away.

"No. I really don't want it. Please."

She cocked her head, studied him for a bit, and put the bill back in her bag.

"Then let's go."

Chapter 6

She led the way to the door and they walked to the car.

Charles opened the passenger door. As it creaked, he cringed at the thought of this beautiful woman getting in his junker. He cleared papers off the seat and stood back as she got in. Her skirt hiked up, revealing a perfectly formed thigh. Charles swallowed hard and took a slow, deep breath. He slowly closed the door, trying to keep it from squeaking. It did anyway. He got in and started the car.

"Where to, ma'am?" He wondered what her name was.

"Well, get to Lake Shore Drive and head north for starters."

Charles swung into traffic, embarrassed by the noisy muffler and the bumpy ride on worn-out shock absorbers. She didn't seem to mind. It took ten minutes to get to Lake Shore Drive, the highway that ran along the lake. In the distance, the lights of the skyline of Chicago sparkled against the dark sky. Charles wanted to glance at her, but knew his eyes would go right to her legs and thought that wouldn't be polite. She'd know he was staring.

"Are you warm enough?" he asked politely.

"Yes, fine. Thank you. So what do you do, Charles Lamb?"

He thought about how to answer that. She wouldn't know if he made something up. For the moment he could be anything he wanted, but he decided on the truth.

"I don't really do anything. I'm out of work."

She turned to face him, crossing her right leg over the left. He stole a quick glance. The skirt wasn't hiding much. The top of the nylons showed along with the end of a garter belt.

"I'm sorry," she said with sympathy. "How do you get by?"

"Oh, it's okay. My wife has a job and I work odd jobs. You know, fixing things, cleaning things. Whatever somebody needs. I was a maintenance man before they laid me off."

She didn't respond.

They drove past downtown and along the curve past Navy Pier. Out of the corner of his eye, Charles saw the red flash of the Chicago Harbor light standing like a sentinel watching over the entrance to the harbor.

The Drive continued north past Lincoln Park and the high-rise buildings that lined the west side of the road. Traffic was light.

Charles was wondering how far they were going when she said, "Make the turn at the end onto Hollywood and then turn right onto Sheridan. Stay in the right lane. You'll turn right again onto Glenlake. It's up four blocks."

He didn't tell her that he was familiar with the north-side neighborhood. He and Sarah had lived near Foster and Broadway when they were first married. And the north side was still where he did most of his drinking. She directed him to the end of a short block and told him to pull in the driveway on the right. The house was a two-story brownstone and was the last house on the block. On the other side was Lake Michigan. Charles turned into a cracked, concrete drive which led to an old, wooden garage that looked to be in bad shape. The house was built like a fortress with huge cornerstones and fancy, carved stone decorations. He stopped the car next to the back door, which was protected by a tiny awning. He turned to face the lady and tell her the ride was over when he realized she was looking at him strangely.

"Here we are," he said simply.

She didn't respond—just kept looking. He felt nervous and wondered if he had done something wrong.

"Is this your house?" he asked hesitantly.

The strange look slowly changed to a smile. "Yes, it is."

He waited for her to get out. When she didn't, he asked, "Is something wrong?"

"No." She pulled her legs under her on the seat and folded her arms across her chest. "No, there isn't." She paused for only about ten seconds while she looked at him again, but it seemed like ten minutes. "Charles Lamb you are a very nice and a very strange man. You remind me of my brother."

Charles felt his face get hot. He was sure he was blushing. "If you mean because I gave you a ride home, that's no big deal."

She shook her head. "That *is* nice. I appreciate it very much. But that's only a part of it." She folded her hands in her lap. "You found my fifty dollars on the ground. You could have walked off with it, but you returned it."

He smiled. "Well, I tried to."

She returned the smile. "Yes, and that's the important part. Then you refused to take money for the ride home. You open the door for me, call me ma'am, and have behaved like a perfect gentleman."

Charles didn't understand what was so special about all that. He was simply doing something to earn the fifty dollars and told her so.

"That's sweet. Would you like to earn some more money?"

Charles didn't know what he had to do, but he could always use more money. Sarah didn't give him much, and most of that went for beer. It wouldn't hurt to find out what she had in mind.

"What would I have to do?" he asked hesitantly.

"Nothing you can't handle." She shifted on the seat and the skirt slid way above the nylons. There couldn't be much more leg left.

"This place is old and hasn't had much tender care. Needs a lot of repairs and I'm helpless. So, if that's what you do, you've got a job."

He couldn't believe what he was hearing. To make some money would be good. To work for this woman would be wonderful. "What do you want me to do?"

She pursed her lips and raised her shoulders. "I really don't know. Why don't you come in and look around and we can make a list."

Charles glanced at his watch. It was almost ten o'clock. If he didn't get home before ten, Sarah would be mad. Now he wouldn't be home until after eleven. Sarah would accuse him of being in a bar all night, or worse. On the weekends, she would let him alone when he came home drunk and late. But a weeknight would be different. She didn't care if he went out, but there was a line at ten. Charles had no idea why.

He sighed. "I really should get home. It's very late and my wife is going to be very upset as it is."

She looked concerned. "Oh, I'm sorry. I didn't think. This isn't late for me. Well, how about this? You come back in the morning and we'll start then. No, wait. I have appointments tomorrow. Could we make it Friday?"

He felt relieved. *Ten* something was one thing. After eleven would be quite another. "That's fine. But how do I know what tools to bring?"

"Bring your basic ones. There's a tool room in the basement where you should find what you need. They may be a little dusty, but I'm sure they work. The man who owned this house was a carpenter. He went into a nursing home and left all his tools."

"What time would you like me to come?"

"How about ten?"

He nodded. "And if I may ask, what's your name?"

She laughed with a sound full of bells. "Of course you may ask. Which name would you like?"

He was puzzled. "You mean first or last? Could I have both?"

This time her laugh was louder and stronger and she shook a bit. He felt like she was laughing at him and looked hurt.

She stopped immediately and touched his arm. "I'm sorry. I'm not laughing at you. You're just not what I'm used to. No, I mean I use several different ones. I'll give you the one on my birth certificate." She held out her hand. "Hello Charles Lamb, I'm Amanda Brock. Call me Mandy."

He looked at her hand and slowly reached out and shook it. This woman confused him. He didn't understand most of what she said and had no idea why she had more than one name. He wanted to ask, but didn't want to be nosy.

She picked up her bag and opened the door. "So, I'll see you Friday morning?"

"Yes, ma'am."

"Mandy."

"Okay, Mandy."

She pushed the door open. He cringed again as it squeaked. She started to get out and then turned back to him. "It has been nice meeting you, Charles Lamb. You are an amazing man." She got out without adjusting her skirt. "Ten o'clock Friday?"

He nodded. "Ten o'clock Friday."

She waved and made her way around the car. He waited until she got the door open. She waved again and he started backing out of the drive.

As he drove home, Charles tried to make sense of the evening. He was fifty dollars ahead, had met a beautiful woman who didn't seem to be repulsed by him, was going to see her again, and was going to work for her. It had been his lucky night.

Chapter 7

Benjamin Tucker had ranked in the top ten percent of his law class at Harvard. Top ten meant somewhere between six and ten. If it was five he would have said five. With a little more work he could have been at the top. But he hadn't wanted to work that hard. And he still didn't. That was one of the reasons he worked for the state and had chosen the public defender's office. While his richer, but more stressed-out friends worked late nights and weekends, Benjamin went to the club and played golf. The other reason was, he truly believed that people who could not afford a high-priced attorney should still get someone who was competent.

But Thursday morning he knew he was going through the motions instead of putting a hundred and ten percent into his job. He was thinking about Laura and hoping Spencer would be able to come up with something. He had no idea why he wanted information or what he would do if he got it, but it would make him feel better. He was tired of shuffling his clients through the system and pushing them back onto the streets where they would end up doing something that brought them back to him. Didn't make any sense. Maybe this time he could help.

Chapter 8

Spencer's phone calls hadn't added any more information about Laura Douglas other than what he got from Ben, and that wasn't much. Blond hair, blue eyes, and five-foot six. That roused his interest. It was rare that he couldn't find background on someone. He decided to make a trip to 247 Wilson.

That afternoon, he let himself into the lobby of Laura's apartment building. Fifty years ago this was probably a classy building, but it had seen better times. The lock on the front door was no longer operable. The door didn't latch, but was heavy enough that it stayed closed. The floor was gray marble. It was rugged enough to hold up over the years. The rest of the lobby was rundown and dingy. The mailbox tags showed Laura Douglas on the second of three floors, apartment 2D. The stairs were covered with worn green carpet and the railings were solid oak. A wide staircase led to an expansive landing at the second floor where Spencer entered the hallway and turned to the right. 2D was at the end on the left. 2C was right across the hall.

Putting his ear gently to the door, Spencer listened for signs that she was home. It was a little after two p.m. The television was on. He listened for a few minutes and heard nothing else. He was a bit nervous. The longer he stayed, the greater the chance of being seen. If he was going to follow Miss Douglas, being seen was something he certainly wanted to avoid. But he also wanted to get into the apartment and needed to know if she was home. Benjamin didn't have a phone number for her, and she wasn't listed.

Realizing that he was holding his breath, and was tensed up in anticipation of trouble, Spencer took a deep breath and walked down the hall and back. A minute later he listened again and heard nothing. The television was off. She was home.

He hurried down the stairs and got into his Mustang, which was parked across the street about fifty feet west of the building. From there he could see the front door. Ten minutes later, Laura left the building and walked slowly east. She was easy to spot from Benjamin's description. Blond hair in a pony-tail, about five-foot six, looked like your average college kid. She wore jeans and a loose, yellow sweater over a white blouse and looked very much like she should be heading for class. Spencer cringed when he thought of her walking the streets. She would attract every pervert in sight. He watched her walk to the end of the block and halfway down the next before he got out of the car.

Leaves fluttered in the warm breeze blowing out of the south. Spencer quickly crossed the street and re-entered the building. An old woman was try-ing to open her mailbox. She didn't even look up as Spencer walked by. He glanced back at her as he turned the corner onto the stairs. She was still fum-bling with the key.

As he walked down the hall, Spencer fingered a set of lock picks in his pocket. The door to Laura's apartment had a dead bolt, but it wasn't locked. He didn't need the picks. Sliding a thin plastic strip between the lock and the jamb released the latch and Spencer was in the apartment in less than ten seconds. He was very nervous.

The shades were halfway down and the apartment was dark and dingy. But even in the subdued light, the despair that filled the room was obvious. It was basically one room with a bathroom in one corner and a kitchenette built into a wall. An open sofa bed took up part of an interior wall. Assorted clothes and a pillow with no cover lay on the floor in front of the bed. A pair of black leather pants, half hanging off the end of the bed, was mixed in with the sheet. Quite a different image from the girl Spencer had just seen. Spencer picked the pants up and went through the pockets. Two dollar bills and some change. He dropped them back on the bed. As he turned to his left, they slid onto the floor. He didn't notice.

A small TV was next to the bed on a stand. The only other pieces of furniture were a beat-up couch with an end table and a dresser next to the bed. There was a picture of Laura and another young girl on top of the dresser. They were posed in front of a palm tree. He guessed the picture was about four years old.

Spencer glanced around the room and decided to start with the dresser. Opening the top drawer, he felt revulsion at what he was doing. It was the second time he had searched through someone else's things. The first had been a fellow who was definitely one of the bad guys, and he had had no qualms then. Now he felt like he was invading someone's life, but he reasoned that he was doing it for a good cause.

The drawers held whatever she felt like throwing in. Underwear was mixed with blouses and sweaters in a confused mess. The underwear, lacy and very sexy, looked expensive. The third drawer down held two pairs of jeans, four red tube tops, a white blouse, a couple sweaters, and a business-sized white envelope. It was addressed in longhand to Laura Justine. The address was Detroit and the postmark was a year old. The return address was a Mr. and Mrs. Harold Justine, Naples, Florida. Expensive turf. Spencer assumed the letter was from her parents. He was right.

The letter started "Our Dear Laura" and went on for three pages. Scanning quickly, he got the gist of it. They had hired a private investigator to find her and wanted to talk. They weren't sure why she had left, but desperately wanted her back and were willing to change whatever she wanted if she would return. They hoped she was okay and loved her deeply. It was signed "Love Mommy and Daddy". The stationery was expensive and was embossed at the top with some sort of family seal.

Spencer sighed at the sadness of a family gone wrong. Whatever was bothering Laura was bad enough for her to leave home, change her name, and live in this lonely room. If it was that serious, you'd think her parents would have a clue. He jotted down the address in a small notebook. After returning the letter to the drawer, Spencer quickly searched the rest of the room, including the refrigerator and the garbage, and found nothing of interest. There was very little sign that a person lived there. What would make a pretty young girl choose to live this kind of life? Whatever it was, Laura still cared enough about home to keep the letter. That was at least one ray of hope.

Spencer had been in the room for about twenty minutes and was anxious to leave. Placing his ear to the door, he listened to make sure no one was in the hall and heard a door open and close. He waited a minute and then reached for the doorknob. As he did so, someone knocked on the door. Spencer jumped back, gasped, froze, and hoped whoever was at the door hadn't heard him. A second knock was followed by a key being inserted in the lock. Spencer looked for a place to hide and saw none. He didn't have time to make it to the bathroom. The only thing he could do would be to try hiding behind the door. As he inched back against the wall, he heard a woman's voice from the hallway.

"Jeanne, what are you doing down there?"

The key was quickly pulled out of the lock.

"Just seeing if little Laura is home. I thought she could pick me up something from the market if she went out."

"Well, she already went out. I saw her up at the corner. She said she's coming right home. You'd better not let her catch you there. You know she told you to stay away from her, old woman."

"Oh, she didn't say that. You're just jealous," snarled Jeanne. "And I'm no older than you. And my hair is real."

The other woman humphed and went into her apartment.

Spencer didn't like the fact that Laura was on her way home. He hoped Jeanne wouldn't like it either. She didn't. He heard her footsteps heading slowly back down the hall.

* * *

Jeanne dropped the key into the pocket of her smock. It was left over from a lady two tenants ago who was the only friend Jeanne had ever had in the building and who had given her a spare. The landlord never changed the locks. What did it matter? Why would anyone want to come back here? She would wait until tonight. Laura usually went out at night. Jeanne would go back and see if she had any new fancy underwear. Such pretty things.

* * *

Spencer heard a door open and close and quickly let himself out of the apartment. He hurried to the stairs. Hearing steps in the lobby, he went up instead of down. Glancing around the corner at the top of the stairs, he watched Laura climb steadily to the second floor and disappear into the hall. He listened for her door and then quickly left the building. The wind had picked up, and he zipped his jacket as he walked across the street and got back in the Mustang.

He had only found one new piece of information, but that was worth a phone call to Florida.

Chapter 9

An old man in an apartment across the street glanced at the alarm clock on the table next to the window and wrote down the time Spencer left the building on a yellow legal pad. He had also noted the times Spencer had first entered and exited and the time Laura had left. For that he got paid two hundred eighty dollars a week, cash. It was an easy job for an old man on welfare. He worked four-hour shifts every day of the week. Some of the others took weekends off and they could arrange among themselves if they needed to miss a shift. Twelve men manned the shifts.

The man who hired them, known simply as Stretch because he was constantly rolling his head or pulling back his arms or reaching toward the ceiling, wanted to know when Laura left and came home, what she wore, and if anyone who didn't live in the building was hanging around. They were given photographs of all the tenants. There were a few rules: no alcoholic beverages were allowed; they had to be alert; and they couldn't sleep. That was why the shifts were only four hours, Stretch had explained. They were to be self-policing. If their relief showed up drunk, they were to call a number Stretch had given them and stay until he arrived. They would then work the drunk's shift and receive an extra fifty dollars. The drunk would be fired. So they all hoped their relief would show up drunk. The refrigerator was kept full of soft drinks and juices. Potato chips and pretzels were in the cupboard. They could ask no questions and, as long as they were paid, none of them had any questions.

The man in the window was Billy. He thought Stretch had some kind of attraction to the girl but kept that to himself. He also thought Stretch was not the big boss and kept that to himself, too. He had noted Spencer's license number and written *brown hair, medium build, navy jacket* when Spencer went into the building the first time. He wrote *same guy* the second time. Billy watched with great interest as Spencer got into the Mustang and then didn't leave. He wrote that down too. Billy hoped Stretch would be as excited as he was. Maybe he would get a bonus. They weren't told the girl's name, but her picture was taped under the window. They all referred to her as *the girl*. They were all very fond of her. She was their meal ticket.

The apartment was bare except for the table by the window and four wooden chairs with thin cushions. Stretch didn't want them getting too comfortable. If the relief man found one of them asleep, the same bonus system applied. Billy thought one of them might lie and say they found someone asleep just to get extra money, but Stretch had let them all know they were also being watched so he would know if they were lying.

Stretch would stop every day to look at the yellow pad. He dropped in at random hours just to keep them on their toes. Sometimes he brought pizza. They had no complaints about the working conditions. The place was heated through the winter and that was more than most of them were used to.

Stretch wanted to know if anything strange happened or anyone out of the ordinary stopped by. The tenants in the building, of course, would have guests. Everyone who went in and out was recorded. But this guy sitting in the Mustang was definitely out of the ordinary. He had come out of the building just before the girl left and then had gone back in. Then someone had entered the girl's apartment.

Billy picked up the telephone and dialed Stretch's number.

Stretch asked Billy if he would stay an hour past the end of his shift so he could talk to him. Billy would be paid accordingly. Billy agreed. He had nowhere to go and would have stayed all day as long as he got paid.

When Stretch showed up, Billy filled him in. He had already told the story to his relief man, Al. Al was impressed. Billy showed Stretch the Mustang that Spencer was still sitting in. Stretch told Billy he had done a good job and paid him for his time plus an extra fifty. Al watched with wide eyes as the fifty changed hands. He would be glued to the window for the next four hours. But Al soon lost his excitement; Stretch was going to stay and watch for himself. Without complaining, Al sat on one of the chairs and picked at his fingers. He would settle for getting paid for doing nothing.

Five minutes after Billy left, the phone rang. Stretch answered.

"Yep. Still there," he said and read Spencer's license plate. "Let me know when you get it run." He hung up and stretched both arms back over his head without taking his eyes off the window.

Since Stretch was doing Al's watching job, Al watched Stretch. None of them had ever paid much attention to him before. He was meaningless. He was given the respect due the person who hands out the money, but other than that they didn't care who he was or what he did. Normally, the only time they saw him was when they got paid.

Al soon got tired of studying Stretch. There was no point to it. There was nothing else to do except sleep, and Al was smart enough to know that wasn't a good idea. He tried to stay awake by twiddling his thumbs, first in one direction, then the other.

Twenty minutes later the phone rang again. Stretch slowly rolled his head in a clockwise direction and just listened. He now knew the man sitting in the car was Spencer Manning. He also knew where he lived and that he was a private investigator. Stretch said nothing to Al, who had gotten up to get a bag of potato chips and a can of Coke and was settling back onto his chair.

Chapter 10

Laura immediately noticed the leather pants on the floor. She knew she had left them on the bed. There had been other times when she thought someone had been in her room. Sometimes it was just a feeling. Another time she thought her underwear was not the way she had left it. But her drawers were so messy she couldn't be sure. That was the look she wanted; a poor, lost, down-and-out soul. Aside from a black-and-white TV, there was absolutely nothing in the room anyone would want. A burglar looking for something to sell for drug money would be very disappointed. One of the old ladies on her floor, Jeanne, had warned her about security and had pointed out the broken lock on the front door. Jeanne was very concerned about Laura's safety and raved about how useless the landlord was. Couldn't even fix the lock.

Jeanne would have been surprised to learn that the broken lock was one of the reasons Laura had chosen the building. If someone found her, she wanted to know. And if that someone was concerned about how she lived, she wanted to know that too. That was why she left the deadbolt unlocked. The only time she locked it was when she was in the apartment. Once, when she returned, she found it locked, but thought she had locked it without thinking. Jeanne had been in for a visit and thought she was doing Laura a favor by turning the deadbolt.

Holding the refrigerator door open with her hip, Laura placed a quart of orange juice and four containers of fruit yogurt on the bare shelf. She kicked the door closed and threw the bag in the garbage. She walked to the bed, pulled off her sweater, and slowly unbuttoned the plain white blouse. Shrugging it off, she let it fall to the floor and turned to the mirror above the dresser. She arched her back slightly and looked at her breasts covered by a plain white bra. Smiling, she thought they were just right; large enough to be noticed from a distance, but not too big to be saggy when she hit eighty.

After stretching her calf muscles, Laura closed the blinds, planning to lie down for a couple of hours of sleep before hitting the streets. With the blinds closed, the room was dark enough to sleep during the day. She regretted the lack of sunshine, but usually closed the blinds when she was home. She knew about the men in the apartment across the street, and she was not an exhibition-ist. She knew about them because she was the one who hired them.

As she walked to the bed, the phone rang. It was Stretch. He told her about Spencer Manning and asked, "Does this have anything to do with what you're doing?"

"Can't see how it does, but it doesn't make any sense."

"Maybe we should call the cops."

"Sure, just what I need."

"Well, he *is* breaking into your apartment."

"Yeah. Strange. But there isn't anything here for him to take. He must want something, but whatever it is is beyond me." She sighed.

"So what do you want to do?"

She took a deep breath and said, "Keep watching and see if you can find anything else about him."

"Will do."

Chapter 11

Charles Lamb woke up early Friday morning. He was awake when Sarah left for work at 6:30, but pretended he was asleep so he wouldn't have to deal with her. He usually slept until after seven, but this morning was excited about starting work at the lady's house. He pulled on worn jeans and a work shirt and went downstairs. He constantly asked Sarah to throw the paper up on the porch as she left. How hard could that be? She never did.

The days had been getting longer. The sun was shining brightly in a cloudless sky and it would be a warm day. Charles loved summer. As he walked back up the drive, he thought he saw movement from the side of the house where the neighbor kid had a tree house. Slowing his pace, he watched out of the corner of his eye, but saw nothing. Maybe just the glint of the sun. His eye moved slowly back to his house and he sighed as he saw the obvious signs of neglect. Sarah was right—the old frame house needed a lot of work. He made a mental list while the sun warmed his back. Light brown paint was peeling and cracked; pieces of fascia were rotted and others were partly missing, revealing roof joists in a few spots; window sills were rotten; and one pane of glass next to the front door was cracked, but still holding together. Sarah had threatened to hire someone to do the work if he didn't. Charles found that funny, since he could do it all himself. But darned if he was going to give in to her and do it. And he knew she would never hire someone; there wasn't any money, and she wouldn't be able to bitch about it.

He made a pot of coffee and unfolded the Chicago Tribune: two shootings the night before; why the aldermen think they need a raise and why they would get it; and hope for the Cubs, more in Sports. As he sipped the coffee, he decided to leave at 8:30. That would give him plenty of time, and he would miss most of the rush-hour traffic. He finished the coffee, rinsed his cup, and headed for the basement to collect his tools.

Chapter 12

Jimmy sat in his tree house and watched as Charles Lamb picked up the newspaper and walked back to the house. He held his breath when Mr. Lamb looked in his direction and thought for a second that he had been seen. But Mr. Lamb didn't know he was there. That was important. If you're going to gather information on the enemy, they can't know you're there.

Like Charles, Jimmy also loved summer. From his perch in the green leaves he had seen important things and they were all in his notebook. Someday he would enlist in the army and apply for intelligence school. He would be able to show them he already had the skills they were looking for. Neatly documented by date, his notebook listed many neighborhood events.

The Lamb house was only twenty or so feet from his lookout perch, and he had a clear view of the kitchen and the bedroom. Other neighbors were further away, but a pair of binoculars brought them closer. His mother was a bird watcher and had given Jimmy the binoculars along with a book about northern birds. He kept a list of birds he had seen, and, after he was in the tree house, he'd show his mother the list. He would be especially excited if he saw a new bird. Actually, the names had come from the book. It was a lot more fun spying on the neighbors.

There was the night he had missed dinner last fall. He had told his mother he was tracking an oriole, rarely seen in these parts. She had let him stay out. Actually, he had been watching Charles and Sarah Lamb in their bedroom. Mr. Lamb had come in while she was undressing. He had put his arms around her from the back. She pulled away, grabbed her blouse, and covered her chest. But Mr. Lamb had taken ahold of the blouse and pulled it away. He had grabbed her and thrown her on the bed. She rolled to the other side and ran out of the room. As Jimmy watched, Mr. Lamb punched a hole in the wall.

Then there was the Saturday afternoon in October when the police had come. Jimmy didn't know what was going on, but he had heard yelling and ran to the tree house. There was often yelling from the Lamb house. But this time there had also been sirens. Two police cars stopped in front, and after about ten minutes the policemen had walked out of the house with Mr. Lamb in handcuffs. Jimmy knew that would be very important to Army Intelligence.

After that afternoon, his parents had warned Jimmy to stay away from Mr. Lamb. They said he was a very bad man and Jimmy should never ever go on his property or say anything to him. They wouldn't explain. Jimmy never understood why Mr. Lamb had been taken away or what his parents had been so concerned about. Mr. Lamb had always been nice to him. When his ball had gone over the fence and Mr. Lamb was in the yard, he would throw it back with a smile and say *nice catch*. He was certainly not as mean as Mrs. Crow, the neighbor on the other side, who would keep his ball and scream about her vegetables and what a naughty boy he was. *She* was the one he should be staying away from.

The police had come again during the winter, but Jimmy hadn't had a good view because he couldn't go in the tree house. Jimmy had noted each event in his notebook.

Chapter 13

Spencer called his Uncle John first thing Friday morning. He lived on a golf course just north of Tampa that included a small lake that was the home to an alligator named Arnie. Spencer briefly told John about Laura.

"I'm looking for more information about her and want to talk to someone down there. Don't you have a neighbor with the Tampa Bay Times?"

"I do," said John. "Martin Becker. Should be in the office." He gave Spencer the number. They chatted for a few more minutes. Spencer said he'd be down soon for a visit.

* * *

Martin Becker was in a meeting, but his secretary transferred Spencer to the society editor, Tim Burke, who picked up after one ring, probably hoping for some juicy gossip.

What Spencer had to say wasn't that juicy, but Tim was interested.

Spencer gave Tim what he had and asked what he knew about the family.

"The Justines are one of the richest families in Florida. Very well respected. Lots of money from real estate. Two daughters, Laura and Katherine. About a year and a half ago, the parents reported Katherine missing. At the time, she was twenty, in her junior year of college. Good student, but hung with a wild crowd. Katherine had trouble with the police, but never anything daddy couldn't take care of. The police never found anything concrete, but there were rumors. Daddy hired a P.I. but nothing came of it. Laura is three years older and has a degree in business."

"What was the trouble that got covered up?"

"Wild parties. Disorderly charges. Minor drug charges. Nothing very serious, but sex was involved."

Spencer was getting tired of that thread. "I wonder if that has anything to do with Katherine's disappearance."

"Well, there were rumors about prostitution in the group Katherine hung around with. Put that together with drugs and who knows what falls out. I wanted to run a story suggesting that perhaps she had been kidnapped and sold into the sex trade, but that never got off the ground. From what you're telling me, I've gotta think Laura is looking for her sister and has some reason to think she was in Detroit and then Chicago."

Spencer agreed. "Makes sense. What do you know about the family? Everyone get along?"

"Nothing unusual in a rich family. One daughter is perfect, the other a handful. Katherine was the wild one. Didn't seem too happy with all of daddy's money. Laura was the good daughter. She was being groomed to take over the real estate business."

"Was the business doing well?"

Tim said something to someone in the office. "Very well and very high-end. We're talking houses over a million. The business was started by Mr. Justine's father."

"And Laura?"

"A year ago, daddy reported Laura missing. Evidently didn't show up for work for two days. Usually reliable as clockwork."

"Police found nothing, I assume."

"Right. The same P.I. managed to track Laura to Detroit, but she suddenly disappeared. It was very bizarre. The P.I. wondered if it was because of a letter the parents had sent. Sounds like the one you found."

"How do you know about the P.I. information? I would think that's not public knowledge."

"My wife plays bridge with Mrs. Justine."

"Did you print that information?"

Tim laughed. "Hell no. I don't want a divorce."

"Must have been hard to sit on that."

"Yup, but you don't know my wife."

They both laughed.

"I wonder why Laura is living in that apartment," said Tim. "She has a boatload of money."

"Maybe she doesn't want to touch daddy's money."

"She doesn't have to," answered Tim. "Both girls have trust funds they came into when they reached twenty-one. Seven figures."

Spencer whistled. "Maybe Katherine's disappearance wasn't about sex. Maybe it was about money."

"Yeah, I thought of that. But the family was never contacted about a ransom. And Katherine's trust fund hasn't been touched."

"Bridge?"

"Bridge."

Spencer laughed. "They never mentioned bridge in detective school."

"You'd be surprised at where I get some of my information. Does all this help?"

Spencer sighed. "More pieces to add to the puzzle. Pretty strange."

"Yes, it is. Do I get a story when you figure out the puzzle?"

"Absolutely. Thanks for your help."

Spencer hung up, wondering what Ben had gotten him into.

Chapter 14

Charles Lamb pulled the old Chevy into Amanda Brock's driveway at five minutes to ten. He got out of the car and admired the view of the lake. Waves lapped up onto the edge of a sand beach. The sky was bright blue and banks of off-white clouds hung over the water a few miles offshore. An older couple walked hand-in-hand across the sand. It was a life Charles could only dream about.

He opened the trunk and lifted out his tool box. Then he slammed the trunk several times trying to get it to latch. He finally gave up and walked slowly to the side door, partly afraid to ring the bell and have this bubble pop.

Using his fat thumb to ring the bell, Charles held his breath. In less than a minute he saw movement inside the hallway. He let out his breath, but was disappointed when a short, plump, middle-aged woman answered the door.

"Yes?" she asked.

He looked past the woman, but saw no one. "I'm Charles Lamb," he finally said. "Mrs. Brock asked..."

The woman responded without emotion. "Oh yes, Mr. Lamb. Miss Brock said you would be coming. I am to show you into the kitchen. She will be down in just a minute."

The woman led the way down the hall past a large pantry and showed him into a sunny kitchen. "You can wait here."

Charles took off his cap and set his toolbox on the floor next to a large wooden table and sat in a straight-backed wooden chair.

He was happy that she was expecting him. And she was a *miss*. She wasn't married. Not that it mattered. *He* was. And she wasn't interested in him anyway. She just wanted him to do some odd jobs. And he was lucky to have that. While he waited, he looked around the kitchen. Bright, cheerful decorations hung on the walls, and two flower baskets were on the table. An old stove and refrigerator were against one wall. Another was lined with shelves and cupboards up to a doorway that opened into a dining room. The door was half open and Charles could make out a large, polished table of dark wood and a picture window looking onto the lake.

Even if it hadn't been right on the lake, the house had to be expensive. He wondered what Miss Brock did to earn that much money. She said she had appointments. He decided she must be a doctor and was trying to decide what kind when she walked in. She looked absolutely wonderful.

Amanda walked confidently right up to him and held out her hand. He stood and took it. "Hello Mr. Lamb. I'm so glad you're here. This house needs a man's touch. Did Margaret offer you some coffee?"

Charles fumbled with his cap and looked down. She made him very nervous. Not wanting to get Margaret in trouble, he hesitantly said, "Well, I don't want any coffee, thank you."

Mandy looked at him questioningly with raised eyebrows. That was a strange answer. He didn't talk much, this Charles Lamb. And he was pretty shy for a big man. But he seemed nice, and he was willing to work.

"Shall we walk around and see what needs to be done?" she asked.

"Yes, that would be fine," he answered, feeling more comfortable at the prospect of doing something. He wasn't good at small talk.

Mandy turned, opened a drawer, and handed Charles a yellow legal pad and pencil. "How about you take notes as we go? Then you can make a list and we can figure out what's most important."

He nodded and took the pad.

* * *

They took about forty-five minutes to tour the entire house. There were three bedrooms and an office and bath upstairs. Charles would call the office a den. But even though there was a large, heavy desk, the room was decorated with feminine tastes: flowery curtains and upholstery, a copy of Redbook lying on an end table, and a picture of some good-looking young man. An impressive stereo system was built into a niche in the back wall. A large wood desk faced the picture window overlooking the lake. Instead of drawers on the left-hand side, there was a swinging door that looked on the front like pull-out drawers. The door was partially open and Charles could see a safe inside the door. Two of the bedrooms were frilly and smelled like a woman. The door to the third was closed and Mandy didn't bother to open it.

Charles kept a list as they walked, but didn't see much that needed doing. The house was in very good shape. Mandy pointed out things like nicks in the walls that needed patching, trim she wanted replaced, a window pane that needed glazing, and carpet to be tacked. The largest job upstairs was in the den, which was done in dark woods. Mandy said she was ordering a new desk that was light oak and wanted the baseboard replaced to match. She wanted to stay as close to the old style as possible. That wasn't going to be easy. The baseboard was very old and ornate. Part of it was missing. Other things looked like they were partially completed, also.

"Can you handle this, Charles?"

He said it was not a problem but would take some time.

She smiled and said she knew it would.

On the way down the carpeted stairs from the second floor, they passed Margaret, who was vacuuming the landing. She paid no attention to either one of them as they squeezed past and stepped over the cord.

In the kitchen, Mandy swept her arm across the room and declared, "This place is a mess. I want it all repainted and new cabinets. Bright and cheery!"

She led him outside where she pointed out window trim that needed scraping and painting. Then, laughing, she said, "And you can knock down the garage if you want."

Charles laughed.

The last stop was the basement. As they were walking, Charles mentioned the things that were unfinished and asked if someone else was working there.

Miss Brock seemed angry all of a sudden. "Well there was, but not anymore." She opened the basement door, ending the conversation.

Charles expected dust and cobwebs. Instead he found a clean, organized room. The tools were stacked neatly in a corner. His own tools were not kept this nicely. Aside from the standard hand tools there was a table saw, a miter saw, a router, and several drills of different sizes. They all looked fairly new.

Mandy stood behind him and watched as he looked through the tools. "Do you think you can use these for what you need to do?"

Charles bent and lovingly touched the blade of the miter saw. Someone had taken good care of these tools. "Sure. This is great. I'll need some supplies, like spackle and nails, and of course the trim and baseboard and paint."

"Of course. Why don't we go now? We can shop and Margaret will have lunch ready when we get back."

Charles cringed at the word *shop*. Men didn't go to manly places to shop. He wasn't sure what word he would have used but it wasn't *shop*.

Following her up the stairs, he asked if Margaret was there every day. Mandy's hair was pulled back in a pony tail, and a trendy sweatshirt didn't cover much of what filled a tight pair of jeans.

"No. She comes three days a week, usually Monday, Wednesday, and Friday." She waited for him to reach the hallway and then turned out the basement light. "How long do you think all this will take?"

Charles thought hard about that. He didn't want to have her think it would take too long and cost too much. But he also didn't want to underestimate and have her mad later. "Well, it's a lot of detailed work. There's a lot of sanding and painting and the baseboard has to be removed carefully so the walls aren't damaged. And there's the kitchen. It's hard to say really."

Mandy smiled and patted his arm. He caught his breath. "I know. I'm not trying to pin you down to the day. Just wondering generally. Would you say two to four weeks?"

Nodding, Charles agreed that was a safe bet.

"Good. Well, let's get going. We'll take the Cherokee."

* * *

They loaded up the Cherokee with supplies, returned home, and ate lunch. They talked about nothing in particular over ham sandwiches. Charles was amazed at the willingness of this pretty lady to talk to him.

Charles spent the rest of the afternoon unloading and organizing and planning. He found her in her office when he was ready to go. He had been there for seven hours but hadn't done much. He was going to charge her for three hours. She swung open the door of the small safe that was built into the left side of the desk. The safe wasn't locked. She pulled out an envelope full of money and counted out one hundred forty dollars in twenties and held it out to him. It barely made a dent in what was left in the envelope.

"What's that for?"

She laughed. "For working today. What did you think?"

"I just meant that it's too much. I didn't work that much."

"You were here for about seven hours. I know we hadn't talked about pay, but is twenty an hour okay?"

"That's fine," he said with amazement. "But I didn't work seven hours. We spent an hour just looking around, and shopping, and there was lunch."

"Your time is valuable no matter what you're doing."

Charles couldn't believe his ears. He had never made this much money in one day. "Okay. But I shouldn't get paid for eating, especially when it was your food."

She laughed again. "Okay, if you'd feel better, give me back twenty dollars for lunch."

He did. Charles said goodbye and was halfway to the door when Mandy called him back.

"Oh, Charles. Here." She rummaged through one of the drawers and pulled out a key. "Take this key. It's to the back door. If you're coming every day you may have to let yourself in sometimes." She held out the key.

Charles hesitated. "You trust me with a key to your house?"

Mandy smiled. "Sure. Why not? You're trustworthy aren't you?"

"Well, yes," he stammered. "But you hardly know me. I..."

Gripping his arm tightly she said, "Charles, I know you as well as I need to. Sometimes you can tell about people right away. You know?"

He did. He knew about Amanda well enough. She was the nicest woman he had ever met. But no one had ever trusted *him* that much. That was a strange feeling.

Driving home, Charles thought that Sarah would never believe how he got this money. She thought he was worthless. But maybe if he told her, she would change her mind. He and Amanda had made plans for him to return on Monday. For the first time in his life he wished the weekend would go by quickly.

Chapter 15

Spencer fought the hunger that was rolling in his stomach. He felt stupid for not having thought ahead. It was close to nine. The sun had set and the night was starting to chill. Turning on the engine to run the heater, he wondered how long he would have to wait. If Laura was going out tonight, he wanted to follow and make sure she lived through it.

The neighborhood had gone through two spurts of activity while he sat and watched. Most of the traffic was on foot. This was a public transportation neighborhood. The el was not far to the west and buses traveled every fourth street. Parking was just too tough in the city. The workers had come home between five and six. The early evening dinner crowd had streamed out around 7:30. The next rush would be the nightlife bunch after ten. He figured that was when Laura would hit the streets. The city didn't really come alive until eleven. At 9:20, he got out to stretch his legs.

* * *

Stretch watched as Spencer walked down three buildings and back. He had accepted the nickname his crew had strapped him with and he kind of liked it. It was the third time Spencer had gone for a walk since Stretch had arrived at five. He was sure this Manning fellow was interested in Laura, but he didn't know why. And *why* was something he wanted to know. This fellow was worrisome. Stretch would meet Laura later and fill her in.

Standing at the side of the chair, Stretch went through his exercises while keeping an eye on the P.I. strolling down the sidewalk. He glanced at Al and chuckled to himself as he watched him struggling to stay awake. He cleared his throat and Al jumped and then yawned.

Stretch was paid too well to ask questions, but he couldn't help wondering what all the secrecy was about and what Laura was doing. In the beginning, two cities ago, he had asked why and she had said if he needed to know why she would find someone else. He then asked why she had hired him. That she *did* answer. He was highly recommended as a man who could keep his mouth shut if the price was right, and the price was more than right. So he kept his mouth shut, played the game, and did a damned good job of keeping his employer informed and safe.

His only orders had been to let her know if anyone seemed to be interested in her whereabouts and to keep her safe. He found her apartments, set up the extensive security, and reported anything strange. Anyone following her or asking questions of the neighbors was suspect.

Stretch had questioned her when she told him about the plan to join the ladies-of-the-evening club. That seemed crazy, especially for such a wholesome-looking young woman. But she responded by telling him that was none of his business either. He had dropped it until the murders started in Chicago. Then he had again voiced his concern. She laughed and told him that was why she hired him, to protect her. She trusted the men around her enough to not be concerned about the murders. She was never out of their sight. And if he didn't think he could do it, she would find someone else.

Despite the money, there might come a day when Stretch would quit. He considered it off and on. No amount of money could pay for the guilt if she ended up dead in an alley. But she wasn't concerned. He had hired four more men to help out at night. One of them—he called himself Root—was as big as a house. And he could run like a thoroughbred. She was as safe as she could be considering the situation, but Stretch still worried. You just never knew what was around the corner, and he wasn't arrogant enough to think he had all the answers. He stretched his fingers as Spencer got back in the car.

Al threw an empty pop can toward the garbage and missed. It rolled to the wall. When Al didn't move, Stretch ordered, "Pick it up. This isn't a dumpster."

Al looked around. It wasn't a dumpster, but it wasn't much of anything else either. He hauled himself out of the chair and did as ordered. The can landed with a loud clang.

Chapter 16

Charles sat down in a booth at Lights Out at 8:15 and finished his second beer by 8:30. There were only twelve people in the bar but it was early. The place would be full in a few hours. And tonight, with money in his pocket, Charles would be the one buying a round, and people would be raising a glass to *him*. He ordered another beer and a shot of tequila.

Chapter 17

Every time the front door of the apartment building opened, Spencer straightened in the seat and reached for the door handle. Each time it wasn't Laura, he slumped farther down in the seat. He was trying hard to stay awake. He had listened to all the radio he could stand. He was about to go for another walk when Laura came out. But if Spencer hadn't seen the clothes in her room, he might not have recognized her. It simply was not the same girl he had seen earlier. Black leather pants that squeezed every inch of her legs, a black jacket, and the red tube top that did the same for her bust, helped change her look from a college coed to a hooker. With black heels, bright red lipstick, and hair pulled back harshly, she fit the part well.

* * *

Stretch's team used hand-held radios to communicate, and he checked to make sure Laura's bodyguards were in place. They were good at disguise, so from one week to the next, no one would suspect they were the same person. It was all a show choreographed by Laura. To anyone looking, she was a hooker. She was never in danger, at least not in her opinion. But there was always an unknown danger on the streets. Laura didn't seem to understand that, but Stretch did and he worried about it. The show was so real that Laura had even been arrested. She was thrilled—said it made the show even better. He had asked who the show was for, assuming she wouldn't answer. He was right.

Stretch got the distinct feeling she was enjoying the game, and that worried him too. She wasn't being as careful as he would like. She said that's why she had hired him, to take care of her. He was worried before the murders started. He was even more worried after. That's why he was never far away whenever she went out. The times were prearranged. The rest of the team was already on Broadway. Stretch would follow Laura on the opposite side of the street, and tonight he had added an extra man to watch Spencer.

* * *

Laura was walking quickly and Spencer had to work a bit to keep up. As he crossed Kinley Street, waiting for a car that turned right in front of him, it started to drizzle. He turned up the collar of his jacket and pulled the visor of his baseball cap down. A growling stomach reminded him that he had missed dinner. He walked on, hoping there would be a chance to grab something on the run once they reached Broadway. He assumed that's where she was going. If she was, it would make keeping track of her a bit easier. Broadway was a crowded, brightly lit street and he would be able to follow Laura easily. She reached Broadway, glanced in both directions, and turned right, with Spencer following about a hundred feet behind.

The street was crowded with cars and the sidewalk with people. The steady hum of traffic blended with music from apartments above the stores and clubs along the street. Spencer threaded his way through the crowd, completely unaware that he was being followed by two men, one on each side of the street, who were also keeping an eye on Laura. Spencer took off his cap and shook off the raindrops that were starting to drip off the brim.

At the corner of Broadway and Webb, Laura turned into a hot dog joint, the Last Wiener. Spencer decided he was too hungry to worry about her wondering if he was tailing her and followed her in. There were two lines and he stood in the one she wasn't in, hoping he got served first. He did, and ordered two dogs with mustard, relish, and onions. One he stuck into a jacket pocket, the other he wolfed down on the way out as he grabbed a pile of napkins and stuffed them into another pocket. Taking up a position in a bus-stop shelter across the street, he waited for Laura, who came out a minute later holding a wrapped hot dog. Spencer watched as she looked around, threw the hot dog into a metal trash basket, and, unbuttoning her jacket, continued south on Broadway. The dogs weren't the best he'd ever had, but they weren't *that* bad. He took another bite and pulled out a napkin to wipe mustard off his chin. As he threw the napkin into a trash can, he noticed a yellow LW in the corner. He pulled out another. It had a red LW. Last Wiener done in mustard and ketchup. Cute.

* * *

The hot dog man tucked the fifty dollar bill Laura had given him into his pocket. He was the contact man between Stretch and Laura. His only responsibility was to relay the information to Laura that everyone was in position. Fifteen minutes ago Stretch had passed along that information to him with a nod. He thought he was part of some undercover police sting operation and was told to keep his mouth shut or they would find someone else. If they were willing to pay him fifty bucks for doing basically nothing, he was willing to keep his mouth shut.

Despite what Stretch thought, Laura was very concerned about her safety and wasn't about to walk out on the street without knowing she was closely watched. There had never been a serious problem, but she wanted help close at hand. The elaborate system was expensive, but money was not a problem, and she would not go out on the street without an okay from the hot dog man.

Chapter 18

Stosh got home at eight and sat in front of the TV, slowly nursing a beer and hoping this would be a quiet night. He had done all he could with the manpower he had. There was a greater presence on the streets, both uniforms and plain clothes. But the women they were trying to protect were also doing everything they could to evade the protection. Dark alleys were a favorite spot. After all, they couldn't exactly make a living while Chicago's finest looked on. Stosh wondered if perhaps they were just forcing them deeper into the dark corners of the city where they were even more at risk.

At 10:15, Stosh fell asleep watching the news. Knowing he would spend the night in the chair, Stosh hadn't bothered to get undressed. If anything *did* happen he would be ready, and he was used to the chair. It really wasn't that uncomfortable. And it wasn't quite as lonely as the bed. At some point, he would wake up and turn off the TV.

Chapter 19

Spencer kept abreast of Laura on the opposite side of Broadway. With frequent glances in her direction, he pretended interest in the store windows as he slowly ate the second hot dog.

"Hey gorgeous, like some company?"

The voice came from a dark stairwell to Spencer's left. He stopped, and a woman who looked to be in her thirties, and was not wearing her age well, stepped out of the shadows.

"You look like you could use a friend on a rainy night," she said with an effort to sound sexy. "Want to buy me a cup of coffee?"

Her face was lined and tired, but there was a hint of prettiness that had been worn away by years of drugs and the street.

"No thanks," said Spencer with no attempt to make excuses.

"You don't know what you're missing," she answered with a smile completely devoid of warmth.

Spencer was pretty sure he knew what he was missing, but felt no need to explain. He had to hurry to catch up to Laura.

Halfway down the block he noticed a middle-aged, well-dressed man who came out of a bookstore, turned left, and then, after noticing Laura, turned right and followed her. Spencer had wondered what he would do if she got picked up. He wasn't against private enterprise, but anybody could be the guy with the knife. He had considered making some kind of disturbance that would chase the guy off. He had even considered picking her up himself, taking her for a cup of coffee, and trying to talk some sense into her. But that would end his surveillance, so he just watched.

The man caught up to Laura, and they started to talk as they walked. Spencer wished he was close enough to hear what they were saying. After ten seconds of conversation, the man laughed and stopped and stared at Laura. She shrugged and kept walking. The man turned around and headed north. Spencer wondered why the deal fell through, but was thankful it did. From the laugh, he assumed she was asking more than the man wanted to pay.

At the end of the block, Laura waited for the light to turn red and then walked across Broadway, heading straight for Spencer. He turned and stared at a dresser in the window of an antique store. A car honked and someone yelled, "Hey honey," out the window. Ignoring the car, Laura leaned against a brick wall just thirty feet from where Spencer was standing. The rain had stopped, and even in the shadows Spencer could see that Laura was beautiful. She was full of youth and innocence, despite the outfit and the curves. Her hair glistened in the glow of the street lights. He sighed as he remembered the college coed he saw that afternoon.

The sidewalk was crowded and several people leered at Laura as they walked by. She was very alluring.

The woman who had propositioned Spencer was leaning against a street light smoking a cigarette. Laura stopped a few feet from her, leaned against the wall of a coffee shop, and started a conversation.

A bus horn sounded as a brown van squeezed a little more yellow out of a red light. Another honk brought Spencer's attention to the same car that had passed a few minutes before. This time it stopped at the curb. A punk in the passenger's seat rolled down the window and smiled at Laura. Music blared out the window.

"You just holdin' up that wall, honey?"

Laura stared at him without responding. The kid folded his arms out the window and stared back. After a minute of thinking, Laura slowly pushed away from the wall and ambled over to the car. She bent down, giving the punk a good look at what she had to offer. They talked quietly.

The other woman watched intently.

Because of the music, Spencer couldn't hear what they were saying until the kid yelled, "You gotta be kidding! I could get ten broads for that!"

Again Laura shrugged, and walked back to the wall. The punks didn't leave. Evidently not everyone agreed, for the discussion in the car was hot and heavy. The other woman walked to the car, bent down, and had a few words too quiet for Spencer to hear.

After a minute, the car pulled away from the curb and sped down the street, taking the obnoxious music with it.

Spencer moved to a different window of the antique store and watched people's reflections in the glass as they passed by. A squad car drove slowly down Broadway.

An hour went by with no new events. Then a stocky, tall man dressed in expensive-looking clothes walked up to Laura. Spencer joined a group of laughing, drunk twenty-year-olds as they walked past her. He heard the man say, "Girls on this street work for me." An entrepreneur. He had more to say, but Spencer had moved with the group and heard no more. The other woman had disappeared.

The man left, leaving Laura with a decision to make. She would certainly be a good addition to his business. But if she didn't agree to work for him, what was the consequence?

Laura went back to leaning against the wall and seemed indifferent to the crowd until a young man with dark skin and a brown leather jacket walked briskly past her spot at the wall. She followed him with her eyes as he disappeared around the corner. A minute later he returned, walking more slowly. Laura slid one foot up the wall behind her, tightening the leather on her leg. She crossed her arms under her breasts and lifted them just enough to send a message.

The man stopped next to her. She looked up and down the street as they talked. Probably looking for the entrepreneur. This time there was no protest, and the two walked toward Spencer. He watched their reflection in the window as they passed within a few feet of him. The man was about six feet tall with dark complexion and dark hair. Spencer registered a mental picture that he would remember.

Without looking back, Laura and the man turned into an alley that ran beside the antique store. Spencer gave them a few seconds and then walked past the alley. He glanced quickly into the darkness as he passed. But after the bright lights of the street, all he saw was dark. He walked past, and then came back and stood at the corner of the building, staring into the alley. Two phone poles and a few dumpsters stood like eerie ghosts against the walls of the buildings. His stomach turned as he thought of Laura on the wet concrete behind one of those trash bins. As his imagination ran away with thoughts of what might be happening to her, he decided, against his better judgment, to walk through the alley.

Walking a few feet in, he paused to let his eyes adapt to the dark. He was at enough of a disadvantage without being unable to see. He stood quietly and listened, and heard nothing but the traffic in the street. Gathering courage, he cautiously made his way deeper into the alley. He could see that it T'd about eighty feet ahead as it ended at the back of another building where a dim light hung over a door. He could see two dumpsters about halfway down the alley. Other than those, the alley was empty. Expecting to run across the couple behind the dumpsters, Spencer walked faster. He glanced quickly as he passed the dumpsters and saw a small pile of boxes next to the first. As he passed the second, he was startled by a body lying next to the dumpster.

"Hey, shmister. Gotta buck?"

A bum was using this spot to get a night's sleep.

Spencer kept walking. Hurrying to the end where the alley T'd, he looked up and down the alley. Laura and her client were nowhere in sight. He had passed two doors about halfway down the alley, one on each side. Walking quickly, he went back and checked them. They were both locked. He walked back to the T.

To his right, Spencer saw the bright light of the street just one building away, like the sun at the top of a well. To his left, the alley dissolved into darkness as it stretched to the north. If she had walked toward the light, Spencer certainly would have seen her, so he turned left and headed into the darkness.

The moon cast fingers of light that glimmered on pools of shimmering water in low spots of the alley. Past that, the alley was dark. Avoiding potholes,

Spencer crunched along over crumbling concrete. Just before the light, he noticed someone lying in the recess of a rear door. He was holding a paper bag shaped like a bottle. By the dim glow of a bare bulb across the alley, Spencer saw a scar on his neck. He wasn't very old, but he had definitely seen better times. The man gave Spencer a bit of confidence as he walked toward the doorway—he wasn't alone in the alley. Spencer glanced back at the man. A ragged old trench coat, buttoned to the collar, a wool ski cap, and shoes that were not as worn as Spencer would have expected, covered whatever pain and suffering must have been on the inside. What Spencer didn't see was the gun the man was holding in his other hand, tucked behind his right leg. He also didn't see another man who had entered the alley from the south end and was crouched behind a trio of garbage cans.

Peering down the alley into the darkness, Spencer decided he wasn't willing to go any farther by himself and started back toward the street.

The man in the doorway raised his bottle in a drunken salute as Spencer walked by. Spencer nodded and kept walking to the end, glancing back once to relieve the growing feeling that he was being followed. He looked back down the alley. He wasn't. And he wasn't *following* anyone either. Laura was gone. He thought of going back and asking the man if he had seen anyone, but realized the odds of getting an answer were slim.

There was less traffic on the street, but more on the sidewalks. Young couples jostled along on their way to the night's entertainment without a care in the world. But Laura could be lying somewhere in pieces. Wondering if it was worth bothering Stosh, Spencer squinted into the bright light and checked his watch. Almost midnight. He had nothing to go on except a gut feeling, and he wasn't about to walk back into that alley by himself.

Chapter 20

Several girls passed by on both sides of Broadway. But the one he had picked out was working the other side. She was a pretty young thing. After watching several men talk to her and walk away, he crossed the street and started a conversation that quickly turned to money. He agreed to her price and they calmly walked to a nearby alley and turned in. As they walked, she said something about smelling alcohol on his breath. She said most men needed alcohol to do what he was about to do. He didn't answer.

They walked down the dimly lit alley toward the end where they turned left into a dark section lit only by a little moonlight that filtered between the building tops. It was a world away from the bright lights of the street just a few hundred feet away. The girl stopped next to a dumpster and asked how he would like to start.

Without saying a word, he reached out and gently caressed her cheek with the back of his right hand. What beautiful skin. As she started to smile, he clamped his left hand around her throat and strangled her until she passed out.

After letting her slump to the pavement, he pulled out a knife that was in a sheath under his jacket and plunged it a few inches into her stomach just below the ribcage. With one quick movement, he made a cut down to her waist. He stood back and admired his work as blood poured out onto the concrete pad the dumpster sat on.

The shock of the cut had awakened her, but only long enough for her eyes to register the fear of something she could do nothing about.

He pulled the skin apart and then grabbed her intestines, pulled them out, and hung them over her left shoulder.

Taking a paper towel out of his pocket, he wiped off the knife and returned it to the holder. He threw the paper towel on the ground next to the body.

With no emotion, he stared at the girl for a minute and then pulled a small, plastic baggie out of his pocket. Inside the baggie were five coins. Holding them carefully by the edges, he arranged them neatly and placed them next to her shoulder. He then walked out of the alley and blended back in with the crowd on Broadway.

Chapter 21

Stosh was dreaming he was in high school and late for class. Hurrying down a hall that had no end in sight, he heard the period bell ring over and over again. "Okay, okay, I'm running as fast as I can," he yelled angrily as he lost hold of his books and they scattered across the hall. Then he woke up. The bell was still ringing. Slowly, he realized it was the phone and got up to answer it. The phone was on top of a table next to a clock. Twelve-fifteen. This would not be good news.

"Yeah."

"Stosh, it's Spencer." No response. "You awake?"

"If I'm not, I'm havin' another nightmare. Either way, it's not good."

"Stosh, I think I've got a missing person." He explained the last hour's events from a corner pay phone.

Stosh yawned and rubbed the back of his neck which was stiff from two hours of sleep in a chair. "Just cuz you can't find her doesn't mean she's missing."

"But she just disappeared, Stosh."

"Spencer, has it occurred to you that girls in that line of business don't exactly want to be found? They know how to disappear."

"It was too fast, Stosh," Spencer argued. "It was like she vanished into thin air."

"You're worried?"

"Yeah, I'm worried."

Stosh chose his words carefully. "About a girl you don't even know."

"Right. What's your point? She's a human being too, you know, and I think she's in trouble."

Stosh put the phone on the other ear and rubbed the side of his neck. "My point is, you fear for the safety of a complete stranger. Okay, that's commendable. But what about yourself? Ever stop to think about that? You walk into a dark alley in the middle of the night all by your lonesome. How smart is that? And what about me worrying about you out there doing stupid things? What do I gotta do, put one of those kiddie leashes on you and tie you to a tree?"

"Can we skip the lecture, Stosh? I know it wasn't a smart thing to do. I promise never to do it again. Now can I get some help here?"

"I'll get you a patrol car to look through the alley. That make you happy?"

"Yeah, thanks."

"Where are you?"

"Corner of Broadway and Webb. Southeast."

"Okay, sit tight. Should be somebody there in a couple minutes if they're not busy."

"Thanks Stosh, I owe you."

"Yeah, you do. Spencer, you don't have a gun on you, do you?"

"No."

"Good. But walking into a dark alley by yourself without one wasn't too bright either."

The phone went dead. Spencer hung up. He sat down on a concrete stoop and waited. In five minutes a patrol car pulled up to the curb. Jamie Hernandez rolled down the passenger window. Jamie and Spencer had been in the academy together.

"Hey, Spencer. Hear you've had a busy evening."

"Hi, Jamie. It's been interesting."

Nodding to the back seat, Jamie said, "Hop in, we'll go take a look."

Jamie introduced Spencer to his partner, Mike Wells, and they drove to the alley as Spencer explained what had happened. He described Laura and told them about the man in the doorway.

Jamie twisted and looked into the back seat. "I assume you already got a lecture from the Lieutenant, so I'll keep my two cents to myself."

"Thanks, I appreciate it."

Mike turned on the spotlight and slowly drove into the alley. After the first building, Mike drove and Jamie and Spencer got out and walked. They looked down stairwells, walked up passageways between buildings, and checked in dumpsters. Jamie held his gun at his side. Spencer held his breath every time they opened a dumpster, expecting to find something, or someone. Laura had to be somewhere, and there just wasn't enough time to have made it out of the alley. They had to have walked down the dark part. The man could have knocked her unconscious and hidden in one of the passages until Spencer left.

When they reached the doorway, Jamie inspected it but found nothing. There were no signs that anyone had been there recently.

Jamie opened the door of the squad car and got in. "She's not here, buddy."

Spencer nodded. "No, I guess not. But that's good. Cuz if she was, she'd be in trouble."

Pulling the door closed, Jamie said, "Tell you what I'll do—I'll put her description out and keep a lookout. You got a number if we find something?"

Spencer took a card out of his wallet and handed it through the open window.

Jamie took it and nodded.

"Thanks guys."

"No problem. Part of the job. Hey, I'll give you a call, we'll have a few beers. And stay out of dark alleys."

Spencer managed a smile. "Sounds good, Jamie. Take it easy." He knocked on the side of the door and they drove off.

It took five minutes to walk back to his car. There was no light in Laura's apartment window. Spencer quietly entered the building and made his way back to her apartment. Listening at the door, he heard nothing. A gentle knock brought no answer. He jimmied the lock again and slowly opened the door, still expecting to find the worst. She wasn't there. A minute later he was back in his car. He started the engine and let it run until it was warm and ran the heater until the chill wore off. Then he sat and watched some more, but she didn't show. An hour later he drove home. He called Stosh, who answered with the same gruff "yeah", but this time he sounded more awake.

"Stosh, it's me. We didn't find her."

"I already know that. You got something worth keeping me awake?"

"No, guess not. But would you run her name and see what you find?"

"Already asked for it. I'll have it in the morning."

"Both names?"

"Both names. I've been doing this a few years now, Spencer. Come on over this afternoon. We'll watch the Cubs and I'll fill you in."

"Okay. Thanks Stosh."

* * *

As Stosh shuffled back to his chair, he mumbled to himself "I don't get paid enough." He sat down and got comfortable. Before he fell asleep, he thought at least Spencer's was the only interruption of the night.

Chapter 22

Stosh slept soundly until six a.m. when the phone rang again. Two officers, responding to a call from the owner of a Chinese laundry, had found the body of a girl in the alley behind his shop. She was lying next to a dumpster on north Broadway.

Stosh was out the door in three minutes. As he turned the corner, he got on the radio and asked dispatch to get the officers on the horn. Officer Jenks responded within one minute.

"How old, Jenks?"

"Hard to tell, Lieutenant. I'd say twenties."

"How's she dressed?"

"Black pants, black jacket."

Stosh turned onto Western and headed north. He didn't need the siren. There wasn't any hurry. The city would wake up slowly and quietly as it stretched out the aches and pains from the night before. "What color top?"

"Well, brown. Far as I can tell."

"Far as you can tell. What's that mean?"

"That means it's a little messy. Whatever color it was, it's now the color of dried blood, you know?"

He knew. "Okay, thanks, I'll be there in ten."

* * *

Stanley Powolski had been a sergeant for many years, working under Captain Manning in the 35th precinct on the south side of Chicago. He had been offered promotions regularly, but Stosh had turned them down. He was happy being one of the boys and wanted to stay that way. The extra money was not a lure. Francie, his wife of thirty-two years, thought he was crazy. But Stosh knew he would not have been happy higher up the ladder.

Then Francie had been diagnosed with ovarian cancer, and all of a sudden their lives changed. The prognosis was not good. She was given a year at the most to live. Medical bills piled up, and one day Stanley asked if he could still accept a promotion. It was granted retroactive to the last review, which was two months prior.

The extra money helped, and Francie was so proud. The precinct had a special ceremony and a dinner. There wasn't one person on the force who didn't like Stanley Powolski and wouldn't have given an arm to keep Francie alive.

Stosh lived on the north side of Chicago. So did Captain Manning. The 35th precinct was on the south side. After the Mannings died in a car crash, Stosh asked for a transfer to a precinct on the north side. In September of last year, he was transferred to the 18th precinct amidst many tears and hugs from members of the 35th. The 18th welcomed him with open arms. Two months later, Rosie joined him. But Stosh had always been happier as a sergeant.

* * *

Stosh made it to the scene in eight minutes. He joined the crowd of people behind the laundry, which included two detectives, six officers, and two paramedics. The body was still on the ground between two dumpsters. A large puddle of blood darkened the concrete pad the dumpsters sat on.

* * *

Detective Spanell filled him in. Mr. Woo had found the girl when he had taken the trash out shortly before six. The coroner had been called. Stosh parted the crowd to have a look at the body.

Stosh's stomach turned when he saw the girl. Her upper body was a bloody mess and there wasn't much left that was recognizable. Deep blue eyes may as well have been glass marbles lying in a dish. Her hair lay matted in drying blood on the concrete, and what was probably once a pretty face was frozen in a twisted contortion of pain. Her organs were exposed, and her entrails had been pulled out and slung over her left shoulder like a string of sausages in a butcher's display case. The top she was wearing was brown from the dried blood. It could have been any color. Stosh saw a button. Spencer had said his missing girl was wearing a red tube top. He also saw a stack of coins behind the girl's left shoulder and what looked like a bloody paper towel next to her feet.

He asked Spanell, who was wearing gloves, to pull the top out of the pants. He wanted to see part of the top that wasn't covered in blood. Spanell, who acted as though he didn't care if his wrinkled and stained suit got any dirtier, stooped and gingerly pulled the top away from the pants.

"Okay," said Stosh. "That's enough." It was white. Stosh felt some relief, but not enough to take away the horror of what had happened. He would never get used to it. He sighed and moved with Spanell away from the body.

"You got an ID?"

"Yup, Jane Deltine, Twenty-eight. Address on Lawrence."

Noticing a sickly, yellowish puddle on the pad, Stosh asked, "What's that?"

"Breakfast. Our laundry man doesn't have a very strong stomach."

Spanell moved a bit closer and studied the mess.

"Kinda looks like Cheerios, don't you think?"

Stosh looked at him with disgust. "Jesus Christ, Spanell. You check out the coins?"

"Yup. Same five coins. Nickel, penny, dime, half, quarter."

Stosh nodded. That fit the pattern. It was what they expected. The coins by the first body were stacked in order of size with the half dollar on the bottom. The stack by the second body moved the top coin, the dime, to the bottom, and the current stack, next to the body of Jane Deltine, had continued the pattern with the penny moved to the bottom. That left only two more combinations before the murderer got back to the starting point. But did that mean something?

* * *

Driving slowly to the end of the alley, Stosh honked and carefully eased out over the sidewalk. He looked both ways, but there was no one in sight. Early morning sunlight bathed Broadway with a false sense of cheer. Driving slowly south, Stosh noticed businesses that hadn't been there just a few years ago. Restaurants, bookstores, upscale taverns, and mini-malls, had taken the place of rundown apartments, vacant lots, and boarded-up businesses long since vacated by their owners. The street used to be one of the highest crime areas of the city, and it had definitely changed for the better, but the change was only skin deep. At night, the bright lights and happy music spilling out into the street and throngs of people bringing money to spend was evidence enough of that change. Driving along past the sleepy storefronts, Stosh couldn't help but feel sad and depressed because there was also evidence that crime still existed. Walk a block east or west, or into the alleys, and the picture wasn't so pretty. He had just seen that picture at its worst. The bright lights and fancy storefronts had just pushed the sadness off the streets and into the alleys and gangways where it was harder to find and control.

Brightly colored canopies hung over doorways of upscale coffee shops and trendy boutiques. Slowing to a stop as a light turned yellow, Stosh surveyed the facade of a used bookstore. The walls were the subdued green color of spring lily leaves, and large glass windows were framed by gold trim. But under the fresh paint was a hint of dinginess. Influenced by what he had seen in the alley, Stosh felt a struggle between the facade and the tired, rotting boards beneath the paint, and he wasn't sure that the paint would win. In front of the store were two black, wrought-iron benches where people could leisurely sit and pass the time of day. Just five feet away from the empty benches, a mangy, brown-and-white dog gnawed at something dead lying in the gutter. A safe distance away, five pigeons waited patiently for the leftovers of the dog's breakfast. As he stared at the dog, an impatient honk let Stosh know that the light had turned green.

Maybe a day of sunlight would burn off the sins of the night before, Stosh thought. Some of those sins were legal, committed by people just out to have a good time. Some weren't. And there were some the sun couldn't fix, like the dark bloodstains that had soaked into the concrete pad behind the laundry.

On a whim, he turned left and headed for the lake. He pulled into the parking lot of the Belmont Street marina and stepped out of the car. A pair of joggers passed on the blacktop path that snaked through the park along the lakeshore. Walking slowly with his hands in his pockets, and turning into the breeze blowing onshore, Stosh made his way to the granite boulders at the north end of the marina and sat on the nearest one.

The marina was dotted with wooden docks, floating in a lonely dance. The docks housed a myriad of expensive toys filling the marina with all the colors of the rainbow like an artist's palette, one blending into the other in an arrogant slap at the world Stosh had just left. He looked out over the lake and took a deep breath of fresh air, trying to force out the stale, heavy air of the alley. The sun was about twenty degrees above the horizon, long thin arrows of light scattering off high cirrus clouds. Looking into the glare, he thought he saw the outline of a freighter far out on the lake, making its way down to the steel plants to the south. As he listened to the waves gently lapping against the rocks, Stosh tossed pebbles into the lake and thought about his first date with Francie.

The years were many, but the memories were vivid. They had left some boring party and walked along the lake. They had ended up sitting on rocks just like these, but it was at night and farther south, and the night had been warm and muggy. They had talked and watched the boats come into harbor and tie up for the night. They had talked long after the onboard lights winked out, and he had known then that he had found the right woman.

A gull screeched and circled down to the beach with wings spread wide. It landed next to a dead fish washed up on the beach and began pecking. Within twenty seconds it was joined by three other gulls. Before long the fish would be torn open. Nature has a use for everything, he thought. A dead fish becomes breakfast for hungry gulls. He watched with growing irritation, and then picked up a rock and threw it at the gulls. They flew off and landed down the beach a ways. They'd be back.

The alley killer would be back too, unless of course they could catch him first. Stosh walked slowly back to the car and headed home, wondering what was wrong with the world.

Chapter 23

Charles woke up with a slight headache, something that he was certainly used to. He knew he had spent part of his fortune, but, after seven or eight beers, he had stopped keeping track. He did want to get the money out of his pocket and into a safe hiding spot before Sarah found it or there would be hell to pay. She would never believe where he got it.

The telephone rang three times before Sarah answered it. Charles wasn't ready to get out of bed yet, but figured if she was tied up on the phone that would be a good time to hide the money. It would be safe under the mattress until he could think of a better spot.

He swung out of bed and sat for a minute rubbing his temples. With the light to his back, the pain wasn't quite as bad. His clothes were in a heap next to the nightstand. Dressed in just his underwear, Charles confirmed that Sarah was still on the phone downstairs. He picked up his pants and stuck his hand in the left-hand pocket. No money. There was only the key to Miss Brock's house. He tried the right side and pulled out a business card from a taxidermist. Where the hell did that come from? His wallet was in the back left, and that had eight dollars folded in the key compartment. The other back pocket was empty.

Starting to panic, Charles sat back down on the bed and tried to think, something he was not very good at under the best of circumstances. There were only three possibilities: he had spent it all, and he was sure that was not the case; someone had picked his pocket; or Sarah had found it. He rocked back and forth and prayed that he had been robbed.

Charles heard footsteps coming up the stairs. Hurrying back under the covers, he turned his head away from the door and pretended he was asleep. He heard her come in the room and held his breath, hoping she would go away. He wasn't that lucky.

"Get outta bed!" she yelled.

He didn't move.

"I heard the floor creaking. I know you're awake."

He still didn't move. This woman, who was two-thirds his height and half his weight, scared him to death.

Sarah Lamb picked a book off the dresser and threw it at his head. It missed, but it got his attention. He jerked away from the pillow and sat up.

"Hey! What the hell is wrong with you?"

"Wrong with me? Wrong with *me*? I've been dragging your lazy ass around for eight years while you bounce from one worthless job to another and you want to know what's wrong with *me*?" She picked up one of his shoes and threw it at him. "I told you what would happen if I ever caught you gambling again," she said with fiery eyes.

Charles scrambled out of the other side of the bed, his head pounding. "Calm down, Sarah. I can explain."

She picked up the other shoe and raised it above her head.

He raised his arm in case she threw it. "I wasn't gambling. Honest."

"Then where did you get the money?"

"I earned it," he said as he kept an eye on the shoe and slowly crept toward her.

"You earned it?" Throwing back her head, she laughed with a wicked cackle. "There's almost a hundred dollars! There's nothing you can do that someone would pay you that much money for one day's work. How stupid do I look?"

Wisely, Charles didn't answer. He desperately wanted to tell her that there was someone who thought he *was* worth that much.

"Sarah, you know I can do handy work. Right?"

"Sure, when you want to and you're not drunk, which isn't often."

"Okay." He moved closer and was only a few feet away. "Well, I got a job doing some handy work." He reached for the shoe.

Sarah pulled the shoe away and spat through clenched teeth, "If you touch me I'll call the cops again. You know I will."

He did know. She had before. "She's paying me twenty dollars an hour to..."

"She! How long does it take you to make up these lies?"

He backed off slowly, carefully eyeing the shoe. "It's not a lie. A lady hired me to work at her house." Charles was close to begging her to believe him.

As he moved back to the bed, Sarah lowered the shoe but she didn't drop it. "Okay, let's say some crazy lady hired you to work at her house," she said in a calmer voice. "Where is this house?"

"On the north side," Charles said as he grabbed his pants and struggled to put them on.

"I assume this is some old lady you're taking advantage of?"

Knowing she wouldn't believe him, Charles decided to try the truth anyway. His lies had never worked. But then he saw the crazy look on her face and changed his mind. If he told her how pretty Amanda was, the shoe and everything else within reach would come in his direction. "I'm not taking advantage of her, she offered twenty dollars an hour." Charles was dying to tell her that she was also beautiful and that this beautiful woman had treated him like a real person.

Sarah dropped the shoe, leaned back against the dresser, and ran her fingers through her long hair. She laughed again and Charles winced as the laugh cut through him like a knife. He wanted to kill her and imagined his hands around her throat.

"So some old lady is paying you twenty dollars out of the kindness of her heart. How stupid is this woman?"

Charles crossed his arms over his chest. "She's not stupid. And she treats me nice."

Sarah shook her head and asked with a frown, "And where did you meet this angel?"

Charles knew he was fighting a losing battle but figured he might as well get it all out. "I met her at a gas station," he said quietly. "She was..."

"I don't care what she was." She stood straight up and pointed an unwavering finger at him.

"Now you listen to me, Charles Lamb. How you even *start* to think I would believe any of this crap I don't know. And I told you what would happen if you started gambling again. I give you a roof to sleep under and food to eat, and I pay for you to go out and get drunk on the weekends, and I don't ask you where you disappear to or how you spend your days. But if you're gambling, that means you're losing more than you make, and I will not finance your habit. And you're even too stupid to take the money out of your pocket."

The phone rang. She ignored it. So did he. Something about what she had said bothered him, but he couldn't remember what it was.

Sitting down on the bed, he got up the nerve to ask, "Where's my money?"

She laughed again. "*Your* money? It's *my* money now."

"I earned it," he said with the last bit of backbone he had left.

"With what? A pair of dice?"

He looked dejectedly down at the floor.

"And you'd have to do a lot of earning to make up for your share of things around here." She turned away from him and began searching for something in the top drawer of the dresser.

Charles bent over, put his elbows on his knees, and squeezed his head on both sides with the heels of his large hands. The pain intensified and then lessened as he dropped his hands. He stared at dust particles floating through a square of light from the window and said, "I was going to give some to you."

Looking over her shoulder, Sarah said strongly, "You'd better give me more than some." Her eyes narrowed. "If I find out you made money and didn't give it *all* to me, you'll be sorry. I pay the bills around here. You're lucky I don't throw your ass out. I control the money and I control you and don't you forget it." She closed the drawer and, as she left the room, Charles figured out what was bothering him.

"Hey, how did you know I made that in one day?"

She stopped in the hall and turned back to him. Placing her hands on skinny hips, Sarah said, "How the hell do you think I know? Jesus Christ, you're stupid." She walked away mumbling something about putting up with him.

Her sister often asked her why she did. What she didn't tell her sister was that Charles had a rich brother who was dying, and Charles was his only relative. That's why she had married him in the first place.

Charles touched his pocket and thought about the money. He decided the only way she could have known was if she went through his pockets every night, and for some reason that shocked him. When he thought about it, he figured that was something she would do, but they were *his* pockets and he wanted some privacy. He was thinking of giving her some of the money, but there was no way she was getting any of it now.

But what would he do with it? Where could he put it so she wouldn't find it? By Monday, he would find a good hiding place and Sarah could go to hell.

And, thankfully, she hadn't found the key to Amanda's house.

Chapter 24

He told her he was going to run errands. She asked why he waited until Saturday to run errands when stores would be less crowded during the week. She didn't consider him a genius. He really didn't have any errands. He just wanted to get out of the house.

While driving, he listened to the news and the account about the dead girl found behind the laundry. He was as disappointed as he was the first two times. They reported the incident but didn't talk about the real problem, the immoral activity on the streets. The police arrested women once in a while, but they always came back. There were now three who would *not* come back. And still no mention of the coins. He slammed his fist on the dashboard.

He drove along the lake with the windows rolled down. He liked the wind and the freedom of driving along the shore next to the water where there was no hint of the sins on the streets just a few blocks inland.

Chapter 25

Spencer wheeled the Mustang into Stosh's driveway at 2:15. The Cubs were in the second inning, losing four to one. After parking on the gravel next to the concrete drive, Spencer rang the back doorbell and waited. No answer. He walked around the side and peeked in the window. The game was on and Stosh was asleep in his chair. Stosh had given Spencer a key after his folks had died in case he needed a quiet place to spend some time. Spencer let himself in the back door and quietly closed it. He knew Stosh had been up early and wanted to let him sleep.

Spencer made a ham and cheese sandwich, grabbed a bottle of beer, and tiptoed into the living room. He set the bottle on the floor, balanced the plate on his lap, and ate while he watched.

WGN went to commercials as Spencer washed the last bite down with a long swallow of Schlitz, the beer that made Milwaukee famous. It was Stosh's favorite beer and the first label Spencer had emptied by himself. He set the plate on the floor and glanced about the room which hadn't changed a bit for as long as Spencer could remember. The front wall was filled with windows with a long table beneath. A vase on the table always used to be filled with fresh flowers. Now it was empty. Spencer meant to bring some every time he came, but never remembered. Next to the vase was Stosh and Francine's wedding picture. The TV was on the wall opposite the couch. Stosh's favorite chair, a recliner, and Francie's rocker sat in front of shelves along the fourth wall, with an end table between them. The shelves held photos and books. The only change in the room since Francie had died was a layer of dust.

In the last of the fourth, the Cubs went ahead with a grand slam. Spencer let out a yell that woke Stosh.

Stosh stretched and looked over the intruder, noticing the plate covered with crumbs and the almost-empty bottle of beer on the floor.

"Hey, just make yourself at home," he said in his best polite but gruff manner.

"Thanks. I already did. But I did it quietly so you old people could get your afternoon nap."

Glancing at the clock, Stosh asked, "How long you been here?"

"'Bout an hour."

"I miss anything?"

Spencer filled him in.

Stosh humphed. "They build you up and then they let you down. I'll bet you they go a hundred years without winning another world series." The last had been in 1908.

Spencer laughed. "If I thought you'd live that long, you'd have a bet." He finished his beer. "You want one?"

"Sure. Grab some chips too, okay?"

"Be right back."

They watched the rest of the game in relative silence, which got even more silent after the Dodgers returned the grand slam in the ninth. The game over, Spencer gathered the empty bottles and started for the kitchen. Stosh handed him the half-empty bag of potato chips.

As Stosh took the bag, Spencer said, "Thanks for the heads-up on the girl, Stosh."

"Sure. I knew you'd hear and be worried."

"I'm still worried."

"Yeah. I figured. But right now you'd better be worrying about me. Get rid of that stuff and get back in here so I can chew you out."

Stosh had called Rosie when he got home in the morning and told her about the white blouse. He knew she and Spencer ran together on Saturday mornings. Telling Rosie served two purposes: she would tell Spencer about the murder so he would know it wasn't Laura, and Stosh wouldn't have to deal with Spencer's questions. Stosh stretched and closed his eyes.

Spencer returned and, hoping that Stosh was asleep so he could get away without a lecture, tiptoed to the couch.

With eyes still closed, Stosh said, "So, what possessed you to do something that stupid? You got more brains than that."

"I know Stosh. I got caught up in the moment. I was worried about her. And it was just an alley."

Frowning, Stosh replied, "Wanna take a ride? I'll show you another alley not far from there."

"Point taken."

"Good. Now what the hell is all this about?"

Settling back into the couch, Spencer answered with a shrug, "Nothing more than I already told you. Ben asked me to see if I could find out something about her. She was picked up for prostitution a while back. Doesn't seem the type." Spencer told Stosh about his chat with Tim. "You find out anything?"

"Nothing on Laura Douglas other than what you already know. No trail, which points to something else you already know—that isn't her real name. Laura *Justine* is indeed from Naples. She's twenty-four. Called a friend down there who tells me the address is in a very ritzy neighborhood."

"Yeah, rich family in real estate. She's got kind of a classy look about her."

Stosh continued. "She was assumed to be kidnapped, but no demands were ever made. They ran the usual and nothing turned up. Parents hired the P.I. who found her in Detroit. They sent the letter you found but got no reply. P.I. said she moved out shortly after the letter would have arrived, and he lost her. He also reported that she appeared to be safe and coming and going as she pleased. And she can continue doing that because she is twenty-four and can indeed do as she pleases."

"Yeah. She certainly wasn't kidnapped. Looks like she left of her own accord. I'm guessing Laura is trying to find her sister."

Stosh nodded. "And here she is in Chicago, still none the worse for wear according to you."

"Except that now she's really missing."

"From you, maybe. But it looks like this girl is good at disappearing and doing so under her own free will. Just cuz you don't know where she is doesn't mean she's missing."

Spencer shook his head. "She disappeared, Stosh. She should have been in that alley somewhere, but she was just gone."

"Maybe she ran. Maybe she knew she was being followed, hard as that may be for you to swallow."

"She wouldn't run. She was with a *john*. He wouldn't have run with her without wasting some time asking questions."

Stosh pulled up the footrest and stretched out in the chair. "Spencer. It's my day off. You get me something to look into and I will. We already swept the alley and there was no sign of her. I think you gotta give her more credit than you are. Face it—she lost you."

With a perplexed look, Spencer said, "She can't lose me if she doesn't know I'm there."

"Maybe that's your mistake. Assume she did know you were there. Then it might make sense. And if you ever do find her again, tell her the next time we run into her she'll face charges for falsifying a driver's license. Now shut up, I wanna watch golf. And I'm gonna smoke a pipe." Giving Spencer a stern look of warning, he said, "And I don't want any crap from you."

Spencer raised his eyebrows in surprise. "Me? Certainly not. You want to kill yourself, go right ahead." He held out his hand, palm up, in the direction of the tobacco tin Stosh kept on the table next to the chair.

* * *

Stosh opened the tin of London Dock and began the tedious process of filling and tamping. Spencer watched with fond memories as Stosh lit the tobacco, drew just the right amount of air through the bowl, and sent a thin gray line of smoke curling up to the ceiling. The smell of the tobacco brought back memories of lazy days when he would sit on the porch with Stosh and his dad, both of them carefully and lovingly working their pipes, and listen to stories about the good old days.

They watched golf in silence, Stosh relaxing with hands folded on his stomach and Spencer fretting over the possibility that Laura might have gotten the best of him. But once Spencer accepted that, he realized that also meant she was safe. Kicking off his shoes, he arranged a couple of pillows behind his head and stretched out on the couch.

At the first commercial, Spencer asked, "You got anything on the murder this morning?"

Stosh rolled his head to the left and stared at Spencer. "What happened to our relaxing afternoon?"

"I'm still relaxing. And by the looks of it, so are you. Just a simple question, like *how you doin'* or *how 'bout those Cubs?*"

"Yeah, sure. What makes you think my information is there for the sharing?"

"It'll probably be in the papers so what's the harm in knowing early?"

Stosh placed his pipe in the glass ashtray and let down the footrest. "And what exactly do you want to know that Rosie hasn't already told you?" he asked gruffly.

Ignoring the jab to Rosie, Spencer answered, "You knew about the blouse. So you saw her, right? So I'm wondering if the coins were there."

"You are, huh? Well, that's still being kept quiet so it won't be in the papers." Spencer started to answer, but Stosh held up his hand and cut him off. "I know you wouldn't tell a living soul, but I'm not taking any chances. I don't even want to know that you already know whatever it is you think you know. If anything ever got out and you were involved, it would come back to me. Most of the force knows you're always hanging around here drinking my beer. They'd assume you got it from me."

"Got what?"

"Whatever. I want to be able to say with a clear conscience that I know nothing about it."

"About what?"

"About whatever we're talking about, that's what."

Spencer thought for a minute and then said, "So you have nothing here?"

Stosh glared at Spencer, turned up the TV, and answered in a voice filled with frustration, "Right, I got nothin'."

"Nothing on the coins?"

After taking a deep breath, and trying to erase the picture of the girl's stomach from his memory, Stosh said quietly, "Spencer, there was very little left of her midsection. It was a bloody mess. I don't know if the coins mean anything or not, but I doubt it. We're dealing with a wacko. For some reason the guy went nuts and ripped her apart."

"Were the others mutilated?"

"Not that bad." He took another deep breath and let it out slowly.

"But they were?"

"Yeah, I guess, if you consider anything beyond a stab wound mutilation."

They sat in silence for a few seconds as Spencer thought about how to carefully phrase his next question. "Seems kinda strange, doesn't it?"

With a wary look, Stosh asked, "What?"

Like a lawyer slowly building his case, Spencer spoke slowly. "Well, on one hand you've got a guy making a bloody mess." He looked at Stosh who was looking back with no expression. "On the other hand, he leaves a pile of coins in a pattern."

Spencer stared at Stosh, hoping to see if his guess about the coins was right.

Stosh stared at Spencer, only slightly moving his eyes. "How stupid do I look?"

Spencer laughed. "Can't blame me for trying."

Stosh grunted. "I need another beer. You want one?"

"No thanks. Gotta get going."

Stosh started to push himself out of the chair.

"Hey Stosh, you know Jack the Ripper was never caught."

Giving Spencer a scornful look, Stosh said with astonishment, "Are you nuts?"

"No, I was just..."

"You were just suggesting that a hundred-year-old man is stalking women in the streets of Chicago and has enough energy to attack them and cut them apart. You *are* nuts!"

Spencer sat up on the couch. "No, don't be silly. I'm suggesting that the victims and the mutilation are the same. And since *he* was never caught, some-one else with the same inclinations might think *they* could get away with it too."

Stosh exhaled loudly through his nose and shook his head. "First of all, he *was* caught. At least they thought he was."

"What do you mean?"

"From what I remember, they knew who the guy was and tailed him. He knew he was being watched and ended up in a nuthouse."

"How did they know it was the right guy?"

Stosh arched his back to stretch out tight muscles and then relaxed. "They didn't, for sure. But the attacks stopped when they started the tail."

"Could've been coincidence."

With a shrug, Stosh answered, "Could've been. But that's a big coinci-dence."

"I agree. Did they have any evidence against the guy?"

"Not really. Technical evidence back in those days was virtually nonex-istent. No fingerprints even. They pretty much had to catch somebody in the act."

"So why did they suspect this guy?"

Stosh scratched his head trying to remember. "There was a witness. Some-body thought he saw the guy with a woman before she was murdered. But he was unwilling to testify."

"How come?"

"I don't remember."

"It might be worth checking Stosh. Look at the patterns."

Stosh nodded. "Sure, you just drop out of the academy and then tell us how to do our jobs."

"Stosh, I didn't mean..."

Cutting Spencer off with a wave of his hand that meant don't worry about it, Stosh stood and replied, "Couldn't hurt. I'll see what I can find." He left for the kitchen thinking that somewhere on the shelf he had a book about Jack the Ripper.

* * *

Spencer was thinking about Jack the Ripper when the doorbell rang. Shocked out of his quiet thought, he jumped. Stosh yelled for him to get the door. Half expecting a thick London fog to roll in, Spencer slowly opened the door. It wasn't Jack. It was the mailman. He had a package that was postage-due a quarter. Spencer pulled a wrinkled bill out of his pocket and paid him. As he closed the door, he wondered why these women would continue to walk the streets when they knew there was a madman wandering around. And that madman obviously didn't look threatening, for women were willing to walk into dark alleys with him. It didn't make much sense. He put the box on the TV.

Stosh returned with a beer. He looked at the package, ignored it, and sat back down.

Spencer watched him sit and asked, "Aren't you going to open it?"

"Nope."

"Mind if I ask why not?"

Stosh set down his bottle and gave Spencer a disgusted look. He got up and left the room, returning in less than a minute with an armful of ten boxes similar in size to the one on the TV.

"Here you go. You want to open them, be my guest."

With a confused look, Spencer asked, "Mind explaining?"

"They're ties from Aunt Bessie who is a little... well, confused. She sends me birthday presents that are the ties I used to send to Uncle Ed when he was alive. After three or four, I stopped opening them, but I couldn't bring myself to throw them out."

"For ten years she has sent you ties?"

Pursing his lips and tilting his head back, Stosh answered, "No, probably for five or six years. She can't remember when my birthday is, so they just arrive at odd times, and always postage due. Her postage meter stopped a while back."

"At least she remembers."

Glad to have the conversation changed from business, Stosh nodded and agreed. He dropped the boxes on the floor next to the chair.

Spencer announced that he was having dinner with Rosie and had better be going, but needed to make a pit stop. When he returned, Stosh was opening one of the boxes. It held a wide tie with yellow and olive diagonal stripes.

"Classy," said Spencer with a smirk.

Stosh shot him a hard look and told him to enjoy dinner and not to bother Rosie about business.

Spencer promised he wouldn't. Business was the farthest thing from his mind. He let himself out the front door. As he walked by the front window he saw Stosh reaching down for another tie box.

Chapter 26

Spencer picked up Rosie and pulled up in front of Gibsons Steak House at 7:15. It was the best steakhouse in Chicago. The doorman opened Rosie's door, and one of the parking attendants wheeled the Mustang off to that secret spot where parking attendants find parking. Rush Street was always crowded, especially on a Saturday night, and Gibsons was packed. People were standing outside waiting to get in.

Joining Spencer on the sidewalk, Rosie looked wide-eyed and said, "Spencer, we'll have to wait hours—look at this crowd."

With a laugh, Spencer said, "Do not worry, madam. We have reservations," and started parting the crowd. He took her hand and she followed closely, driven by fear of being swallowed by the crowd.

"How did you get reservations? I heard they don't take reservations," Rosie said in his ear.

Spencer looked over his shoulder and smiled. "Dad had a special table. He and Mom came here at least twice a month."

"Good evening, Spencer," said the hostess. "How nice to see you again. I apologize, your table is not ready, but we have another available. Would you like to wait approximately twenty minutes or be seated now?"

"Another table is fine, Christy. Thanks."

They were led to a table covered with white linen on the far wall and slid into the booth opposite each other.

"Good evening, Mr. Manning. Would you and your guest like a beverage?" the waiter asked as he placed menus on the table and filled the water glasses.

"Sure, Manny. I'll have my usual, and bring us a plate of the mixed appetizers, please. Rosie, what would you like?"

Too busy gawking around the room at the people, Rosie didn't respond.

Spencer touched her arm and she snapped her head back to him. Trying not to laugh, he asked again.

"Oh, chablis, please."

Manny nodded and disappeared.

Spencer took a drink of water. Rosie turned her attention back to the room.

"Spencer! That's the mayor over there!" Her mouth hung open. "We're having dinner with the mayor!"

"Well, not quite, but now you know why our table wasn't ready."

Her mouth dropped open even farther. "You mean the mayor is sitting at your table?"

Spencer nodded with a smile and spread the napkin in his lap. "More like we would be sitting at *his* table."

Rosie frowned. "Kind of awkward, don't you think?"

Spencer slowly shook his head. "No, over and done with. Life moves on, Rosie."

At that moment, the mayor happened to glance in their direction and nodded with a slight smile. Spencer returned the nod and the smile. The nods acknowledged the pain of a past case. The smiles showed that life had moved on.

Manny arrived with the drinks. He placed the chablis in front of Rosie and a bottle of Peroni in front of Spencer. He poured the beer slowly down the side of a fluted glass and said the appetizers would be right up.

"Are you ready to order?"

"I sure am," Spencer said hungrily. "But why don't you bring the display tray for the lady, please."

Rosie started to protest, saying she would just have a small steak, but Spencer insisted.

"My pleasure, Mr. Manning," Manny said with a bow.

"Spencer, I know what I want. He really doesn't have to go to the trouble."

"It's no trouble. And you have to see this." His eyes twinkled. He was obviously enjoying the suspense.

She shrugged. "Okay. You're the man with the special table."

* * *

anny was back in less than a minute, holding a large silver platter in one hand. The platter was filled with steaks. Rosie's eyes opened wide in amazement as Manny started to describe the cuts of meat. Steaks bigger than salad plates draped over each other in luxurious decadence. Manny lovingly pointed to each cut and described them like he was talking about expensive jewelry. He balanced the tray expertly and said he would return in a moment to take their order.

They lifted their glasses and clinked in the center of the table.

Spencer raised his glass a bit and said warmly, "Here's to good friends."

Rosie stopped the glass an inch from her lips, looked disappointed, and said, "Is that all? I was hoping for a bit more than friends."

After a long drink of beer, and with a great deal of poise, Spencer returned, "I did say *good* friends."

Still holding the glass and looking like a sad puppy dog, Rosie slowly and softly said, "I was hoping for a bit more than *that* too."

With raised eyebrows and a smile, Spencer said, "If I had known that, I would have planned somewhere a bit more private."

She took a sip of wine and set the glass down to the right of the plate. Brushing auburn hair from her face, Rosie said with a coy smile, "I don't think this dinner is going to hurt your chances. A very good source tells me the steaks here are wonderful."

"I promise you a steak that will absolutely melt in your mouth."

Rosie dabbed her mouth with the napkin as Manny arrived with a large wicker basket of breads. He explained the three homemade varieties which included apple nut, marble rye, and whole wheat with just a hint of banana.

"May I take your order?" Manny asked.

They both ordered filets, Rosie the ten ounce and Spencer the sixteen with melted blue cheese.

Rosie took a piece of the apple nut bread and, as she was adding whipped butter, asked Spencer if he had any more information about the girl he was looking for. As Rosie listened quietly, sipping wine and making a pig out of herself in the bread basket, Spencer filled her in on what he hadn't covered during their morning run. Manny placed salads on the table during the conversation.

"Do you have any idea why she left Florida?" Rosie asked.

Spencer shrugged. "I'd have to agree with Tim. Probably looking for her sister, but who knows?"

Rosie tried to make Spencer feel better by telling him the same thing Stosh had—if the girl knew he was there and wanted to lose him, she would. She also told him she didn't want someone who treated her to dinners like this sticking his head in dark alleys and made him promise he would be more careful in the future. He promised. She had asked what Spencer planned to do about Laura when Manny arrived with the steaks and the biggest potato Rosie had ever seen. Manny cut it in half and served it on two small plates.

Staring at Spencer's steak, Rosie said, "That's the largest piece of beef I've ever seen. You can't possibly eat all that."

Spencer sliced a piece off an end, put it in his mouth, closed his eyes, and chewed very slowly. Opening his eyes, he declared he was in heaven. "No, I can't eat all of this, but I'm going to give it my best." He waved the knife at her plate and said, "Dig in."

Following Spencer's lead, and expecting something extraordinary, Rosie took a bite of the filet. He was right. It was not possible that food could be this good. They ate and talked a bit about the weekend murders. Rosie didn't have anything to add that Spencer didn't already know.

* * *

Rosie watched Spencer as he slowly savored each bite of steak and wondered if her hints had any effect or were just falling on deaf ears. Lord knows she had been trying long enough. She had been in love with Spencer Manning ever since she knew what love was. They had gone out in groups and had become good friends, continuing activities together, like running, that they had previously done in groups. She had no doubt that he enjoyed her company, but couldn't for the life of her figure out why he showed no deeper interest. She didn't consider herself beautiful, but she was attractive and had many other requests for dates to prove it. They had cooked together, told each other deep, dark secrets, laughed about silly things, and fallen asleep in each other's arms while talking into the wee hours of the morning. She had done everything but jump in his lap, and tonight she was ready to do that.

Spencer finally gave up trying to conquer his steak, and Manny started to clear the dishes.

Asking where the little girl's room was, Rosie slid to the edge of the seat and swung her legs into the room.

"Up the stairs. You'll see it at the top. Take your time looking at the pictures. And see if you can find the mirror."

"What mirror?"

He smiled. "You'll find it. I'll meet you by the pictures."

Rosie left and Spencer paid the bill. Five minutes later he joined her on the second landing of the stairway. Engrossed in the pictures, she didn't notice he was there till he asked, "See anybody you know?"

"My God, Spencer. This is amazing. Is there anyone famous who *isn't* on this wall?"

"Probably not."

"And this mirror!" She spread her hands and pointed with both to the ceiling and a huge mirror in a hand-carved, ornate wooden frame. Turning toward him and wrapping her arms around him, she said, "Thanks for bringing me here, Spencer. I had a wonderful time."

He hugged her back. "Yes, it is wonderful, isn't it?"

She looked up at him, her eyes about six inches lower than his. "So are you."

It was the perfect moment for a kiss but the kiss didn't come.

Trying to keep the confused look off her face, Rosie looked into his eyes. She believed the reason for his reluctance to get involved lay somewhere deep in those eyes, mixed in the cobwebs of the past. He had lost both parents in a car accident, and common sense told Rosie that had to have something to do with the way a person acted. Maybe it was a big part and maybe it was a small part, but it was something Spencer wasn't facing by himself. He needed help, but she had no idea how to go about suggesting that. One thing she knew for sure—his reluctance wasn't because of her. She wanted to scream at him that she loved him and had for years, but knew that wouldn't work either. So she would continue to drop hints and slowly try to wear away the wall Spencer had around him. It might take time and it might never happen, but she had plenty of time and it was worth a try. She had nothing to lose and plenty to gain. And if this was all she got, she had a wonderful friend to share life with.

Rosie oohed and aahed over autographed celebrity pictures, including Tony Bennett and Ron Santo, and then they headed for the door. There was no longer anyone standing outside, but about twenty people were still waiting for a table. It was 10:25.

Chapter 27

The city lights washed out everything in the sky except for a half moon that hung above the western horizon like a slice of orange. The temperature was in the low forties and Laura was chilly. She wrapped her arms around her chest to try and keep in some warmth. She had spent the last hour avoiding police cars. At a quarter to eleven, she decided it was too cold to stay out on the street.

On the way back to her apartment, she sympathized with the women who tried to make a living at this. It was hard enough to start with. But throw in the fact that some deranged maniac was roaming the streets and the cops were out in droves trying to catch him, and business got much riskier. The *johns* knew the cops were out in bigger numbers and patrolling more heavily, so they stayed away. Maybe that would stop the murders. No tricks, no reason to be on the streets, nobody for the guy to kill.

As she turned onto Wilson, Laura thought about Naples and longed for the warmth of Florida. But the problem that had sent her north was still there.

As she turned into her doorway, Laura watched the moon disappear behind a blanket of clouds.

Chapter 28

The doorman held the passenger door open for Rosie, who held onto the roof of the car and gently lowered herself into the baby-blue Mustang. Spencer paid for the service and headed north on Rush Street, which was packed with Saturday-night traffic, everyone going nowhere fast and not seeming to mind.

Without considering where he was going, Spencer drove north and turned onto Lakeshore Drive.

Rosie moved her hand to Spencer's leg and asked, "We going somewhere in particular?"

"Just thought a drive along the lake would be nice."

It was, but Rosie knew there was more to it than that. She wasn't sure what drove Spencer emotionally, but she knew in the rest of his life there was little wasted effort. When he exited at Belmont, she asked if he wanted some help.

"With what?"

"Looking for Laura. Four eyes are better than two and you're supposed to be driving."

Spencer turned right onto Broadway and drove slowly down the tunnel of neon lights. As he headed north, he described Laura to Rosie. He also wondered if she was smart enough to figure out that he was thinking about Laura or if he was that obvious. Probably both. He pointed out the spot where she had stood and the alley where she had disappeared. People in all stages of drunkenness filled the sidewalks, but there was no Laura. After the third pass of a six-block area, Spencer turned onto Wilson and headed for her apartment.

A half block from the apartment, Spencer spotted Laura walking home. He pointed her out to Rosie and pulled into an open spot next to a hydrant where he could see the rest of the block. She turned into her building and disappeared inside.

"Do you feel better now?" asked Rosie.

Taking a deep breath, Spencer responded with relief, "Yeah. I was worried someone would find her in a dumpster somewhere."

"Well, thankfully that didn't happen. But you know Spencer, even if it had, it wouldn't be your fault."

"No?"

"No. Now let's go home. My place or yours?"

He looked at her with surprise. "Not both?"

"No, not both." She twisted sideways and gave him a coy smile.

He gave in. "Mine." He pulled away from the curb. As they passed Laura's apartment building, Spencer gently placed his right hand on Rosie's leg and said, "You know, I'd hate to ruin a good friendship."

"Ruin how?" she asked innocently. She knew what he meant, but wanted to tease him.

Not wanting to wrongfully assume what Rosie had in mind, Spencer answered noncommittally. "You know, doing things that are, well, beyond the things friends do." He turned onto Halsted and headed south.

"And those would be?"

"Jesus, Rosie!"

She laughed. "It's okay, Spencer. I'm just teasing. We can do or not do whatever you like. I think it would be nice to spend the night with you. We can talk and fall asleep on the couch if you like."

They sat in silence for a few minutes as Spencer drove through the crowded streets.

"Would you like to do more?" he asked as he stopped for a red light. He looked straight ahead.

Rosie touched his arm and said, "I would like whatever you feel comfortable with."

"That doesn't answer my question." He slowly pulled away from the light.

"I've wanted to do more for years."

Chapter 29

Stretch had been following Laura and saw the Mustang park and then leave after she entered the apartment building. He went up to the second floor room across the street and let himself in. The shift man, a skinny, balding runt named Rico, looked up from his chair with sleepy eyes.

Stretch looked over the log. "You see the notice about the Mustang?" he asked irritably. A page with large print, directing the men to watch for a baby-blue Mustang with Spencer's plates, was taped to the wall next to the window.

Rico shrugged. "Sure."

There were two times noted in the log—when Laura left and returned. "No Mustang?"

Rico shrugged again, pursed his lips, and shook his head sideways.

Stretch calmly pulled a roll of bills out of his pocket, peeled off a few, and dropped them in Rico's lap.

"What's that?"

"That's your pay. Get the hell out."

"What for? My shift's not done." Rico said with a sneer.

"It is now." He thumbed toward the door.

"What the hell for?" Rico asked belligerently. "I did my job."

"Your job is to watch the street. A couple minutes ago that blue Mustang drove by so slow you could have counted the dents." He glanced at the money in Rico's lap. "If you don't want the money, I'll take it back. One way or the other, you're leaving."

Rico stared at Stretch for a few seconds and knew he was done. He folded the bills and tucked them in his pocket. As he got up and started walking toward the door, he said under his breath, "Maybe the lady would like to know that you're watching her all the time."

Without a blink or a second to think about it, Stretch responded coolly, "Maybe you'd like to try walking on your hands."

Rico left the apartment without looking back. He didn't mean anything by his threat. He just wanted the last word. But despite his bravado, he had the feeling Stretch *did* mean what he had said.

The last word belonged to Stretch.

Chapter 30

Stosh woke up about four o'clock Sunday morning to what in his dream was a gunshot. In reality, it was a clap of thunder. In his dream, he was running through a dark, foggy alley toward a woman's scream. Hazy yellow light from the end of the alley filtered through the fog like smoke through a veil. No matter how much he ran, Stosh never seemed to get closer to the scream, but for a second the fog cleared and the light sparkled off a shiny steel blade held in an upraised hand. As the hand lowered, Stosh raised his pistol and fired. At that moment he woke up, sweating and breathing hard, as if he had actually run down the alley.

Taking several deep breaths, Stosh wiped sweat off his forehead and sat in the quiet of his living room. The only sound was rain falling softly on the roof. His breathing was returning to normal when a bolt of lightning lit up the western sky, followed about three seconds later by another crack of thunder. The storm was moving toward the lake, and Stosh knew the rain would soon intensify. He looked at the picture on the credenza under the window and thought back to nights when he and Francie would lie in bed, wrapped in each other's arms, and fall asleep to the gentle patter of the rain. The feeling of loss that now kept him out of that bed started to wash over him like a river over a sand bar, lifting from here and shifting to there, leaving him with a confusion of emotions that surfaced at the oddest times, seemingly out of nowhere.

Whether it was because of the dream or the afternoon nap, he was wide awake. Another bolt, followed immediately by thunder, brought Stosh back to the alley and thoughts of Jack the Ripper. The rain suddenly fell in a torrent as he got up to search through his books. In the middle of the third shelf, he found *Famous Unsolved Crimes*, slid it out, and blew dust off the top. He ran his finger along the front edge of the shelf, and thought of all the little things that Francie had done that he had taken for granted. It was the first time he had ever found dust on his books.

Stosh shuffled back to the chair as the rain drove into the picture window. It took him less than an hour to read the chapter on Jack. There was no mention of any coins.

Memory had served Stosh fairly well. Five murders within a ten-week window had been committed in a poverty-stricken area of London known as White Chapel. They all had been low-end prostitutes, willing to sell themselves for only a few pennies. All but one had been mutilated, some more than others. One had been lucky and only her throat had been cut. The girl found by the owner of the laundry was fairly neat compared to one of the victims of Jack the Ripper.

The London police did have a suspect—a Polish Jew by the name of Kosminski. Another Jew by the name of Israel Schwartz had seen Kosminski struggling with Elizabeth Stride, the third victim. Schwartz had run away. He later said he'd seen Kosminski. After the fifth murder, Kosminski had been arrested, but couldn't be held because Schwartz had been unwilling to testify against a fellow Jew and had not seen the actual murder. Kosminski had been released into the custody of his brother and had been continuously tailed. Following that, the murders stopped. Kosminski was later committed to a mental institution.

Stosh noted that the London police had run into the same problem *they* were confronting—how do you keep the women off the streets? The women had kept going back out because it was either earn a few pennies or starve. There was a greater chance of dying if they *hadn't* gone out at night.

He closed the dog-eared book and leaned his chair back. He hadn't read anything that would help, but he would ask for a check on Jack the Ripper copycats. The main part of the storm had moved through, and the rain was now falling gently as the sky turned from black to gray. Lacing his hands behind his head, Stosh let the drumming of the rain on the roof lull him back to sleep.

Chapter 31

Spencer squeezed his eyes tight and then opened them wide. When he realized the ring was the phone, his first thought was *who the hell is calling me at this hour on a Sunday morning*. Then he glanced at the clock and saw it was almost ten. He answered the second ring with a sleepy hello.

"Morning Spencer, it's Ben."

"Hey. I'll call you back." He quietly hung up the phone.

Rosie was still asleep, her body half wrapped in the sheet and her reddish-brown hair sprawled across the pillow. She looked soft and lovely. Rosie stirred as Spencer got out of bed, but she just burrowed deeper into the pillow.

Grabbing a pair of shorts, Spencer headed for the kitchen, poured a glass of orange juice, and then dialed Ben.

"Hello, Spencer. Hope I'm not interrupting anything."

"Nope. What's up, Ben?"

"I read the story about the girl in the alley and was wondering if you've learned anything about Laura."

Spencer gave him a brief overview, including Laura's real name and home.

"Think we should call the parents?"

"You can do as you please. I'm going to watch her a little more. Something about it is odd, but I'm not sure what's going on. And she *is* twenty-four, Ben. Old enough to do what she wants."

"Yeah, but what she's doing might get her killed."

"Ben, the bottom line is, that's her choice. You could say the same about me."

"Jesus, Spencer, why don't they stay off the streets with this nut out there? It's insane."

"Because they have to earn a living. If there was some guy targeting lawyers, would you stay out of court?"

"Well, no, but that's different."

Spencer rinsed out his glass and placed it on the edge of the sink with a few other dirty dishes. "Not much different at all, Ben."

"It *is* different. I have to go into court to do my job."

"And where do streetwalkers go to do theirs?"

"They don't..."

Spencer cut him off. "Hey, it's Sunday, day of peace and rest. I'm just playing devil's advocate. You figure out a way of keeping them off the streets and the Chicago police force will pin a medal on you." Out of the corner of his eye, Spencer saw Rosie walk into the kitchen wearing one of his sweatshirts. "Gotta go, Ben. I'll let you know if I find anything."

"Thanks."

"Welcome." He hung up the phone and smiled at Rosie. "Good morning. You look..."

"Gee, thanks. That bad, huh?"

"No. That good." He wrapped his arms around her and pulled her close. "Just couldn't find a word good enough."

Rosie pulled her head away from his shoulder. "Are you crazy? I can imagine what I look like flopping around in your sweatshirt. I..."

Spencer kissed her, and then picked her up and carried her back into the bedroom.

Chapter 32

On the drive north Monday morning, Charles Lamb thought about which project he would do first. He had trouble deciding because it really didn't matter; they would all be done at some point and there was no urgency to any of them. But as he drove and absently glanced at the sun rising above the calm surface of the lake, he found himself thinking of Amanda's office. That was where he wanted to be; the rich woods, the thick carpet that absorbed even his heavy footsteps, and the view of the lake out the large picture window had been in his thoughts many times over the weekend. He felt very peaceful in her office.

Traffic was light and Charles had left early to avoid having to talk to Sarah. He left while she was still in the shower. It was 8:10 a.m. and he was not due until nine. Leaving the car at the end of the driveway, he made his way to the beach and slowly walked to the water's edge, leaving large footprints in the wet sand. The only vessel visible through the bright glare was a small sailboat slowly heading south.

Charles took several deep breaths of the cool, fishy air and looked around for a place to sit. Twenty feet to the north, the sand narrowed into a ledge made of granite boulders and limestone slabs that stretched for two hundred feet. Charles headed toward the rocks. On the side of the rocks was a chain link fence and trees that hid the ledge from the houses beyond. Climbing the rocks, he neared the fence and noticed a shabby-looking man lying on a small patch of grass behind the rocks. The man was asleep but was tightly clutching a black, plastic garbage bag that was wedged in between him and the rock. Charles hadn't seen him until he stood at the edge of the last slab.

Charles peered into one of many deep cracks between rocks and couldn't see to the bottom.

He climbed back down to the sand, carefully picking his steps. Sitting on the rock nearest the water, Charles tilted his face back into the sun and let the waves gently lap against the tips of his shoes.

A pigeon landed nearby, and Charles lost himself in watching the bird peck about for food. The time went by quickly. Reluctantly, he stood, brushed sand off the seat of his trousers and headed for the house. As he walked, he decided he would come back to the rocks to eat his lunch and wondered if the bum lying behind the rocks would still be there.

Not wanting to just barge in, Charles chose not to use his key and rang the doorbell. Amanda answered the door herself, explaining that Margaret was sick and would come on Wednesday if she felt better. She wore a baggy sweatshirt and her hair was pulled back in a pony tail. Apologizing for the way she looked, she led Charles to the kitchen and offered coffee. He declined, telling her she looked just fine. Actually, he thought she looked a lot better than just fine; he had to make a conscious effort to keep from staring at her.

As Amanda poured herself a cup of coffee and stirred in cream, which she added from a tiny ceramic pitcher, she asked, "What would you like to start on this morning?"

Charles hemmed and hawed a bit like a kid who knew what he wanted but was afraid to ask because he might not get it. Pretending that it really made no difference, Charles answered, "Well, I guess I might as well start with the office upstairs." He fidgeted with the back of the wooden chair he was standing next to as he waited for an answer. When Amanda didn't quickly agree, he added, "You know, replace the molding and the baseboard." When she still didn't answer, he wondered if he had said something wrong and asked if he had.

Amanda took a sip of coffee and answered. "Oh no. I'm sorry. I was just thinking about what I have to do. If you feel comfortable starting there, I can arrange it. But you see, Monday morning is when I settle my accounts from the week before and arrange my appointments for the next week. It's pretty silly, but I'm a creature of habit. I really could wait if you want to work in there."

She paused, taking another sip, and looked up at Charles who seemed nervous. Still wondering why this beautiful woman was being so nice to him, he finally stammered that he could start anywhere, and that the kitchen might be a good spot.

Amanda agreed and said that would be fine.

They chatted for a few minutes about the work in the kitchen. As she refilled her cup, she told Charles to help himself to sandwich meat and rolls for lunch. Cradling the cup in her hands, Amanda took a sip, wished Charles luck, and headed upstairs. Charles watched her walk until she turned the corner at the landing on the stairs, looking longingly at the curve of her jeans. When she disappeared, he turned to the cupboards and thought about his work plan. They had decided that he would remove the old cupboards. Then, when the walls were bare, they would make some drawings and talk about the new cabinets.

As Charles carefully emptied the cupboards, he wondered about what Amanda did for a living. It was obviously something important. This house was old but it was worth a lot of money. Remembering that she had mentioned working on her accounts, he wondered if she was some type of accountant like Sarah. Amanda certainly made more money than Sarah, but Sarah worked for a company and Amanda worked for herself. Charles knew that people who had the initiative to start their own business could make much more money. Sarah worked hard, but she had no initiative. She wouldn't be able to start her own company. They managed to get by, but they could be doing much better if she had initiative. Amanda obviously did, and she attracted important people.

Charles thought back to the man in the limo and decided that, yes, Amanda had all the initiative she needed.

Chapter 33

Staring into the glare of the sun, Spencer pulled into the parking lot next to the Greendale station house. He planned to get to Wrigley Field about noon and meet a friend for the Cubs/Dodgers game at one-thirty. But first he wanted to stop and ask Stosh if he had read up on Jack. It was a silly idea but something about it was gnawing at him.

"So what brings you to the palace?" asked Stosh, as he thumbed through manila folders and slid one of the files he was holding into a drawer.

"On my way to Wrigley and thought I'd see if you had read about Jack."

Stosh continued to file. Spencer watched.

"So?" Spencer asked.

"So what?"

"So, did you read the book? And why do I have to ask twice?"

"Yes. And you didn't ask twice." He looked at Spencer with raised eyebrows and a look that left Spencer feeling he had missed something.

"Yes, I did. I said I stopped in here to see if you had read about Jack."

"Right. At least your memory is better than your grammar skills. That is a statement, not a question."

"Jesus. Your day isn't hard enough without giving *me* a hard time?"

Stosh smiled and closed the drawer. "Giving you a hard time is what helps me get through my hard day."

"Great. Glad to help. What about Jack?"

"Nothing. At least nothing helpful. Both target prostitutes and both like to use a knife. Other than that there are no similarities. And no clues." He shrugged and rolled a pencil across his desk.

"Did they catch him?"

Stosh shook his head. "Not officially. Like I told you, there was this fellow, Kosminski, who was a good suspect—hated women, especially prostitutes. The police arrested him but couldn't hold him. But they were sure it was him and stayed on his tail. He ended up in a nuthouse. And like I told you, as soon as they started watching him the murders stopped."

Spencer thought for a few seconds. "Did the book say why he hated prostitutes?"

"Nope."

"I wonder why. I think we can assume the new guy hates them also. Look for someone with a reason."

Stosh laughed. "Thanks. That narrows it down to thousands who don't like prostitutes."

"Not *don't like*. Hate—enough to kill. Something happened to this guy that's making him do this."

Stosh nodded. "Okay, makes sense. I'll put somebody on records."

Spencer replied, "Hopefully he *has* a record."

Stosh slowly let out a deep breath. "He doesn't."

Spencer's eyes opened wide. "And how do you know that?"

"There's a good print on one of the coins. The guy's not in the system, or it's somebody else's print."

"Bad break. Mind if I borrow the book?"

Smiling again, Stosh pointed to his basket. "Be my guest."

Spencer picked up the book and thumbed through it.

"I hope you have better luck than I did," said Stosh.

"Thanks. I'll take good care of it. Wanna join us at Wrigley?"

"Some of us have to work for a living. Us? What's her name?"

"Not a *her*." Knowing Stosh would wish he could get away, Spencer added, "I'm meeting Donald. You know, just soak up some sun, drink a few beers, and watch over-priced outfielders drop fly balls. See you later." He turned and started out, knowing Stosh couldn't let it lie.

"Hey, Spencer, what time's the game?"

Spencer laughed. "One-thirty, you're screwed." He waved over his shoulder with a big grin and enjoyed leaving Stosh frustrated. Stosh was a huge Sherlock Holmes fan and Donald Starre was president of the Chicago chapter of the Sherlock Holmes Society.

"Say hi to Donald. Give him my best."

"Will do."

Chapter 34

Charles spent most of the morning emptying the cabinets. He was extra careful with a cabinet full of fragile cups and saucers, some of which looked like antiques. He studied the patterns on the sides, thinking that he had never seen anything so beautiful, and carried them gently to the dining room table. He placed them in the middle so there would be no chance of them falling off. Shortly before noon, he decided to stop for lunch and started up the stairs to see if Amanda wanted to join him.

The thick, rich carpet sunk under Charles' heavy footsteps as he slowly and quietly moved up the stairs. He thought he would like to walk barefoot on this carpet. Turning left at the top of the stairs, he walked down the hall to the office and looked in. Amanda wasn't in the room. Charles stood in the doorway and admired the view of the lake through the large picture window. He was a few steps into the room before he saw the ledger book lying open on the desk. He glanced down the hall. Seeing and hearing no one, he walked over to the desk.

The pages were filled with names and phone numbers. Beneath each name were single words like leather, nurse, cop, and others. Charles lovingly ran his hand over the carved edge of the desk top. He never heard Amanda come up behind him.

"Pretty, huh."

Charles jumped and looked startled.

Amanda asked if he needed something.

"Yes. I'm sorry to bother you. I just wanted to let you know I was stopping for lunch and to see if you wanted to join me."

"Thanks, Charles, that's sweet." She touched his arm. "I'm going to work for a while more. Why don't you make something and take it out on the beach. It looks like a gorgeous day."

He said he would. As he walked away, he felt his heart pounding and wondered if it was from the scare or the touch on his arm. When he got to the stairs, his thoughts changed to what he had seen in the ledger. Remembering the black limo, Charles thought about what the words might mean. He didn't want to think Miss Amanda might be a prostitute. There must be another explanation, but he couldn't think of it.

The hot, noon sun was cooled a bit by a gentle breeze off the lake. Charles scuffed through the sand over to the rocks and set his plate and glass on a flat spot on top of a greenish boulder flecked with bits of black. The bum was no longer around. Probably out looking for cans, Charles thought.

Chapter 35

With his glove tucked under his arm, Don was waiting when Spencer got to the ticket booth at the front of Wrigley Field.

After finding their seats in the right field bleachers, Spencer scanned the park while Don looked for a beer man. When he was a kid, Spencer and his dad had come to the park a couple times a month. They had seats in a reserved box, but Spencer's best memories were of days spent in the bleachers. The ivy-covered walls and the perfectly manicured field were best admired from the cheap seats. And if you listened carefully, and the wind was blowing just right, you could just barely hear the cheers of every Cubs fan who had ever slapped his buddy on the back and uttered those famous words, "We'll get 'em next year."

Don passed Spencer a beer.

"Stosh sends his regards," Spencer said, "and his regrets that he couldn't join us." After the grilling Don got when they were last together, Spencer thought Don had no regrets.

"Well, say hello. He certainly is a colorful character."

"Yes, he is that. But beneath that bluster is a heart of gold."

"And the man knows his Holmes. I've been meaning to call and get him to come to one of the meetings."

"Yeah, that's just what you need." Hearing a yell of "hot dogs", Spencer turned and saw the hot dog vendor in the next section above them. He waved. The man nodded. Spencer waited for him to make his way down the aisle. Coming to Wrigley Field wasn't about winning or losing, it was about hot dogs and ivy on the walls of one of the last ball parks in the country that had any character. Spencer snapped back to Don in mid-conversation.

"I think he'd make a great guest speaker with all the stories he has to tell. Sometimes we bury our faces too far in the books. A dose of real life is good once in a while."

"I'm sure he'd love to come," Spencer responded with one eye up the aisle. "But you'd have a hard time getting him to stop."

Don laughed as he watched the outfielders warming up playing catch. "That's preferable to the hard time I have getting speakers." As the players started to trot off the field, the right fielder turned and tossed the ball up into the bleachers.

"Now that's baseball," Don said.

"Yup," Spencer agreed as he reached into his pocket for money. The hot dog man had arrived. Spencer held up two fingers. The grizzled man with one eye half shut tossed two dogs down the row.

As he took a bite and savored the taste, Spencer said, "Nothing better."

"Agreed," responded Don as he unwrapped his dog. He took a bite and asked Spencer what he knew about the prostitute murders.

Wiping mustard from the corner of his mouth, Spencer said, "Not a whole lot more than you if you've been reading the papers."

"But a little more?" Don teased with a glimmer in his eye.

"A little."

"Do I have to beg?"

"No. I'd like your thoughts on a theory of mine. It crossed my mind that these killings are reminiscent of Jack the Ripper. I mentioned it to Stosh and he didn't think much of it."

Don nodded. "I agree. I thought the same thing. But there are a lot of sick people in this world who don't need a mentor to do something like this."

"Unfortunately, that's true," mumbled Spencer through his last bite of hot dog. He washed it down with cold beer and continued. "But I had Stosh check anyway. He has a book about Jack the Ripper. He read it and didn't find anything pertinent. He tells me they never officially arrested anyone but thought they knew who it was."

Don leaned forward. "I don't remember anything that would have fit here other than the method and the victims."

The public address announcer started in on the lineups. Don and Spencer both got out scorecards and pencils and filled in the players.

"You going to read the book?" Don asked.

"I have it in the car; I'll read it tonight. Probably a waste of time, but I'll know more about Jack the Ripper, if nothing else."

Don leaned back and dropped the pencil in his shirt pocket. "So what do you know that I don't?"

Spencer told Don about the piles of coins.

Don's eyes immediately lit up. "How many coins were there?"

Spencer shrugged. "Don't know."

"What coins were they? Any pattern?"

"All I know is there were piles of coins left by the bodies in some sort of pattern. I hinted at the pattern and Stosh clammed up. Why? Does that have something to do with Jack the Ripper?"

Sitting straight up in the chair, Don vigorously shook his head. "Not that I know of, but it does with Sherlock Holmes."

Spencer was catching Don's excitement. "Was there a story about coins?"

"No. But what do you know about the history of Arthur Conan Doyle?"

As the Cubs ran out onto the field, Spencer pursed his lips and answered, "I know he was a medical student and Dr. Watson was based on his experiences to some extent. And Doyle believed in fairies, didn't he?"

Don laughed. "Well, he was a spiritualist, but we'll forgive him for that foray. Yes, Dr. Watson was based on his medical school experiences, but so was Sherlock Holmes."

When Spencer looked puzzled, Don continued. "Conan Doyle had a professor of surgery named Dr. Joseph Bell. He was a strange old fellow who had the magical knack of making deductions from seemingly meaningless bits of information, such as where you'd been by the color of the dirt on your shoes."

"Really? Just like Sherlock Holmes."

Don laughed again and slapped Spencer's knee. "Really. But the accurate statement would be that Sherlock Holmes was just like Bell."

"I suppose so. But how does that relate to the coins?"

"Dr. Bell had a case involving someone who killed people, prostitutes included, with poison."

"How does that apply here?"

"This fellow left a pile of coins next to each victim. So you put Doyle together with Jack and you have someone copying history."

"And mixing it up."

"Not necessarily. Perhaps just picking his favorite parts. It would help to know what the pattern is."

"Was there a pattern with Doyle?"

"Not that I recall. But it seems your fellow is adding his own personal touches. Understanding the method tells you a lot about the person."

Spencer watched a long fly to center end the top of the first inning and said, "I wonder if Stosh knows about that."

"Perhaps not," said Don after swallowing the last bite of his hot dog. "You can know a lot about Sherlock Holmes and not much about Doyle."

Spencer made a mental note to ask. More dogs, two more beers, and a Cubs' two-run homer for a win in the ninth made for a great day at the ballpark.

Chapter 36

By the end of the afternoon, Charles had removed all the old cabinets and moved them out into the garage. Amanda came down for a cup of tea just before five and asked how much she owed him. He counted nine hours, minus one for lunch, and slowly figured it out in his head. One hundred and sixty dollars. Sarah would be shocked.

The hell with Sarah.

Amanda dropped a tea bag into a cup of hot water. "Hang on, I'll get it for you."

"Would you mind putting it in an envelope?"

"No problem." She smiled and headed up the stairs.

While he worked, Charles had thought about where to hide the money. He had decided that nowhere inside the house was safe. He had taken a plastic baggie and stuffed it in his right pants pocket. The money would go in the baggie, and he would find a spot under a bush, at least till he could think of something better.

Amanda returned with a white envelope full of money and handed it to Charles. He folded it in half and stuffed that in his pocket, also.

"Aren't you going to count it?" She pulled the tea bag out of the cup and tossed it into the garbage.

Charles looked surprised. "Oh no. That's no problem. I know you counted it."

"You're a nice man, Mister Lamb. But you shouldn't always be so trusting." When she saw how nervous he was, she changed the subject. "Well, we're ready to think about new cabinets, I see. I'll draw a layout tonight and think about what I want. Something brighter and maybe glass fronts. Tomorrow morning we can go to the home center and see if I fall in love with anything."

"Anything you say, Miss Amanda. I'll be here first thing."

"Oh, I won't be here till about ten, so just let yourself in. I'll leave the drawing on the table and you can look it over."

"Okay, Miss Amanda."

* * *

Amanda watched him back out of the driveway and slowly maneuver between the parked cars. And she wondered, with all the jerks she dealt with, how she had met such a nice man.

* * *

Traffic wasn't bad going home and Charles made good time. He thought more about the words in the ledger and realized his hands were clenching the steering wheel and his knuckles were white. But it didn't make sense. Miss Amanda was one of the nicest women he had ever met. She couldn't be a prostitute.

This was what bothered Charles more than anything in life. No matter how much he thought about some things, he just couldn't figure them out. That was why Sarah had the advantage over him. She was smart enough to see right through him. And he couldn't see through her. Well, this time he would fool her. He would hide the money where she wouldn't even *think* of looking.

He parked on the pad next to the driveway. Sarah's car was already in the one-car garage. He sat in the car for a few minutes, looking at the bushes, trying to find a good spot. The waist-high evergreens on the south side of the garage looked to be as good a spot as any. He would just push the envelope down beneath the dense boughs, and it would be protected from the rain inside the plastic baggie. He walked around to the side of the garage and picked a spot in the center of the row.

* * *

Sarah had heard the low rumble of the muffler as Charles came up the street. She stood behind a curtain in the living room and wondered why he was sitting in the car. She saw him get out and stare at the house and wondered what he was doing. Then he disappeared around the side of the garage.

* * *

Charles needed a marker so he could find the baggie again. He looked around and saw a rock the size of a softball half-buried in front of the bushes. The branches scratched his arm as he stretched into the bush up to his shoulder and placed the money as far into the bushes as he could reach. Then he stood back and tried to find the baggie. He couldn't. It had disappeared.

* * *

Sitting in his tree house, Jimmy heard the car pull into the driveway and ducked down. He wondered why Mr. Lamb was looking around the house and watched between the boards as Charles pushed a plastic bag into the bushes. Jimmy glanced at his watch and made an entry in his book.

Chapter 37

Sarah was waiting for Charles in the kitchen when he came in the back door, but he didn't know she had seen him. It looked like she was rinsing the breakfast dishes. It wasn't something Sarah usually did. Usually she yelled at *him* for not doing it. It was his job after all, as were most of the chores around the house. As she often pointed out, she was the breadwinner in the family.

He tried to slip through the back hall without her seeing him, but didn't make it.

"I heard you pull in the drive."

"Oh, hi. Yeah, it needs a new muffler."

"Hmm. That was five minutes ago. What were you doing?" She started calmly putting dishes in the washer.

Charles was stumped. He didn't think he'd need a lie. "Well, I, uh, was checking out the muffler. Wanted to make sure it wasn't falling off or something."

She nodded. "Around the side of the garage?"

She had seen him. But she wouldn't have seen him by the bushes. So she didn't know about the money. "I went to talk to Jimmy."

"Jimmy? Since when do you care about Jimmy?"

"I talk to Jimmy sometimes."

She turned to face him, a dinner plate in her right hand. Charles stared at the plate. "So if I go talk to Jimmy he's going to tell me you two had a nice chat?"

Charles' palms turned sweaty and a cold chill ran up his back. He wasn't used to this many lies in a row.

"I, uh, didn't see him. He wasn't there."

Her eyes burned a hole right through him. "You went to talk to Jimmy even though he wasn't there."

It sounded pretty silly coming out of Sarah's mouth. "I thought I saw him, you know, up in his tree house. But he wasn't there." He wondered if he needed to keep talking, but she looked like she wasn't listening anymore. Charles turned and walked quickly down the hall. Sarah didn't yell or throw anything. He would have rather that she did. She knew he was up to something and he knew she would do something. But he had no idea what. He was sure of one thing, though. If she walked around the side of the garage she wouldn't find the money. Unless you knew where to look, the baggie was safe.

Sarah noticed Charles' left arm and let him walk away without asking about the scratches.

* * *

Jimmy looked into the kitchen window and saw Mrs. Lamb at the sink. After Mr. Lamb went inside, she looked like she was talking to someone. It must have been Mr. Lamb. He watched for a minute after she moved away from the sink and then he climbed out of the tree.

Walking directly toward the spot in the bushes where Mr. Lamb had stuffed something, Jimmy tingled with excitement. He stood in front of the bushes, but couldn't see anything. When he parted the low branches at the front, he saw part of a plastic bag. But his arm wasn't long enough; he couldn't reach it from the edge of the bushes. He looked around for a stick but saw none. He had to hurry. Mr. Lamb might be back. Jimmy stepped into the bushes, almost tripped on a branch, and again parted the branches. There was a plastic baggie with a white envelope inside. Jimmy opened the baggie, carefully holding it only at the top, pulled out the envelope, and let the baggie drop to the top of the bushes. He opened the envelope and froze with his mouth half open. Inside the envelope was more money than Jimmy had ever seen.

Jimmy thought of taking the money. Mr. Lamb would never know who took it. If Mr. Lamb was hiding it, he wouldn't want anyone to know about it, so if it was gone he couldn't say anything. But why was Mr. Lamb hiding it there? If Jimmy had gotten some money and wanted to buy something, he spent the money. But if there was nothing he wanted, he saved the money in his football bank. Maybe this was Mr. Lamb's bank. And that would mean he would be putting in more money.

Sliding the money back in the envelope, Jimmy put it back in the baggie and put the baggie back in the bushes. He would leave it there, but tomorrow he'd be watching.

Chapter 38

Spencer got home at 6:30, ordered a pizza, took a shower, opened a bottle of Schlitz, and started reading the chapter on Jack the Ripper. By nine, he was on his second bottle and trying to decide whether or not to eat the last three pieces of pepperoni, even though he was stuffed. He was halfway through the chapter for the second time.

The first time through had yielded nothing that helped. But Spencer was still hopeful and decided to read it again. When he was done, he admitted grudgingly that Stosh was right. There was nothing of use in it.

He leaned back in the chair to think and fell asleep within minutes, having succumbed to the sun and the beer.

* * *

Tuesday morning, Spencer stood beneath the shower head trying to massage out the kinks from sleeping in the chair. When he moved into his parent's house, he replaced the old shower head with a new-fangled sprayer that had six settings guaranteed to send you to shower heaven.

As he was drying off, the phone rang. Stosh's booming baritone voice filled the receiver.

"Hey kid, so you find anything?"

"Find anything?"

"Listen, I know you read the book. I was hopin' you'd find somethin' I didn't, cuz I could sure use a break here."

"I didn't, but I'm wondering what the pattern is to the coins."

"And you think I'm going to tell you?"

"Well, kinda hard to solve your crimes with one hand tied behind my back."

Spencer had set the cordless phone on the counter and could still hear as he finished drying.

"Spencer? Spencer!"

"Sorry. I was in the middle of something."

"Are you done?"

"Yup. All dried off."

"Got time to talk to me now?"

"Sure. I won't bother to put a robe on, you being family."

The phone clicked and went dead. Stosh was the only person Spencer knew who could give you the finger over the phone and get his point across. But he was right. If Spencer had found something, he would have called before this and Stosh knew it. He didn't have to wait for an answer. Spencer tightened the towel around his waist and thought about Jack as he poured a glass of orange juice. He still didn't want to give up on the Jack angle, but he couldn't tell Stosh that. As far as Stosh was concerned, it was a dead issue. But he did want to tell him about the coins and Arthur Conan Doyle.

Using the orange juice to wash down a piece of cold pizza, Spencer called Don, who answered on the sixth ring.

"Hi, P.I. You solve the murders yet?"

"No. Dead end. But there's still something bothering me about it."

"Could be just a coincidence, Spencer."

"A coincidence that this guy leaves a pile of coins? Not exactly something that makes any sense. Who the hell would think of that by himself?"

"I agree. But whether or not it is a coincidence, it's an ironic statement."

"Meaning?"

"Meaning, he leaves money for women who risked their lives for a few dollars."

Spencer thought and let the silence hang like a bank of fog. "That's really sad, and weird. I gotta believe he copied the coin thing. If he did, maybe he copied Jack the Ripper, too."

"Maybe."

"But there's no thread that ties the two together. I hoped I'd find something with the Friday killings, but Jack was pretty random. And two were on the same night."

"So, maybe that's the wrong thread."

"And maybe this is damned silly."

"Did you call for advice or to entertain me while you beat yourself up?"

Spencer shook his head. "Point taken."

"As long as you have nothing to lose, I'd go with your hunch. Give it another shot. If there's something there, you'll find it."

"Well, if I don't, would you mind reading it?"

"No problem. But I'm in the middle of writing a book about the Holmes Society for our fiftieth anniversary. I'd appreciate it if you'd find it yourself."

Spencer laughed. "Doing my best."

"You tell Stosh about the coins yet?"

"Uh, no. We talked but he didn't give me the chance. I'll call him later. I'll let you know if I get something."

"Right. Good hunting."

"Thanks."

Chapter 39

As usual, Sarah left an hour before Charles. He waited for ten minutes after she had left and then went outside to make sure the baggie was still there. He had woken up several times during the night worrying about it. He panicked when he didn't see it right away, but then found it after spreading apart several branches. It would be very safe if even *he* couldn't find it. He was very proud of himself for finding the perfect hiding place.

Charles ate a bowl of cereal and dressed for work. He had planned to get to work early and spend more time on the beach, but it was overcast and looked like rain.

Whistling along with the radio, Charles felt in control of the situation. He had outsmarted Sarah for the first time. She had always seen through his lies before. But this time she had no idea and he wanted to keep it that way. He drove up Lake Shore Drive, watching the clouds piling up over the lake. He turned onto Amanda's street and pulled into the drive a little before nine. He never noticed the car that had been following him since he left home.

* * *

Sarah parked a few houses down from where Charles was parked. From there she watched as he got out and rang the side doorbell. After a minute, he reached in his pocket, pulled out a key, and let himself in.

About ten after nine, a jeep pulled into the drive behind Charles' beat-up Chevy. A very attractive woman got out. She was dressed in a fancy white gown and was carrying a small bag. She also let herself into the house. Sarah was more shocked than angry. It must be costing Charles a small fortune to get a woman like that to sleep with him. And he must be getting the money from gambling. After all she had done for him. The lying bastard would pay dearly.

Chapter 40

After breakfast, Spencer called Stosh and said he was still wondering about the coins.

"And why are you wondering that?" asked Stosh.

Spencer told him what Don had said about Dr. Bell.

"So you're making some connection between Bell and Jack?"

"Not really. But it seems strange that there are two historical events here. And you once told me information is power." Spencer twisted the phone cord around a pencil.

"Yup. But withholding information can be powerful too."

"You're not going to tell me?"

"What good would it do?"

"Couldn't hurt." He pulled on the ends of the cord, trapping the pencil like one of those Chinese finger puzzles.

"I know my detectives have already looked at that angle and come up empty."

"So you're not giving me anything valuable."

"I'm not giving you anything at all. Be home tonight. I think Rosie said she needed to talk to you."

"Thanks, Stosh."

"Don't thank me. This is the only way I can get rid of you. We never had this conversation."

"Right."

"And kid..."

"Yes, sir."

"Call me if you come up with something."

He hung up. Somebody needed to teach Stosh some phone manners.

Chapter 41

Charles arrived home a little before six that evening. He knew Sarah had watched him last night and was probably watching again, so he had hidden the envelope with the money in the trunk. It was Sarah's night out with the girls. He would put the money in the baggie after she left.

* * *

Jimmy was waiting with great excitement and was disappointed when Mr. Lamb didn't appear. But Jimmy was very patient—and very lucky. He ate dinner and again took up his position in the tree house. Fifteen minutes after Mrs. Lamb left, he was rewarded for his patience. Mr. Lamb came out the back door and went straight to the spot in the bushes. He looked around, retrieved the baggie, and put in more money. Jimmy was right. This was Mr. Lamb's bank.

Jimmy again fished the baggie out of the bushes and was amazed at the amount of money in fifties and twenties. Deciding Mr. Lamb would never miss a little, he took two twenties and added that to his notebook in code. He drew a little picture of a bird for each twenty.

* * *

There was now three hundred dollars in the baggie. On the way back into the house, Charles wondered what he was going to do with the money. He couldn't buy something expensive or Sarah would know. But he would have money for gambling that Sarah would never know about. He could bet all he wanted. And he would be able to buy drinks for his friends. He would be the most popular guy in the bar.

If only he wasn't stuck with Sarah. And then, suddenly, he thought of the safe in Amanda's desk and the pile of cash. That would buy him freedom—freedom from Sarah. He could go somewhere she would never find him. If only that money were his.

Chapter 42

Rosie called Spencer about nine. She asked no questions—just said she had the information he wanted.

There were five coins: a half dollar, quarter, dime, nickel, and penny. The first pile was arranged in order of size with the half dollar on the bottom and the dime on the top. The next piles simply moved the top coin to the bottom. So the second pile had the penny on the top and the dime on the bottom. The third moved the penny to the bottom.

"Any thoughts, Rosie?"

"I wasn't told to share thoughts. I was just told to tell you what I just told you."

"Rosie! This is me you're talking to."

"I know, Spencer, I'm sorry. I'm just following orders."

"Okay. I understand." He paused. "So, any thoughts."

"Jesus. No, none that make any sense."

"Thanks. I owe you."

"Yes you do." She hung up. Stosh must be coaching her on phone etiquette, Spencer thought.

* * *

Spencer called Don and told him about the coins and the pattern.

"Do they have any ideas about the pattern?" asked Don.

"No. Or none that they're sharing."

"Do you?"

"Well, no, but I haven't given it much thought yet. I called you right away."

"Run through it. What do we have?" asked Don.

"Well, five coins." Spencer hesitated. "And five victims of Jack."

"And three current victims," Don added. "So, if he *is* a copycat, the good news is there are only two more victims."

"That may not be good news," said Spencer.

"I didn't mean two more people dying is good."

"Not what I meant," said Spencer. "Maybe two left in the Jack pattern. But if this guy likes to kill, he may find another pattern, or no pattern at all."

"So, we may have two more chances to figure it out."

Spencer sighed. "Maybe, maybe not. Who knows?"

"If the guy is playing a game, there may be more to it than just the number match."

"Maybe. Any suggestions?"

"Read the book again, Spencer."

"And if I still don't find anything?"

Don took a deep breath. "Well, then maybe it's just a game. A literate murderer messing with your mind."

"And that's a game we can't win."

"Probably not."

"So, what then?"

"Then you rely on good old-fashioned police work. Good luck. See ya."

"Yeah, see ya."

Spencer felt like he was backed against a wall. But it was nice to talk to someone who said goodbye.

Chapter 43

Laura went out Tuesday night and was on the street by nine. She was hoping the man who gave her the warning would be back. He might have seen Katherine.

The night was warm and she was comfortable without a jacket. She had also told Stretch she was going to walk farther down Broadway than usual. Her team was ready to follow wherever she went.

It was easy for her to identify women who were working the street and she sought them out for a brief chat. Some wanted to talk, some didn't. She didn't blame the ones who didn't.

Only three men stopped her in the two hours she was out. None were buyers.

* * *

Stretch watched from across the street. Team members would move around the street but there was always a member of the team within twenty feet of Laura. Stretch noticed a large man talking to a couple of the girls Laura had talked to. He didn't approach Laura. And he didn't hire either of the girls. It was a slow night.

Stretch watched Laura talking to other women. He saw her show them what looked to be a picture and wondered what it was. She had done this before and Stretch had wondered what she was doing. But he had stopped thinking about it—he wasn't paid to think.

Chapter 44

Spencer got a bottle of beer and picked up the book again. He told himself not to think about it, just to read it like he had never read it before. Maybe something would pop out at him. The phone rang as he got up to shut off the TV.

"Spencer, Ben."

"Hi, Ben. How's life treating you?"

"Well, a bit tired. You read about the Spiney case?"

"Sure. The little girl who was abducted and found dead. They caught someone, didn't they? And they have a good case. As I remember, they found some of her clothes in his apartment."

"Yeah, and guess who's defending him?"

"Man, you need a vacation, not a big case."

"No argument there, Spencer. But my boss has other ideas. Anything on Laura?"

"No. I'll pick her up again Friday night."

"Bad choice of words."

"I guess," Spencer said with a laugh. "I'll give you a call Saturday."

"Thanks. Don't work too hard."

After hanging up the phone, Spencer settled back into the chair with the book.

* * *

Spencer took a swallow of beer and wished he hadn't. He liked cold beer and it was now almost room temperature. He gave up on the beer.

As he read, he scribbled on a notepad. The string of five murders accredited to Jack the Ripper had begun on August 31, 1888, a little after midnight. The body of Polly Nichols had been found in an alley about three a.m. with two deep cuts along her neck that nearly severed her head. She'd been viciously butchered, with knife slashes from her groin to her breastbone. In the early morning hours of September 8, the police were summoned to a back yard on Hanbury Street by a neighbor who had heard noises and had found the mutilated body of Annie Chapman. Her throat had been cut and she had been disemboweled. Her entrails were wrapped around her neck. Various organs, including her heart and womb, were lying next to her lifeless body. There was a public outcry, but the police were left without a lead. The gruesome murders, just a stone's throw from the seat of the British government, were to continue.

In the 1880s, crime detection was limited to eye witnesses and informants. There was no blood typing. The police couldn't tell the difference between human and animal blood. Even fingerprints were more than a decade away. The murderer, covered in blood, could be staring at his victim, and the police would have no way of proving he did it. So the police were limited to putting on more constables and crossing their fingers. Prostitutes were certainly afraid, but needed to make a living and warily continued. They just assumed the attitude *it won't happen to me* and trusted in luck. But three more weren't to be so lucky.

On September 30, Jack had struck again in what was termed the double event. At one a.m., a man named Israel Schwartz had witnessed a struggle between a man and a woman near Berner Street. Israel had run away. A short while later, another man had come upon the lifeless body of Elizabeth Stride and called the police. Her throat had been cut, but there were no other marks on her. That led police to believe that the second man had interrupted the murderer, who may have been scared away by the arrival of the second man. The murderer may even have been watching from the shadows of a church across the street. The church had become known as *prostitute church*, and the area was called the *round-about* because the prostitutes would walk around and around the church. If they stopped walking, they were arrested for loitering. Israel Schwartz later identified a man named Kosminski as the man he saw struggling with Elizabeth, but refused to testify against a fellow Jew. Kosminski was released.

Forty minutes after the murder of Elizabeth Stride, a police constable had found the butchered body of Katherine Edows just a few hundred yards from the church. The police had theorized that the murderer had been interrupted with Elizabeth, hadn't been able to finish his butchery, and had needed another victim to satisfy himself. Katherine Edows' throat had been cut all the way to her spine. The tip of her nose had been cut off, her kidney and womb removed, and her intestines ripped out and slung over her right shoulder.

No one had heard or seen anything, but this time there had been a few clues. A piece of blood-stained apron, belonging to Katherine, had been found on a path a few blocks away, and a message was scribbled on a brick wall near the murder site. The message read: *The Jews are the men that will not be blamed for nothing.* Amazingly, Commissioner Warren had ordered the message removed without even taking a photograph. He had said he wanted to avoid a race riot against the Jews.

Even Queen Victoria had voiced her concern, but still the police were helpless. Extra constables were put on the streets, some dressed as women. And still the prostitutes had gone out at night. They said their only other option was suicide.

On October 16, another clue had arrived at the home of George Lusk, a member of the vigilante committee that had been formed to patrol the streets. George had received a letter and a small packet. The letter had taunted him, saying *catch me when you can* and stating that the murderer would "rip" again. The packet had contained a small piece of kidney. The sender had said he'd fried a piece of the kidney and eaten it—it was very tasty. The letter and piece of kidney had been assumed to have been sent by the murderer, but there was no proof. There'd been no way of tying the piece of kidney to Katherine Edows. But from then on, the murderer was known as *Jack the Ripper*.

After the last Chicago murder, the cops named their suspect *Friday.*

Trying to forget about Laura, Spencer put down the book and thought about the general pattern of the London murders. Of course they were all prostitutes. But they were also all alcoholics. Maybe that was something to check. Maybe it was a thread. But it wasn't surprising that a prostitute would be an alcoholic. All the murders occurred in the early morning hours and they were all found in accessible areas. The murderer made no attempt to hide the bodies. He wanted his crime to be discovered. And all the murders were within a mile of each other. The current murders matched the old murders in some of these respects, but there was nothing there that gave a clue to the murderer. One fact still remained. It was very difficult to catch someone who picked victims at random.

* * *

After some information about police efforts, the book got to the fifth and last murder, the most vicious of the bunch. In the early daylight hours of November 8, a rent collector, sent by the landlady, knocked on the apartment door of Mary Jane Kelly. Getting no answer, he walked outside, peered in the window, and then ran for the police. He would never forget what he saw. Mary Jane Kelly was lying on the bed, her head severed from her body. Her face had been skinned and her throat cut all the way down to the groin. This time the murderer had taken plenty of time. He had known that he would not be interrupted. Again there had been no good clues. At three a.m., a witness had seen Mary Jane leave a pub along with a man but could give no good description. A little before four a.m., neighbors had heard someone yell *murder*, but had ignored the shout and had gone back to sleep. Mary Jane Kelly had been left to her fate.

That had been the last murder. And, as Spencer already knew, after that murder the police had started to follow Mr. Kosminski, who ended up in a sanitarium. Whether or not Kosminski was Jack the Ripper would never be known, and it really didn't matter to Spencer.

He thought about the Chicago murders and realized there was another similarity. Even though crime detection had certainly come a long way, the Chicago police had no more clues than the London police. The current murderer was just as free to commit his butchery as Jack was, but with one advantage. As far as anyone knew, no one had seen him. But there was one difference that seemed important. The Chicago murders were all on Friday nights, or Saturday mornings. They were at least a bit predictable. Spencer wondered why.

* * *

Spencer sat quietly, trying to shake the helpless feeling that filled him. He wanted a plan of action. He wanted to be doing something. But, other than following Laura, there was nothing to do. Following Don's advice, he started reading again.

On August 31, the body of Polly Nichols had been found at three a.m.

Spencer sat straight up in the chair and put down the book, as he thought of Laura's sister, Katherine. The fourth victim of Jack was Katherine Edows. He was pretty sure the last Chicago victim was named Jane. He flipped back through the chapter. Jack's last victim was Mary Jane Kelly.

Spencer called Rosie.

"Hello."

"Hi, Rosie. Spence."

"Hi, cowboy. You find something about the coins?"

"No. I have another question."

"You're going to make me work on my night off?"

"Should be pretty simple. But if you're busy..."

"No, not too. What is it?"

"What are the names of the three victims?"

Spencer jotted down the names as she said them, thanked her, and hung up.

Placing the names on top of his book notes, Spencer compared them. Jack's first victim was Polly Nichols. The second Chicago victim was Paula Stannard. Jack's second victim was Annie Chapman. The first Chicago victim was Ann Benning. Jack's third victim was Elizabeth Stride and the fourth was Katherine Edows. Jack's fifth victim was Mary Jane Kelly. The third Chicago victim was Jane Deltine. There was no Chicago victim named Katherine or Elizabeth—yet.

The first and third Chicago names were the same as Jack's victims. The second was similar. Two matches could be coincidence. Three had Spencer wondering. If it wasn't coincidence, then *Friday* was picking his victims by their names. That meant he had to know their names, and it would take some legwork to find out the names of prostitutes without attracting attention. Drumming his fingers on the arm of the chair, Spencer thought about the possibility. If the killer was doing this, then the next victim might be named Katherine or Kate or Kathy, or it might be Elizabeth or Liz or Ellie. That gave the police a slight advantage. But first they would have to find all the prostitutes with the right name and alert them to the danger. And prostitutes didn't exactly register with the cops or use their real names.

They could get out the message on the news and in the papers, but then *Friday* would also be alerted, and if *Friday* knew *they* knew, he may not follow the pattern.

Spencer called Rosie and explained what he had found.

"That's crazy, Spencer."

"But possible?"

"Possible. But even if it *is* happening, what do we do about it?"

"I've been wondering that myself. I have no idea. But it might explain why he takes some Fridays off. He's searching for the right girl."

Silence.

"How about if we set up a sting?" suggested Spencer. "Put someone out on the street and make it known that her name is Kate or Kathy, and set up surveillance."

"Pretty risky. It only takes a few seconds to cut a throat. And what are the odds of him hitting on your decoy? There have to be other Kathys out there. It's a pretty common name. And the killer's territory spreads out over a mile."

"Well, we could put someone in each of the neighborhoods he's hit so far."

"And provide all that surveillance? Doubtful. But I'll talk to the lieutenant in the morning."

"Okay. Rosie?"

"Yeah."

"Friday is three days away."

She sighed. "Right. I wonder why he only strikes on Friday nights."

"Your guess is as good as mine. Maybe something turns him into a were-wolf."

"Like what?"

"Booze, drugs. Maybe he only goes out drinking on Friday nights. You think we should mention this to Stosh tonight?"

"No, he'll think it's crazy enough in the morning. Get some sleep."

Spencer left his notes on the chair, carried the beer bottle to the kitchen, and dumped it in the sink. He hoped this would help, but at best he could only be hopeful. There wasn't any more he could do tonight. He needed some sleep. Shedding clothes as he walked through the bedroom, Spencer fell onto the bed without pulling down the covers, wrapped his arm around one of the pillows, and was asleep within seconds.

Chapter 45

Spencer woke up a little after nine Wednesday morning to the sound of raindrops on the roof. As he stretched, the phone rang. It was Rosie.

"Morning Spencer. I presented your thoughts to the brass. They think it's a coincidence. A pretty amazing one, but a coincidence nevertheless. And the parallels aren't perfect. Polly is Paula, and Jane is the middle name, not the first. They won't devote the manpower. If you can get me something more concrete..."

"How about a dead girl named Katherine or Elizabeth?"

"That's not fair, Spencer. We're trying. This just isn't enough to spend all that time and money on."

Spencer silently shook his head. "I hope I'm wrong."

"Me too. I'll talk to you later. Behave yourself. And stay out of dark alleys—I care about you."

"Sure, I'll try."

They hung up. Spencer had to admit his theory wasn't perfect. But it was better than anything else they had. He decided he would try and stick closer to Laura on Friday night just in case his theory was wrong. But she was elusive.

Chapter 46

Charles got home Wednesday night and saw two mahogany cases lying on the dining room table. He knew one held silver dinnerware and the other, two silver daggers. If they were out, Sarah wanted them polished. He eyed them suspiciously and climbed the stairs to change. Sarah was in the kitchen, but was ignoring him.

She had inherited the silver from her parents and made him polish it twice a year, like she had done as a girl, just in case they had anyone over for dinner, which they never did. As long as they were married, they had never actually used the silver.

Charles hated polishing the silver. As far as he was concerned, it was the most tedious, boring chore there was. Sarah usually would do it and make him help. She would yell at him the whole time. He never did it right. He did have to admit he didn't put a lot of energy into it.

He thought about the silver all the while he was changing his clothes. By the time he got back to the kitchen for dinner he was nervous. She knew something *he* didn't. He wondered if someone was coming to dinner.

Slowly pulling out a metal chair, Charles sat down at the table. Sarah ignored him. He decided this was an improvement over the normal yelling that went on. She would always find something to yell about. He never did anything right according to her. He was dying to tell her about Amanda. Amanda thought he did everything right and was glad to have him around. He was also dying to ask about the silver, but concentrated on eating and kept quiet.

She served the noodle casserole and sat down.

Halfway through dinner, Sarah announced that she was going out and wanted Charles to polish the silver.

He asked why.

She just glared at him. She never gave a reason, and he had learned not to ask again. But this was something unusual. She had never let him do it alone. His curiosity was driving him crazy. Accepting that he would not get an answer, and thankful that she would not be there to berate him, Charles stopped asking questions and finished his dinner.

Sarah left about a half hour later. She didn't say a word. She didn't remind him about the polishing job. No reminder was needed. He knew it had better be done by the time she got home, and he knew she would inspect the job, and it had better be done right.

After adding money to the baggie, Charles turned on the TV and opened both cases. The silverware consisted of a twelve-piece place setting of knives, spoons, forks, and serving utensils. He carefully picked up one of the daggers that had belonged to Sarah's grandfather. The blade was about four inches long, and the handle was about six. The handle was in the shape of a snake with the body curving back at the top and curling around, forming a guard around his hand. The snake's head, with its mouth open, was at the bottom of the guard. They were beautiful pieces and probably worth a good deal of money. A can of silver polish and cotton gloves were also on the table. Charles started with the daggers. When he was through with each one, he lovingly held it up and watched the light dance off the sparkling blade as he twisted it.

Sarah always made Charles wear gloves so he wouldn't mar the silver with his fingerprints. But the gloves made his hands sweaty. When he'd pointed out that you couldn't see the fingerprints, she had said that she would know they were there. This time he smiled like a kid stealing a cookie, and a feeling of power ran through him as he gripped the cold steel in his bare left hand. Sarah would never know the difference. He gently placed it back in its velvet bed.

Chapter 47

At 9:25 Thursday morning, Jimmy watched Mr. Lamb get into his beat-up Chevy and back out from the pad next to the driveway. Mrs. Lamb had left an hour before. From his perch in the tree house, Jimmy couldn't see the car after it pulled into the street, but he could hear the roar of the bad muffler as Mr. Lamb drove away.

When the noise had stopped, Jimmy climbed down to the ground, walked between the houses, and peered around the corner of the Lamb's house. There was no one in sight. He quickly returned to the side of the house and parted the bushes. The baggie was still lying on the ground, tucked beneath the sturdy boughs. Jimmy opened the baggie, holding it carefully by the top edges as he had before. He took two more twenties and counted the rest. Five hundred sixty dollars. He counted it twice. Exactly the same.

Jimmy thought about taking all the money. But Mr. Lamb put more in every day. There would be more. For the moment he was happy with his growing stash.

Chapter 48

Before leaving for Laura's apartment Friday evening, Spencer called Ben and asked about his new case.

"Can't talk much about it, but the evidence is good. Actually my job isn't too tough in a case like this. Neither is the prosecutor's. If the police do their job correctly, it's just dotting the *i* and crossing the *t*. Goes smoothly and nobody complains. In most cases, even the accused knows he's guilty and is ready to do the time. What's happening with Laura?"

"Heading over there now. I'll call you tomorrow."

They hung up and Spencer made a sandwich to take with him.

* * *

Spencer pulled up at 6:20, parked almost in the same spot as the week before, and waited for Laura.

Less than a minute later, Stretch let Laura know that Spencer was back. Actually, what he said was, *that crazy son of a bitch is back.* And he asked Laura if she still wanted to go out. She said there would be no change in plans. But she decided to make Spencer wait until 10:30.

Slowly eating a ham and cheese sandwich on rye washed down by Coke, Spencer tried to stretch his legs and hoped he wouldn't have to wait too long. When she hadn't shown by 10:15, he started to worry and considered another trip to her apartment.

Spencer breathed a sigh of relief as Laura finally appeared, dressed exactly the same as she was the last time. A glance at his watch showed him it was 10:32. He got out of the car and trailed her.

* * *

Laura didn't change her routine. She stopped at the hot dog stand, then made her way to her post just south of the antique store and the alley where she had lost Spencer the week before. Several men stopped to talk but kept on walking. She evidently hadn't lowered her price.

The evening was balmy and the crowds were in a good mood. Weekly paychecks had already started turning into alcoholic smiles and bawdy laughter. Bright lights and music and honking horns overshadowed the possibility that a vicious murderer might be part of that happy crowd, waiting for the right moment to continue his butchery. As Spencer scanned the crowd, he realized the task of catching this modern-day Ripper was next to impossible. It could be anybody. It could even be a woman, but that was unlikely. For some reason, men had the undesirable distinction of committing most brutal murders.

He noticed two other women who appeared to be working the street. He also noticed a rather large man talking to both of those girls. But that's all he did was talk. One of the men who had talked with Laura went off with one of the other girls. Spencer wondered if she would end up as a headline. He thought of following them but didn't want to leave Laura. And he didn't want to interfere with free trade.

* * *

He had started at a bar where he had several beers and thought about his new name. The papers were now calling him *Friday*. He liked it—showed respect. His name would be in the history books.

He did his heavy drinking on Friday nights. He would spend an hour or so talking to girls on the street and then go back to the bar.

Friday had talked with several of them before and now scanned the street for new faces. There were three he hadn't seen before. He walked slowly past one of them and made eye contact.

"Hi, honey," she said with a pasted-on smile. "You looking for some fun?"

He smiled back. "You never know. What did you have in mind?"

"Well. That's up to you. Depends on how much fun you want to have."

"I've been known to have a *lot* of fun. My name's Jake. What's yours?"

"Belle. So, let's take a walk."

"Well, I'll tell you, Belle—I think I'll pass tonight. Perhaps another time."

She shrugged. "I may not be here another night. I can send you home with a smile on your face."

"I'll take that chance." *Friday* turned and walked away.

He looked at the other two girls. One of them was busy. He approached the other and had the same conversation. When he turned away, he didn't see the third girl with the red top. There would be other nights. He would find her again.

* * *

Stretch also noticed the man talking to the girls on the street. One of the girls dropped her shoulder bag. The man bent down, picked it up with his left hand, and handed it back to her. He saw the man glance at Laura several times but he didn't approach her.

* * *

A young man stopped next to Laura and started chatting. He stayed and they talked. In less than a minute they both started toward the alley. Spencer crossed the street and fell in behind them.

They turned into the alley. Spencer saw Laura and the *john* walking slowly about fifty feet ahead. This time he wouldn't lose her. He gingerly stepped into the alley and let them get a little farther ahead. They passed the dumpsters on the left, and ten seconds later he did, too. A bum was lying against the wall, but this time he was between the dumpsters. And this time he was asleep, or so Spencer thought.

Spencer continued to follow Laura, who had not looked back. He had taken four or five steps past the dumpster when he felt a sudden, searing pain in the back of his head.

Briefly aware of Laura floating off down a spinning alley, Spencer crumbled to the ground.

Chapter 49

Amanda Brock got home at four a.m. Saturday. She had spent the evening at a dinner at the Palmer House, the guest of the president of Viscor Dynamics. After dinner, she accompanied him to his penthouse apartment where she earned a thousand dollars. Because of the alcohol and the exercise, he had fallen asleep a happy and tired man. Amanda spent a few minutes admiring the view of the skyline, then called the chauffeur and met the limo at the front door. She instructed the chauffeur to drop her off on the corner of Sheridan and Glenlake. She knew from experience that the stretch limo would never be able to turn around in her dead-end street.

She made some tea, put the mug on a tray with some cookies, changed her clothes, and then moved to the office. She placed the tray and the stack of ten, hundred dollar bills on the desk.

Amanda unlocked the cabinet on the left side of her desk and slid back the panel that hid the safe. Agile fingers spun the dial without thinking. The safe door swung open. As she reached for the money, she saw lights far out on the lake. She placed the money into the safe, leaving the door open, and went to the telescope at the window. She couldn't make out the name in the dark, but could see the boom on the deck of the ship. She knew it to be one of the old-style, self-unloading bulk freighters. She loved watching the ships.

Warming her hands on the ceramic mug, Amanda used the remote to turn on the stereo, choosing WFMT, a classical FM station. As a piano sonata played quietly in the background, Amanda swiveled her leather chair to look out the picture window. She took a sip of the herb tea, which was from Paraguay and supposedly had all kinds of amazing healing properties. She really didn't care about that. She drank it for the taste. Hints of honey and licorice weaved through an overall flavor of wood smoke.

Amanda stretched and yawned. Watching twinkling lights out on the lake was very relaxing. She would watch until night started to fade into dawn, then take a shower and go to bed. Amanda always felt a kind of rebirth as the horizon started the slow change from black to gray, almost as imperceptible as the beginning of the wrinkles she so much feared. If there were clouds banked over the lake, she would stay for the sunrise. The view was spectacular. She sat in the dark and enjoyed her favorite part of the day.

As she stared at the light on the northernmost water intake crib, Amanda tensed up when she thought she heard a noise. It was a kind of muffled click. She listened, heard nothing else, and turned back to the lake. The old house made many noises, most of which she had grown accustomed to. But there was always something new. The radiator clanged and the heat came on. She relaxed. Because of the thick carpet on the stairs, Amanda was not aware of the person who had entered her house.

Catching movement out of the corner of her eye, Amanda jerked her head and saw a blur springing up from the floor near the corner of the big desk. As she dropped the mug in her lap, she saw the flash of a silver knife blade held at the end of an upraised arm. Before she could react, Amanda felt a searing pain as someone plunged the knife into her chest. She tried to kick and push the person away, but the knife struck next in her left eye. It all happened so fast. Amanda lost consciousness as she slumped into the chair.

* * *

The intruder picked up the money off the desk, removed the money from the safe, left the house, walked onto the rocks, and, after looking around to see if anyone was in sight, carefully dropped the knife down in a deep crevice between two rocks as the first hint of dawn appeared on the paper-thin horizon between sky and water.

Chapter 50

A faint odor of coffee hit him before he even opened his eyes. Spencer grimaced from the pain at the back of his head. He tried to rub it, but his hands were tied behind him. He thought he could feel some sort of mask over his eyes.

His feet were tied together and his toes were numb. He was sitting upright on a hard surface with his back against a round post. The floor was cold, probably concrete. All he touched was air when he wiggled his fingers. Every muscle in his body ached. And the pain at the back of his head would be a reminder not to walk into dark alleys again, if he survived.

The last thing he remembered was seeing a bum asleep between the dumpsters in the alley. He had no idea how much time had elapsed between then and now, but it was enough to cramp his muscles and numb his extremities. His mouth wasn't gagged, so he assumed yelling would do nothing but anger his captors. He tried taking deep breaths, but that just hurt his head. Giving in to exhaustion and pain, he passed out.

Spencer woke to footsteps in the room above him. A minute later he heard a click and the sound of a door opening, and then footsteps coming down stairs. He could see a little light around the edges of his mask. He strained to hear more sounds but heard nothing. His whole body was tense.

He thought he heard a brief noise behind him and then felt a sharp stab in the back of his neck. He yelled and his body involuntarily jumped. The room was cold, but Spencer was instantly sweating.

"Who the hell are you?" he gasped.

There was no answer.

And then another stab. His body jumped again. Two more stabs left him dreading the next stabbing.

Minutes went by before he felt another sharp point under his chin. This time the blade stayed. He froze, vividly remembering the chapter about Jack.

Trying to regain some composure, Spencer hesitantly said, "Okay, I don't care who you are. Why are you doing this?"

Still no answer. He couldn't imagine being more scared and thought this was a helluva way to spend your last hours. But if all they wanted was to kill him, he would be dead by now. They wanted something, but what? And if they got it, would he still be alive? After the knife jabs, he was pretty sure he would give them whatever they wanted. And then they would kill him.

After what seemed like hours, he heard two more sets of footsteps coming down the stairs. So now there were three people nearby.

Spencer heard what sounded like a radio crackle. A male voice said, "He's awake."

Someone pulled off his mask.

Even the little light there was sent pain to the back of his head. Gradually, his eyes adjusted. Spencer opened them a slit and turned toward the man who was standing over him with arms crossed, a radio in one hand. The man was as big as a gorilla.

"Can you untie me?" Spencer asked with lips that stuck together and seemed to be moving much too slowly.

No answer. Okay, this guy was just a flunky. Whoever was on the other end of the radio would be down soon.

Less than a minute later they were joined by another man. Compared to the first, he was a midget—shorter than Spencer's six feet and not very weighty. Hard to make him out in the dim light.

This guy Spencer could handle with one hand tied behind his back. Of course, both hands tied was a problem. And then there was the gorilla.

"Untie him."

The gorilla knelt behind Spencer with a knife. One flick and the ropes were loose, leaving Spencer free to fall sideways onto the floor. He landed on his left shoulder and tried to move his right arm around to the front, but it wouldn't budge. He couldn't even feel it. There was also no feeling in his left arm, which was wedged under his body. Spencer stayed on his side while the gorilla cut the rope on his ankles. He noticed his watch was gone but decided that was the least of his problems.

"Should I help him boss?" asked the gorilla.

"No," said the boss, calmly.

While Spencer struggled, the boss read the information from Spencer's driver's license. Holding it up to the light, he asked, "You Spencer Manning?"

Spencer wanted to tell the guy to look at the picture, but figured he wasn't in a position to be a smart ass. Someone who couldn't free his own arm from his own weight wasn't in a very commanding position. But Spencer was making progress—feeling was coming back. Pins and needles let him know his arms were still there. A small roll to the right took off enough weight to pull his arm free. That took all his energy.

"Hey, the boss asked you a question."

Not wanting to anger the gorilla, Spencer took a deep breath and answered, "Yeah, I'm Spencer Manning."

The boss nodded. "I could tell. Nice picture." He threw the license and Spencer's wallet onto the floor at Spencer's feet and said, "You got five minutes to get to where you can walk up those stairs." He turned and walked back upstairs.

The gorilla stayed.

Not wanting to find out what would happen if he didn't make it, Spencer started moving his legs and rubbing some feeling back into his arms. The gorilla kept checking his watch and gave a one-minute warning. Spencer had no idea what time it was, but all that mattered at the moment was that one minute.

He stopped rubbing his arm. Ignoring the stabbing pain in his head, he used the pole to help pull himself to a standing position. Saying nothing, the gorilla simply pointed toward the stairs.

Spencer went first and willed his legs to move up the stairs. When he pushed open the door at the top, bright light sent a pain from his temples to the back of his head that felt like someone had driven in a spike. He covered his eyes with his left hand and turned away.

"Headache?" asked a strong and matter-of-fact female voice.

Squinting through his hand, Spencer didn't answer. He couldn't see the speaker.

She continued. "Michael. Turn off the light. We don't want Mr. Manning to think ill of his hosts. We can do with the window light."

Through his squint, Spencer saw the gorilla move to the wall and flick a switch. He immediately felt like his head had been let out of a vice.

"Better?" the voice asked.

Spencer turned and slowly nodded at Laura Justine.

* * *

Have a seat." From her perch on the edge of a rickety desk, she waved at a group of four wooden chairs in the center of the room. Other than the desk and chairs the room was empty. A bulletin board hung on a wall covered with graffiti.

Happy to be sitting, Spencer looked around the room as he did so. Besides Laura and the gorilla there were three other men; one was the short one who gave the orders in the basement. Spencer massaged his temples and let his gaze come back to Laura. She was calmly watching Spencer with no emotion.

They watched each other for a good two minutes before Spencer spoke. "You knocked me out?"

She crossed her arms over her chest and shifted both feet to the floor while leaning against the desk. "Well, not personally, but a friend of mine did."

"Can I ask why?"

"Sure. But I think I'm more in a position to ask the questions."

"Yup, the person holding the gun is always in a better position," Spencer agreed.

Looking directly at him with raised eyebrows and a tiny smile, Laura asked, "Do you see any guns, Mr. Manning?"

"Figure of speech. With that guy on your side you don't need guns." Spencer nodded at the gorilla. "But I'd bet just cuz I can't see them doesn't mean they aren't here."

The smile disappeared. "Why were you following me, Mr. Manning?"

"I wasn't..." Out of the corner of his eye, Spencer saw the gorilla step away from the wall. That stopped him in mid-sentence.

"Mr. Manning. We are not here to play games. Your headache proves that. Following me once may be a coincidence. Twice is not. Don't play games with me and you may be able to recover from that headache. Now, why were you following me?"

Holding none of the cards and deciding that the truth couldn't get him in any worse trouble, Spencer answered. "A month or so ago you were arrested for prostitution." He didn't get the verification he was expecting. But then he didn't need it—it was a fact. "You were represented by a friend of mine, Benjamin Tucker."

Her eyebrows raised slightly.

"He asked me to check up on you, make sure you were okay."

"Why?"

Spencer spread his hands, palms up. "Because he was concerned. He didn't want you caught up in the system or lying in an alley."

"That's a bit hard to believe, Mr. Manning. Your friend doesn't know me and would have no personal interest. Why would he go to that trouble?"

"Because he thought you were different. You didn't belong in that crowd. You didn't belong on the streets. And you didn't belong in jail."

She smiled again. "We must have slipped up somewhere. I thought I was doing a pretty good job of belonging."

Laura was quiet for a few seconds. "And your friend's concern included breaking into my apartment?"

Spencer squirmed in the chair. "No, that was my doing."

"Why?"

"Because there was no information on Laura Douglas." He shrugged. "Seemed strange."

Locking eyes with Spencer, she said, "Really. Strange enough to commit a crime?"

As Spencer started to respond, Laura held up her hand and stopped him. She looked to the side, nodded slightly, and one of the men left the room.

The door led to another room. As it closed, Spencer asked, "Do I get to ask any questions?"

"Maybe. At the moment you get to wait." She lifted herself into a sitting position on the desk. "Unless you'd like to use the washroom."

"I would."

She nodded toward a door to her left.

Chapter 51

Ben was wrapping up paperwork at the office Saturday morning. At a quarter to eleven, his telephone rang. He was on his way out, but went back to answer it.

"Hello?"

"Benjamin Tucker?"

"Yes?"

"Do you know a Spencer Manning?"

Ben wondered what was up. With Spencer it could be anything. He hoped it wasn't bad. "Yes."

"And did you ask him to become involved with Laura Douglas?"

"Who is this?" Ben set down his briefcase.

"I'm waiting, Mr. Tucker," the man said politely.

"That is privileged information. Why is it your business?"

"Let's say that Mr. Manning is in a position that depends on your answer."

Something in the man's tone made Ben decide that playing tough was not a good idea. He also decided that the man on the other end of the line already knew the answer. So the truth seemed like the best bet. "I did, yes."

"In what manner?"

"I asked Mr. Manning to follow her and keep an eye on her."

"For what purpose?"

"To make sure she was okay." As he said it, he realized how stupid it sounded. There was no way this guy was going to buy that.

The line went dead.

Chapter 52

Spencer had been massaging his neck for five minutes when the door opened. With a sideways glance, Spencer saw the man who had left the room nod at Laura.

She took a deep breath that swelled out her chest. "Okay, Mr. Manning. Suppose for the moment that we buy your story. That earns you a question."

"Okay. What the hell is going on?"

"Could you be a bit more specific?"

"Why clobber me and drag me in here?"

"Because you were following me and we didn't know why," she answered as she moved around behind the desk and sat. "Would you like coffee?"

"Please. Black." Another man left the room. "You could have stopped me on the street. You didn't need all this."

"My apologies if we've inconvenienced you, but, where my safety is concerned, I like to be in control of the situation. And I'd say I'm pretty well in control here."

"For the moment. But you're not in control out on the street. And if you haven't noticed, it isn't too safe these days."

The man returned with the coffee. As Spencer took a sip, a phone rang in the other room. It only rang once. So there was at least one other person in the next room.

"Thank you for your concern, Mr. Manning. But as I said, I like to be in control. That goes for the streets, too. For instance, last Friday you entered my apartment building. You later followed me to Broadway and bought two hot dogs. Enough?"

He slowly looked her over. With her hair pulled back in a ponytail, no makeup, and wearing a baggy sweatshirt, she again looked like a college kid. She was certainly a long way from a prostitute.

"So, why the prostitute act?"

"That's a long story and not one you need to know. Let's just say I needed a cover that brought me down into the lower edges of society."

Spencer shook his head. "I don't know what kind of game you're playing, but it's a very dangerous one."

"First of all, it's not a game, and second, yes it is. But it *is* necessary. The next question is what do we do with you?"

"How about thank me for coming and point me toward the door?"

Laura laughed. It was a pretty laugh. A different time and place and that laugh may have been inviting. No one else was laughing.

"I like you, Mr. Manning."

"Then why not call me Spencer?"

"Okay. But I can't allow my personal opinions to get in the way of business. And at the moment you are a liability. I can't afford to have anyone I don't trust know my whereabouts. And I can't afford anyone poking their nose into my business, no matter how well-meaning. You and Mr. Tucker have stuck your noses pretty far into my business. So how can I be sure you will remove your noses?"

Spencer's head was starting to clear. He answered, "Mr. Tucker's motivation was to make sure you were okay. I think I can tell him you are. I'd say you are more than okay. You may just be more okay than the mayor."

"And that will satisfy him?" The phone rang again. One ring.

"It should."

"And how about you, Spencer? Would that satisfy you?"

He hesitated a second and that was too long.

Laura stood behind the desk. "No, it wouldn't. You'd still be wondering what's going on. And you just might get the urge to stick your nose back in—just to be helpful, of course." She stared at him. "I don't need any help, Spencer. I have plenty."

Stretching his arms behind his head, Spencer said, "You're right, I have no idea what's going on in your personal life, and that's certainly your business. But I am involved in what's going on in the streets, and that's something you're not equipped to deal with. Do you read the papers?"

Leaning over, she put both hands flat on the desk. "I know exactly what's going on. And I assure you that I'm as safe as I am in this room."

Spencer couldn't believe the naiveté of the woman. "How can you say that? Last Friday I saw you go into the alley with a man. That man could have been the killer. How did you know you would walk out of there alive?"

She smiled slightly. "Because I'm in control."

Spencer threw his hands up in frustration. "You don't get it! You aren't in control in a dark alley with a stranger. Okay, you have people watching. But when you turned into that alley, you were alone with him. On the streets your people can get to you. But in the alley it would take one second for someone to pull out a knife and end your life. No one could get to you quick enough."

She nodded. "Right. That's why I don't go into alleys with strange men."

"But you did! It only takes one..."

She held up her hand. Spencer stopped talking.

"Mr. Manning."

"What happened to Spencer?"

"You're pissing me off."

Spencer closed his eyes and rolled his head. It still hurt, but not as much. He tried to be calm, but the frustration still gave his voice an edge that sounded like anger. "I am *trying* to keep you alive."

"Thank you. But I can do that myself."

"Not if you insist on..."

She held up her hand again. "Okay, let's try this. Can you describe the man you saw me go into the alley with?"

"Sure. I can still see his face."

She sat down. "So you could identify him if you saw him again?"

"Yup," Spencer said with assurance.

"Turn around."

Spencer looked confused. Laura twirled her finger and nodded.

Standing behind Spencer was the man she went into the alley with. Massaging his forehead, Spencer turned back to Laura. He tried to get his brain to register. It did, but slowly. And as it sunk in, Spencer's respect for Laura Justine expanded enormously. He looked at her and saw a very smart, very shrewd woman looking patiently at him, waiting for it to sink in. Her eyebrows raised, her shoulders lifted almost imperceptibly, and her head tilted slightly to the side as if to ask, *Got it now*?

Spencer opened his mouth but the words stuck in his throat for a few seconds. "You hired all these people."

She nodded.

"You put on a pretty good prostitute act and then disappear down an alley with someone you hired."

Another nod.

"So you hire men to not have sex with you?"

Another alluring laugh. "I guess you could say that. But what I really hire them for is to protect me."

Spencer stared. "You are either insane or very shrewd. And if you aren't insane there must be a reason behind the shrewdness."

"Everything has a reason, Mr. Manning."

"And what is the reason for all this?"

"For me to know."

"And these gentlemen?"

"They don't know either." Seeing his look of disbelief, she continued. "I pay them well to take care of me. They don't care why."

Spencer looked around at the four men against the walls. They certainly looked like they didn't care.

"That's pretty hard to believe."

She shrugged. She didn't care if he believed her or not. "Maybe just as hard to believe as your friend caring so much about my well-being. How often does someone care about a complete stranger, especially someone caught up in the legal system?"

"Hard to believe or not, it's true."

"See, sometimes things that are hard to believe *are* true," she said with a smile. She was totally relaxed and seemed to be enjoying the control she had.

Spencer edged to the front of the chair. "Okay, let's assume there's a good reason for all of this and that these people are here solely to protect you. I think there are some holes in your plan."

"I would be grateful to you for pointing them out, Spencer," she said calmly. "I do not have a death wish."

Feeling that he had her, and he really wanted to show her up, Spencer continued. "I saw you talk to several men. They couldn't all be in your employ. You have no control over someone stopping and hitting on you."

"Right. That I have no control over."

"So, what if one of those men hires you?"

"Wouldn't happen."

"No," Spencer said with a smile, "Might happen."

She shook her head slowly. "No man would pay what I ask."

"One might."

"No. No man is crazy enough to pay five hundred dollars for what he could get for twenty somewhere else."

Spencer cringed inwardly at the five hundred dollars. That was higher than he had guessed. "One might."

"Okay. If one did, we would be intercepted by one of my group before we walked five steps. But it has never happened."

"Okay. But there's one more thing." Spencer had saved his best ammo for last. "Do you remember walking through the alley and going past dumpsters on your left?"

"Sure. So?"

"So, the last girl killed was found by a dumpster. The papers didn't tell the whole story. What happened to her body was not pretty. I'll spare you the details."

"Thank you. But what does that have to do with me?"

"As you walked through that alley, there was a bum lying by the dumpsters both times. Who knows who he was or what he was waiting for."

"In this case, *I* do. Look to your left."

Spencer had already noticed the thin man standing under a window. "So?"

"So? Cleans up pretty nicely doesn't he?"

Spencer felt like a boxer who had come to within one punch of falling to the mat. But he had one punch left, even though he would admit he was grasping at straws.

"There was another bum lying in a doorway."

"Yes there was. And both of those 'bums' had guns in case you did something stupid. The butt of one of those guns gave you that headache. Give up?"

"Not only do I give up. You should be working for the Secret Service. The president doesn't have this much protection." He paused and became serious as he realized that all this protection meant something. "But one doesn't need all this protection unless there is something bad around the corner. You carry an umbrella if there's a chance of storms. But sometimes the storms blow apart the umbrella."

She nodded. "Point taken. Bottom line is, it's my problem and my decision. But thank you for your concern."

"You're welcome." Spencer sat back in the chair and asked, "So, now what?"

"Good question. I suppose you could go back in the basement." She had a slight smirk on her face, but Spencer knew that was a possibility.

"That's not my first choice. Not even on my list," Spencer said.

"No, I imagine not. You, of course, would like to go. But something you said is bothering me."

Spencer waited.

Laura played absently with a pencil on the desktop and looked up at Spencer. "You said you would spare me the details of what happened to the girl in the alley. How do you know those details?"

Spencer felt trapped and he could feel his heart beating faster. He thought about what to say and decided to tell her the truth. "I have connections in the police department."

She didn't look surprised. "Connections that share information about a serious crime?"

He nodded.

"Care to explain?"

"Not much to explain," he said with a shrug. "My father was a police captain till he was killed not too long ago. I have friends on the force."

There was not a bit of friendliness in Laura's look. "That complicates things a bit."

"Why? You're not doing anything illegal. Though they would frown on this, playing a prostitute is different from actually being one."

"That's not my concern."

"Then what is?"

She shook her head. "Not your business. Remember?"

"Yeah. But maybe I could help."

"I have all the help I need."

Spencer looked around the room. The three men were staring at him, not moving a muscle. But he knew if they had to, they would move pretty fast. At the moment he was a problem. He needed to change that if he wanted to stay out of the basement. He had only one thought.

"Okay. If I can't help *you*, then how about if you help *me*."

Laura leaned forward slightly. "I'm listening."

Chapter 53

Ben listened to the dead line for a few seconds and then hung up the phone and stared at it, wondering what had just happened. He picked it up again and dialed Spencer's home number. No answer. Next, he paged Spencer and waited fifteen minutes, trying not to worry as the time went by.

At 11:40, Ben called Lieutenant Powolski.

"Lieutenant, this is Benjamin Tucker. Sorry to bother you at home."

"No bother, Ben. What's up?"

"I just got a very strange phone call." After explaining the call to Stosh, Ben asked what to do.

"Sit tight. Let me know if you hear anything else."

"Okay. Call me if you find something."

"Sure."

* * *

Stosh hung up. "Crap." What the hell had Spencer gotten himself into now?

Chapter 54

C an we talk in private?" Spencer asked tentatively.

"This is as private as it gets."

There was a knock at the door. It opened and a new man stuck his head in. "Lunch," the man said. Everything here was very businesslike. No wasted words. Very controlled. It was obvious that Laura was very much in charge. She had said she was paying them very well, and that certainly had a lot to do with the obedience, but Spencer knew it also had a lot to do with Laura. She was quite capable of being the boss and commanding respect.

Laura nodded. The man disappeared and was back in twenty seconds with a cardboard box full of hot dogs. The four men in the room pulled a chair up to the table and unfolded the wrappers.

"One for you, Spencer. Actually, two. You're probably hungry. Join us."

Spencer looked at her tentatively and hesitated, even though he was starving.

"Come on," she said with a smile. "We're not as bad as you think. Please, eat. It's on the house."

Spencer pulled up his chair and squeezed in next to the gorilla at a corner.

"They're all the same. Jumbo dog with everything. Scrape off what you don't want," said Laura in a voice muffled with hot dog. "Grab some fries."

Spencer unwrapped his dog and picked off the peppers.

Laura nodded and wiped mustard from the corner of her mouth. "Great hot dogs." The napkin she used had a yellow LW in the corner.

That's your first mistake, thought Spencer. He knew he was close to Last Wiener.

Chapter 55

Charles had little recollection of what happened Friday night. He knew he started out at his local bar, but what happened after that was lost in an alcohol fog, brought on by far more than his normal drinking. With money in his pocket, he had bought round after round, reveling in choruses of *For He's a Jolly Good Fellow*.

Sarah spent Saturday afternoons shopping with her sisters, and Charles looked forward to the time alone to relax and watch sports and recover from Friday night. He got out of bed and stretched. It was almost noon and he was hungry. And he was already looking forward to Saturday night.

Chapter 56

Everyone ate. No one said a word until Laura asked, "So, what do you have on your mind?" Spencer knew she was talking to him because it was obvious she didn't care what was on anyone else's mind.

Spencer finished the last bite of hot dog, wiped his hands on a red LW napkin, and told Laura about the first three murders and the tie-in of the names to Jack the Ripper. Everyone finished eating. Laura at least *looked* at him while he talked, so he knew she was listening. The others seemed to not have any interest in what he was saying.

"The fourth victim was Katherine Edows and the fifth was Elizabeth Stride."

Spencer had been carefully watching Laura as he talked. When he mentioned Katherine, she flinched and her eyes widened. But she quickly regained her composure.

"So, what does that have to do with me?"

"Nothing, directly. But if he sticks to the pattern, the next victim will be named some form of Katherine or Elizabeth."

Laura stood up, pulling her sweatshirt down over her hips. "And your plan is?"

Spencer explained his idea of setting up a trap using a Katherine or Elizabeth as bait.

Laura paced back and forth while Spencer talked. The three men sat quietly. When he finished, she stared at him for a few seconds, then sat back down and screeched the wooden chair back from the desk.

"What about the police?"

"Not interested. Lack of manpower, expense, and the fact that it's kind of a shot in the dark."

"To say the least. And why do you think I would want to help?"

Spencer didn't tell her he knew about her sister.

"From what I've seen, with your protection, you have the perfect setup to give it a try. But it *is* dangerous. It's not really something anyone should be doing."

"I agree. Remember I told you I don't have a death wish." She started to pace again. And she didn't ask anyone in the room for their thoughts. "Let's assume your theory is correct. First he'd have to find girls with the same names. How do you figure he did that?"

Spencer was impressed with the way she thought. That was the first question to ask. "I'm not sure. A number of ways, I guess. Follow them home and look at mailboxes. Ask them on the street."

Laura nodded.

Spencer took a deep breath. "So, are you thinking of doing this?"

Stretch and the gorilla were watching Laura. Spencer had their interest. The other man was picking at his nails and looking indifferent. If he was working for her, he probably wasn't indifferent. He could probably pull out a knife in an instant.

"Thinking. But thinking and doing are two different things. And the odds of your plan working are slim. Michael, please get Mr. Manning's things."

Spencer was baffled. The conversation didn't seem over. Michael returned with Spencer's change, watch, keys, and pager, and laid all but the pager on the table in front of Spencer. He picked them up.

"So?" he asked.

"So, you can go. You will be delivered to your car. I hope you take no offense at being blindfolded."

"Is my other choice being knocked on the head again?"

She nodded.

"In that case I take no offense."

"Good. Michael will return your pager when you reach your car."

"What about the murders?"

"I'll give it some more thought. I have your card."

"And what if I don't hear from you?"

She looked puzzled. "Then I'm not interested and we won't see each other again. Right?"

Spencer didn't answer.

"Mr. Manning, your other option is back in the basement."

That didn't take much thought. "Right."

"Good. Michael will see you back to your car."

The gorilla placed a blindfold over Spencer's eyes, led him to a car, and helped him in. He heard a garage door rise and the car windows close. The car pulled out and Spencer swayed to the right as the car turned left. His legs straddled the hump in the back seat and he felt a person on either side of him.

Spencer tried to pick up street sounds, but the car was almost soundproof. He started to keep track of the turns. If they started from the area of Last Wiener, he should be able to trace the path back to the apartment. But, six turns later, Spencer lost track of the path and they were driving much longer than the time it should have taken to get back. They were obviously driving out of the way and then doubling back. He lost track of both the path and time. Once in a while he heard a faint horn or other traffic sounds, but they were of no help. Considering that he didn't want to end up back in the basement, he finally decided it didn't matter where Laura was—he would have to be satisfied with letting *her* find *him*.

* * *

Stretch had heard everything Spencer had to say. It sounded dangerous. But it wasn't *his* life on the line and he was making much more money than he could ever hope for anywhere else. He didn't know how long that would last, but while it was here he was going to take advantage of it. And he wasn't going to do anything to screw it up. Laura had bought his loyalty, and he was willing to give her all his effort. He had some thoughts about what was going on, but she had made it clear that she wanted a job done with no questions, so he had stopped asking. As time went by, he had gained more and more respect for her, and it was not all about the money. She knew what she was doing, and he was happy to work for her. He would do everything in his power to keep her safe.

Chapter 57

The car finally stopped and backed into a parking space. Spencer felt someone lift the blindfold from his face. As his eyes adjusted, he saw the gorilla holding out his pager. Spencer took it and the gorilla got out of the car and held the door for him. No one said a word.

The vehicle was a silver BMW and was parked across the street and a few cars down from Spencer's Mustang. He got the license plate but knew that would get him nothing. The BMW pulled out and sped down the street.

Spencer turned on his pager and hung it on his belt. As he was walking back to his car, the beeper vibrated.

Pages from Stosh and Ben. He found a phone and called Stosh first.

Stosh breathed a sigh of relief. "Are you alright?"

"Sure."

"Good." Then the anger came out. "Jesus Christ, where the hell have you been?"

"Well, if you want an accurate answer to that, I don't know."

"And what the hell does that mean?"

"It means I was detained, but I'm not sure where. How do you know I had been somewhere?"

"Because I got a call from Benjamin Tucker who'd received a strange phone call and then couldn't get ahold of you. That was two hours ago."

"Oh."

"Oh?" Stosh said with a raised voice. "That's all you've got to say? You've had two friends worried about what hole you'd fallen into and all you say is *oh*? What the hell is going on?"

Hating to admit what had happened, Spencer filled Stosh in on the events since Friday night.

"Jesus, Spencer. Maybe you should think about another line of work. Or maybe you should hire Miss Justine, or whatever she's calling herself these days. She's better at what you do than you are."

That hurt, but Stosh was right. Spencer realized his mistake was in underestimating Laura and letting his guard down—twice.

"She is good."

"What's going on there?"

"Only thing I can figure is the sister angle."

"Anything illegal?"

"Don't think so, but who knows. Even the people working for her have no clue. She's a very shrewd woman. Whatever it is, she knows exactly what she's doing."

"Anything you need me for?"

"No. Everything's fine."

"And is everything over?"

"Over?"

"Yeah, over. Is this the last time she's going to lead you into an alley?"

"Yes, sir. Whatever she's doing isn't my concern."

"That is correct. But that doesn't mean you won't *be* concerned."

"No, I guess it doesn't. But I'm pretty sure. Anything happen last night?"

"Nope, *Friday* stayed home. Do me a favor. Call Ben and let him know you're okay."

The phone went dead. Spencer drove home, called Ben, and, after filling him in, made plans to meet for breakfast at Sunnyside Up on Sunday.

Chapter 58

Spencer was already at a table sipping coffee when Ben walked in.

"So, done in by a woman. Tsk tsk tsk."

"Yeah, funny. Wait till you get my bill."

Ben laughed. "You think you'll hear from her?"

"No clue."

Ben ordered coffee. "Any idea what she's doing?"

Spencer told Ben about his chat with Tim and the sister possibility.

"Makes sense," said Ben. "But how likely is it?"

"Just a possibility. But it's the best I've heard so far. The police came up empty."

They ate and Ben picked up the bill.

Chapter 59

Detectives Lonnigan and Steele turned onto Glenlake and stopped behind the three squad cars and a fire department ambulance at the end of the street. Nice way to start the week. Two officers were stringing yellow tape from tree to tree. A small crowd of curious onlookers had already formed across the street.

"Nice view," mumbled Ronny Steele around the fat, unlit cigar that was stuck in his mouth. He nodded toward the beach.

"Yeah, great," returned Rosie. She walked to the sand at the end of the street and looked out onto the beach. Ronny breathed as much as he could of the cigar through his mouth and longed for the days when he could smoke in the car without complaints.

Rosie Lonnigan rejoined her partner in the driveway and waited for Officer Chambers to reach them with the yellow tape.

"Morning, Chambers," she said with a friendliness she didn't waste on her partner.

"Morning, Detectives."

Steele grunted.

"Mike, when you finish the front here, would you tape the beach too? Up to the end of the rocks at the north and down to that breakwall to the south. One of you watch the beach and make sure no one gets out there."

"Sure thing, Detective." He glared at Steele.

The police had received a call at 7:25 Monday morning from a hysterical lady with a Spanish accent. She claimed a lady was dead. Two squad cars responded at 7:30 and verified that the lady of the house was indeed dead. Lonnigan and Steele were early for the day shift, but were the only detectives in the station and agreed to take the call. They arrived on the scene at 7:50. A third squad arrived just after them.

"What've we got, Mike?" asked Rosie.

Letting the tape droop, he answered, "One dead female up in the study. Amanda Brock, owner of the house. The housekeeper, Margaret Rivera, found her shortly after she got to work this morning."

"Any sign of what happened?" Rosie glanced at Steele, wishing he would show interest in something besides rolling his cigar between fat fingers.

"Yeah. Looks like she was stabbed. It's not pretty. Face is all bloody."

"Thanks, Mike."

He nodded.

Rosie started toward the house with Steele dragging a few yards behind. A female officer Rosie didn't recognize opened the door from the inside. Steele gave her more of an inspection than he had the crime scene. Rosie introduced herself and Detective Steele to Officer Lee while they were led into the kitchen where a woman and another female officer sat side-by-side at the kitchen table. A quick glance showed the kitchen to be in the middle of a remodeling project. Half the wall was covered by new cabinets. An empty tea cup sat on the edge of the sink. Officer Lee introduced her partner, Officer Martin, and the housekeeper, telling Rosie that two more officers were upstairs in the study with the body.

Rosie noticed a wedding ring on Margaret's finger. "Hello, Mrs. Rivera. Can you answer a few questions?"

She nodded and sniffed. Her face was streaked with tears, and she was trembling. Officer Martin had one hand on her shoulder.

"Can you tell us what happened this morning?" Rosie asked gently.

Margaret nodded again but took almost a minute before she started.

"I came here about quarter to seven. I like to come early and have a cup of tea before working."

Rosie nodded and smiled. Steele chewed on his cigar and spat part of a leaf onto the floor. Rosie gave him a look that could have melted lead. He shrugged and looked around for a paper towel.

"Detective Steele, why don't you go see to the upstairs," Rosie suggested in a firm voice. He picked up the leaf, threw the paper towel in the garbage, and left with a sigh of relief.

Turning back to Margaret, Rosie asked, "How long have you worked for Mrs. Brock?"

Margaret vigorously shook her head. "Oh, no. It is not Mrs. Brock. It is Miss Brock. She has never been married. I have been here for two years in July." She looked proud.

"And what type of work do you do?"

"Oh, just the normal housework. Cleaning mostly. But it is a very clean house. Miss Brock is a very clean woman."

Rosie felt she was defending her employer. "I'm sure. So what happened this morning?"

"Well, I had my tea and went upstairs to work."

"When you got here did you know if Miss Brock was home?"

"Pardon?"

"Did you call out hello or something to let her know you were here?"

"Oh no. I do not do that. Miss Brock is out late on the weekends and sleeps late. So I just start with quiet cleaning so I do not wake her. I always start in the study upstairs and clean up the dishes."

"Dishes?"

"Yes, when Miss Brock comes home late she has tea and some snack in the study and leaves the tray for me to pick up. She is very tired."

Margaret obviously felt sorry for Miss Brock. But, other than the fact that she was dead, Rosie had trouble feeling sorry for someone who had the resources to party into the late hours.

"So normally Miss Brock is sleeping?"

"Yes."

"And this morning what did you find?"

Margaret started to tremble again and her eyes welled up with tears. Slowly shaking her head and looking off into the distance, Margaret painfully said, "I see Miss Brock lying back over the arm of the chair. Her face was..."

"That's okay," said Rosie softly as she patted her arm. Rosie took a kleenex from the box on the table and handed it to Margaret, who dabbed at her eyes. "Would you like to rest a bit?" asked Rosie.

Margaret nodded.

"Okay. I'll be back. Martin, would you stay with Margaret please? Maybe fix some more tea. Lee, show me the way."

Rosie had not been able to shed the feeling of despair that overwhelmed her as she approached a murder scene. She much preferred to do the interviews and let Steele handle the bodies. Some of the older detectives—Ronny Steele was a good example—had no problem at all looking at dead bodies, no matter what their state; it was just another part of their day. They had told her not to think about it; just treat it like a stolen car or a broken window. A dead body was just another entry in a report. She thought she did a pretty good job of hiding the sick feeling in the pit of her stomach while she was on the scene, but it was there nevertheless. And the first four or five had come back to haunt her in the middle of the night and resulted in quick dashes to the bathroom. As time went by and cases added up, Rosie got somewhat used to the blood, but she decided she would never get used to the pain one person was willing to inflict on another, and the glaring lack of respect for another human life.

* * *

As she followed Officer Lee up the stairs, Rosie tried to concentrate on the wood paneling and the fine molding. The house was in good shape, but had lost the grandiosity it must have had when it was first built. Their footsteps sank noiselessly into a thick, plush carpet that continued into the upstairs hall. Officer Lee turned to the left and Rosie followed. Her stomach tightened and so did her jaw muscles. She reminded herself not to think about it.

Officer Lee motioned Rosie into a large, sunny room with a sweeping view of the lake that would have been a wonderful place to spend a few hours if it wasn't the site of a murder investigation. Lee asked if she could go back downstairs. Rosie nodded.

Steele and two male officers were chatting in the middle of the room. Hobbs and Jackson were in their thirties and both said hello as she came in. Hobbs politely asked how she was doing. She lied and said fine.

"So, whadda we got?" she asked with more matter-of-factness than she felt. She could see the top of a head and an arm hanging from the left side of the swivel chair at the desk that faced a picture window.

The top of the desk was almost bare. A tray with an empty cup was next to a closed ledger book with a dark green cover. A silver pen was on top of the book. Two piles of papers were near the book and a phone was at the back right corner.

Steele puffed out his chest and said, "Looks dead to me, but I'll wait for the coroner to make the call." Hobbs and Jackson laughed, stroking the ego of Ronny Steele.

Forcing her legs to move, Rosie walked around the left side of the chair and stood next to the desk. Feeling both revulsion and anger, Rosie looked down at the face of what once must have been a pretty young woman. Rosie guessed early thirties. The skin on the right side of her face was perfectly smooth. Her right eye was open and colored brown. Her left eye was gone, or at least was no longer recognizable. The eye socket was a messy hole, and a gash laid open the skin from the socket to the jaw. The left side of her face was covered in dried blood and her hair was stuck together and crusty. Her left arm, spattered with blood, dangled over the side of the chair and pointed to a dark spot on the green carpet.

Moving her eyes down from the head, Rosie saw that Miss Brock wore a yellow cotton pullover with matching jogging shorts. Looked like an outfit just as good for sleeping as jogging. Margaret had said Miss Brock liked to come in late, have some tea, and then go to bed. So this must have happened in the early morning. Rosie guessed at Saturday morning. The yellow top was torn and stained with blood a little below the left breast. Forcing herself to breathe, Rosie felt better thinking about the details and mentally making notes.

She turned to Steele. "Which do you think killed her?"

Steele shrugged with indifference. "Not what I get paid for. Doc'll tell us."

Rosie bristled with frustration at Steele. "I know. Just asking. I thought maybe you might want to take your brain out for a walk and give it some exercise." That got a chuckle from Hobbs and Jackson.

"Nope. It gets all the exercise it needs thinking about smokin' a cigar," he said with a glare. More chuckles.

"Okay. Have some respect. Any word on the doc?"

Hobbs answered. "Should be here within a half. Tech is on the way too."

"Right. Thanks. How about if you two go out and help secure the beach. I don't want any visitors."

Showing that he did put some effort into thinking, Steele said, "This happened at least twenty-four hours ago. If there were any footprints on that beach, they'd be trampled on by now, or washed away."

Rosie walked to the window. "Probably."

Hobbs nodded and he and Jackson left.

Standing with her arms folded, Rosie considered how the world could be totally different depending on what you chose to look at. Trying to ignore what was behind her, she looked out at the lake sparkling in the early morning sun. Fresh and cleanly washed by the waves, the sand glistened as the sun caught the millions of grains of quartz. When she turned around, Steele was bent down on the left side of the body. She hadn't heard him move to the desk. She had noticed an open safe and walked around the other side of the desk and behind the chair so she didn't have to look at the face again.

"Empty," Steele offered.

The safe was built into the desk and it was indeed empty.

"Wonder if the murderer got what was in it, or if it was empty all along?" he asked of no one in particular.

"I thought you avoided thinking," Rosie said with sarcasm.

Standing, Steele said, "Sometimes it just happens all by itself. You know, like hitting your knee with a hammer."

Rosie had never hit her knee with a hammer, but she knew what he meant.

"I wonder what she did to afford a joint like this. Must be worth a bundle with this view."

Steele was doing far more than his share of thinking. "Must be," Rosie agreed. "Margaret may have the answer to that."

"Margaret?" asked Steele.

"Yeah, Margaret, the housekeeper."

"Oh yeah. Margaret."

Rosie was constantly frustrated at Steele's habit of forgetting details and often wondered how he got to be a detective. But he was, and he seemed to do enough to keep his job and not make waves. And sometimes not making waves was more important than doing the job.

Rosie scanned the top of the desk, stopping at the phone with a built-in answering machine. The red light was flashing in bursts of four. Four messages.

Steele saw her looking at the phone. "Sure like to know what's on that tape."

"Yeah, me too." Rosie took a pocket-sized recorder that she used for verbal notes out of her jacket pocket, turned it on, and placed it next to the phone. Using the end of her pen, she pushed play on the answering machine. The machine rewound and then started automatically.

There were no dates or times on the tape, but one of the messages helped. The first message was from a male with a deep voice asking her to call. He had some information about a friend from London. The second and third were confirming dates for next weekend. The last was a very formal male voice explaining that Mr. Smith had asked him to call due to the fact that they had a date at eight and it was now ten.

Busy girl, Rosie thought. Miss Brock had missed a date, but was it Saturday or Sunday night, or Saturday or Sunday morning?

Rosie pushed the *save message* button with her pen, switched off her recorder, and sighed. Already knowing the answer, Rosie asked, "You wanna stay with the scene? I'm going to look around up here."

"Sure. I'll holler when we get company."

She nodded and gratefully left the room, wondering how someone got so callous that they didn't mind staying in the same room with a dead person, especially one so brutally disfigured. She had also wondered what Miss Brock did for a living. But, after listening to the messages, she thought she could make a good guess.

Chapter 60

Charles Lamb approached Glenlake a little after 8:30. He planned to sit on the beach again before starting work and wondered if the old man would still be sleeping behind the rocks. But he soon forgot about the beach when he saw the street crowded with people. They were standing on the grass and in the middle of the street, and Charles couldn't see to the end of the road. Wondering what had happened, he figured someone had drowned.

He found a place to park on the other side of Sheridan Road. It only took a minute to walk back to where the crowd was. There must have been a hundred people. Slowly inching his way between people, Charles finally made it to where a yellow tape was stretched across the street and the front of Miss Brock's house.

He quietly asked if anyone knew what had happened. No one did. Everyone was whispering and wondering. Charles counted three squad cars, one with its lights still flashing. Three policemen were standing behind the tape looking very serious. Charles considered asking one of them what the problem was, but he had never been one to approach a policeman. He thought every policeman knew about every person who was arrested in the city and that they would remember his face. Even though he had done nothing wrong, it didn't pay to go looking for trouble. So Charles stood and waited like everyone else. Except no one else was worried about Amanda.

Chapter 61

Rosie didn't find anything of importance in the rest of the upstairs rooms. She told Steele she was going back down to talk to Margaret again. Steele nodded. Halfway down, she met Officer Lee leading Doc Naggy up the stairs. Half a flight behind them was Jim Head, the evidence tech.

"Well, glad you all could make it," she said with a smile.

"Mornin' to you too, Detective," sputtered the doc as he caught his breath between each word. Between his weight and the cigarettes, he didn't handle stairs too well. He rested on the landing.

Taking up the doc's rear, Jim Head smiled at Rosie and rolled his eyes.

Rosie smiled back, shook her head, and made her way back to the kitchen where Margaret was sipping tea and telling Officer Martin about her grandchildren.

Rosie winked at Martin and sat down across from Margaret. "Sounds like you have a nice family, Mrs. Rivera."

"Yes. I have three grandchildren," she said proudly.

Rosie shook her head. "I'd better get started if I'm going to catch up to you." They all laughed.

"Mrs. Rivera, would you mind if I ask a few more questions?"

She straightened in her chair. "No. I am much better now. And please, just call me Margaret."

"Okay. Thank you, Margaret. I won't be long, and then you can get back to your family. When was the last time you saw Miss Brock?"

"That was on Friday, when I worked."

Nodding, Rosie continued, "Did anything strange happen?"

Margaret shook her head slowly.

"What time did you last see her?"

"I left at quarter to six so I could catch the six o'clock bus."

"Did Miss Brock seem normal?"

"What do you mean?" asked Margaret with a puzzled look.

Rosie spread her hands, palms up. "Was she the same as usual? Or did she seem like there was a problem with anything?"

Margaret thought for a few seconds. "No. No, she was just the same. She told me to have a nice weekend and she would see me Monday—today." A look of sadness came over her face.

Rosie quickly asked if the door was locked when she arrived this morning.

Margaret took a deep breath and pulled back her shoulders. "Yes, it was, just like always. I opened the door with my key."

Ronny Steele walked into the kitchen. Rosie didn't want him to disturb Margaret, and his presence alone was usually disturbing.

"Detective Steele, Margaret tells us the door was locked when she got here this morning. Would you mind checking the front door and the windows and see if there might have been some other point of entry?" She was explaining not for Ronny's benefit, but for Margaret's.

Steele nodded. As he turned to leave, he pulled the half-smoked cigar out of his suit coat pocket. Rosie knew it would be lit before he stepped onto the driveway. And she wondered how he avoided catching on fire.

She turned back to Margaret, who seemed very calm and collected. "Margaret, did Miss Brock tell you anything about her plans for the weekend?"

"No," she stated firmly. "She does not discuss her plans."

Rosie watched Margaret involuntarily fingering her cup. "There were four messages on her answering machine. One was from a man who had a date with her and she didn't show up."

Margaret's face lost all emotion. "I do not know about that," she said sternly.

"You say she was usually out late on the weekends. She must have been very popular."

Margaret said nothing.

"Did she have a boyfriend?"

"No," Margaret said slowly. "I do not think so."

Rosie softened. "She must have been very pretty."

Margaret's lip quivered. "Yes, she was. Very pretty."

Rosie switched topics. "Did you know about the safe in her desk?"

Margaret nodded.

"It's open and empty. Did she keep much money in there?"

"Sometimes. There were many times when I came to work and the safe was open with much money in it. Miss Brock would forget and leave it open. She would be very tired and need to go to bed."

Rosie cocked her head to the right. "How much is *much* money, Margaret?"

"Oh, I do not know. Many bills."

"Cash?"

"Yes."

Pushing a strand of hair out of her eyes, Rosie crossed her legs under the table. "This is a beautiful house."

"Yes, it is very nice."

"Do you have any idea how much it's worth?"

"Oh no, I do not know that. It is not my business."

"I'm wondering what Miss Brock did for a living to own a house like this."

Margaret again said nothing. She was a very careful woman. And, because she was so careful, and because her mood had changed from sadness to hardness, Rosie felt there was something Margaret wasn't talking about.

"Margaret, do you know anyone who might do this to Miss Brock?"

Margaret's eyes welled up and she shook her head.

"Do you know if there is family? Anyone who might have a key to the house?"

"No. She did not have any family that she talked about. No one ever called."

"Hmm. That's too bad. It's nice to have family."

Margaret nodded and wiped her eyes with a Kleenex. "But there *was* someone with a key."

"Oh? Who was that?"

"A few weeks ago Miss Brock hired a man to do work on the house. She gave him a key in case I was not here."

"Did you meet the man?"

"Yes. He was a big man. See the cabinets? He was making them new."

"Was he someone Miss Brock knew? A friend maybe?"

"Oh no," Margaret said fervently. "She never knew him before."

"Do you know where she met him?"

She looked down. "No. I do not ask such things."

"I understand," Rosie said gently. "Do you know his name?"

"Yes. Mr. Charles Lamb."

"How many times did he come?"

"Oh, he came every day. He is still working." She pointed to the cabinets. "See, the cabinets are not finished. He has more work to do."

"Was he coming today?"

"I think. But I am not so sure."

"What time did he start?"

"Usually nine o'clock. But he would come early. I saw him sometimes. He would go sit on the beach before he worked."

"Did anything seem strange about Mr. Lamb?"

Margaret tried to think of something. She was sure Mr. Lamb had killed Miss Brock, but there was nothing she could think of. She shook her head. "I do not know."

"He should be here soon," said Rosie, glancing at her watch. Rosie knew he wouldn't be able to get out to the beach. And, if he was expected and didn't show up, that would be meaningful.

"Do you know if Miss Brock kept his phone number somewhere?"

"No. I think she didn't know his phone number. She just knew his name."

"How did they arrange when he would come?"

Margaret shrugged. "I do not know. He just came every day."

Rosie leaned in closer to Margaret. "Doesn't that seem strange to you, Margaret? Miss Brock hiring someone without even having his phone number?"

Margaret looked down. "What Miss Brock did was not my business."

Rosie knew she wasn't going to get any more out of Margaret even if she did know something.

Rosie folded her hands again and leaned towards Margaret. "Did Miss Brock work, Margaret?"

No answer.

"Do you not know?"

Margaret stared right through Rosie.

"It's okay, you know. Some people don't have to work. I wish I didn't have to. I'm just wondering. Maybe someone she worked with would know something."

Margaret looked thoughtful and brought her eyes back to Rosie. "How about Mr. Lamb?"

"Yes. That's a good lead. We'll talk to Mr. Lamb. Can you think of anything else that might help?"

Margaret said nothing, but looked like she was wrestling with something.

Rosie reached out and rested her hand on Margaret's arm. "Is there something you want to tell me, Margaret?"

Margaret breathed shallowly and quickly and set her jaw. "Miss Brock did work." She sat as solid as a rock.

"Where did she work, Margaret?"

"I do not know that."

"What *do* you know?"

She gave up whatever struggle she was having and said, "I know what she did." She looked right at Rosie. "She had dates. Very late."

"Dates? What do you mean?"

"I mean she had dates—dates that men paid her for."

Rosie wasn't surprised. "Are you saying she was a prostitute?"

She gave Rosie a stern look. "I am not saying. It is not my business."

"Okay. That's okay, Margaret. But you *are* saying that Miss Brock was paid by men to go out with them."

She nodded. It was obvious this was hard for her, and Rosie didn't want to make it any harder. It was also obvious what Miss Brock did for a living.

The screen door slammed shut and Steele came back in. The cigar was nowhere in sight. "Everything is locked up. If somebody got in, they locked up on the way out."

Rosie nodded.

Steele looked nervous, like he was waiting for orders. "Mind if I go back out? I'll take a look at the beach."

"Just a second. Martin, would you stay with Margaret and get her address and phone?"

Martin nodded and pulled a chair next to Margaret.

Rosie walked out in the hall with Steele. "We need to get ahold of Andrews and Spanell."

"Why?"

"Guess what Miss Brock did for a living."

"Yeah, those messages weren't for music lessons. But, by the looks of this place, she didn't play in the same league as our other ladies."

"That's for sure. Pretty high-end. Probably catering to corporate America. But nevertheless…"

"I'll give them a call."

"Right. Would you make a sweep of the beach? I had them tape off beyond the rocks to the north and down to the breakwall to the south. We're missing a murder weapon. Those rocks might be a good drop spot. Or if it was thrown in the water, it may have washed up somewhere."

"Who'd be that stupid?" asked Steele.

"We don't deal with geniuses."

Steele nodded.

Rosie started up the stairs, wondering if Miss Brock was killed in the early hours of Saturday or Sunday.

* * *

Doc Naggy was standing in front of the picture window looking out at the lake.

Rosie joined him.

"So peaceful," he said. "Draw a line a mile offshore and you enter a world free of the human stench."

Rosie was surprised. "Didn't know you were a philosopher."

He just took a deep breath.

"Why a mile?" she asked.

Still looking out as the sun moved behind a cloud, Doc said, "Just an arbitrary number. To some distance offshore, humans are using the lake to kill themselves or dump their violence. Coast Guard finds a bloated, floating body, or they wash ashore." He shook his head.

Rosie had never had a conversation with Doc about anything besides autopsies and was surprised by this look into his personal world.

"What about the fish?" she asked.

"What *about* the fish?" he asked with a confused look.

She shrugged. "Pretty violent even without humans. Fish are being eaten by other fish all the time."

"Survival, not mindless violence. Everything out there has a purpose."

"I guess. But violence has a purpose, even if it's mindless. You have a time of death?"

He gave her a disgusted look. "Why do you guys always do that to me? Drives me nuts. Of course I don't have a time of death. Won't have it till I do the autopsy."

Back on familiar ground with the Doc, Rosie said, "Okay, semantics. You know what I mean. How about a window? It would help to know if it was Saturday or Sunday morning."

"Early morning hours Saturday. I'd say between three and seven."

So the timing fit—but the victim didn't. Perhaps *Friday* had stepped up in the world.

* * *

Rosie returned to the kitchen. Martin and Margaret were again chatting.

"Margaret, did you take the bus today?" asked Rosie.

"Yes."

"Are you okay taking the bus home?"

"Yes, I can walk to the stop."

"Okay, I'll walk you out."

Margaret stood up. "I just have a purse in the dining room. I will get it." Then she stopped and looked down at the floor and started shaking. "I do not have a job anymore."

Rosie touched her shoulder. "I'm sorry, Margaret."

Rosie held the screen door for Margaret who had stopped in the bathroom to freshen up a bit. On the way out, Rosie warned her about the crowd and told her just to ignore them. Margaret paused at the door and glanced behind her. Knowing she was thinking about Miss Brock, Rosie watched her face again fill with sorrow. But, in the few seconds it took to turn back to the door, Margaret was again composed and stern and ready for the crowd. She had known hardship, thought Rosie. And she also knew how to deal with it.

Chapter 62

Charles stood in partial sun and watched the house along with the rest of the crowd. He saw policemen and detectives come and go. One detective checked all the windows and the front door. Maybe it was a burglary, Charles thought. Someone must have known about all the money Amanda kept and broken in. He wondered if they found the money. He wanted to go in and ask Amanda if she needed help with anything, but stayed behind the tape. And every time a policeman came near, Charles turned his head.

At a little after nine, the door opened again and Charles watched as Margaret slowly walked out, stepping very carefully. She was followed by what must have been another detective, a lady. As they stepped down onto the driveway, the detective put her arm around Margaret's shoulder. The detective asked one of the policemen to help clear a path through the crowd.

Trying to catch Margaret's eye, Charles barely raised his hand to wave, but Margaret was looking down at the ground. He decided that when they were gone he would try to get in and talk to Amanda.

As Margaret reached the sidewalk she glanced up, looking almost directly at him. She was still about fifty feet away and he wondered if she saw him because she didn't react right away. He smiled, and then knew that she recognized him. But the look on her face wasn't very friendly. In fact, she looked terrified.

* * *

As she walked down the broken, concrete driveway, Margaret kept her head down, trying to ignore all the people in the street. She wanted to scream at them to go away and leave Miss Brock in peace. She found herself switching quickly between anger and sadness and was thankful for Detective Lonnigan. She let herself be guided down the driveway.

At the end of the driveway, they stepped into a patch of grass and Margaret almost lost her balance. She grabbed Rosie's arm. As she looked up into the crowd, she looked straight into the face of Charles Lamb. A wave of terror immediately swept through her and she tightened her grip on Rosie. The sun was playing through the trees and the breeze was moving shadows across the faces. At first, she wasn't entirely sure it was him. But after a few seconds she knew. It *was* Charles Lamb.

Margaret let go of Rosie and pointed and shouted, "That is Charles Lamb. That is the man who killed Miss Brock!"

* * *

Charles' smile quickly turned into fear. What did she say? Amanda was dead—and Margaret was accusing *him*. He couldn't believe what he had heard. Why would she say that? Miss Brock was the best thing that ever happened to him. It all seemed like it was moving in slow motion. But Margaret was still pointing at him, still glaring at him with a look of horror.

The lady with Margaret was looking where Margaret was pointing—in his direction, but not directly *at* him. He moved back, mixing with the crowd, and tried to move away, but the crowd had penned him in. Not able to afford the time to be polite, Charles started to push. People complained, but he ignored them. And since he was bigger than most of them, they started to clear a path and he was able to move faster. When he got to the edge of the crowd, he ran back to his car.

When he reached his car he was panting heavily. He fumbled with the keys, trying to unlock the door, then banged his head as he got in. What should have been an effortless job starting the car turned into horror. Charles panicked as his fingers took way too long to get the key into the ignition. Finally, the engine roared and he put the car in gear.

Sheridan was blocked by police cars in both directions, so Charles headed west on Glenlake. He had no idea why Margaret said what she did, but did know that the police would soon be after him.

Charles wouldn't be able to remember exactly how many, but he had been arrested three times in the last five years, once for battery in a bar, and two for domestic abuse. Sarah had accused him of hurting her. He was never sure if he was guilty or not. Too much drinking had always left him with no memory of the things she accused him of, or the time she said he did it. But he had spent time in jail.

As he drove west, he decided to stop at the bar where he did his drinking and do some thinking. He hoped the police wouldn't be able to find him. Miss Brock didn't have his address.

The farther he got from Mandy's house, the safer Charles felt. There were no sirens or red lights, no sign of anyone chasing him. As time went by, Charles calmed down and the panic subsided. A beer would help him think. The bar would be open by the time he got there.

* * *

The neon signs in the window of Lights Out came on as Charles drove up. He ordered a beer and took it to a table. He hadn't seen the bartender before. He only came at night—and usually on the weekends.

The first beer was gone quickly, and he ordered another.

He thought of Miss Brock and his hands began to shake. Why would someone kill her? And why would Margaret think he did? It was unbelievable. Maybe she really wasn't dead. Maybe he had misunderstood. But the police were there and an ambulance and all those people.

He thought about Margaret. Miss Brock had made him feel like part of the family, but Margaret had treated him like an intruder. She was never friendly, but Charles didn't know why. He was always nice to her.

He struggled to remember the weekend. He had been out drinking Friday and Saturday night and had no memory of most of Saturday or Sunday.

Chapter 63

Laura sat on her bed with the shades drawn and thought about Florida; sunshine, warmth, her favorite beach, and the view of the bay out of her balcony window. She was tired of living in seclusion.

But she had put herself in this position and had to accept the consequences. It had not been an easy decision. For over a year, she had been asking questions on the street that some people might not want asked. And she was sure those people would have no qualms about getting her to stop. But she wasn't afraid. She was sure the men around her could deal with any threats. There had been a few territory disputes and drunks who simply needed some persuasion. Stretch had wanted to deal with the drunks, but she had assured him she could handle them herself. She had a few rays of hope about what she was looking for, but nothing that led to any concrete results.

Laura actually looked forward to her evening walks. She was sure her team could deal with anything that happened. Spencer Manning was proof of that. But, other than trips to the store for food, that was the only time she got out. She was the one who had set this up, but having to call Stretch every time she wanted to go out at a time that wasn't already arranged was getting old. She longed for the simple freedom of taking a walk down a Chicago street, much less on a hot beach in Florida.

Chapter 64

Rosie scanned the crowd and asked Margaret to point out Mr. Lamb, but he had disappeared. She asked Margaret to stand with an officer and keep looking. She called the station from the house and asked for information on Charles Lamb. A minute later, she had a phone number and an address on the south side of Chicago. Rosie filled in Lieutenant Powolski on the prostitute angle and Charles Lamb. Perhaps they just got lucky. Stosh agreed that she and Steele should head to Lamb's address to question him. Detectives from Area South would meet her there.

"Okay," said Rosie. "We'll be a half hour at least."

"Right. I'll bring the captain up to speed."

Steele was standing at the edge of the rocks.

"Put out the smoke, Steele. We're heading south."

He pushed the cigar onto a boulder and put it back in his mouth. "Nice day for a drive. Any special reason?"

"Margaret says the handyman killed Brock. She spotted him in the crowd and then he took off. Lives on the south side. South detectives are on their way."

* * *

Rosie and Steele drove along the lake to 35th Street and headed west. A half hour later they turned onto Grace and slowed, looking for a white Chevy Impala as they approached the address. It was not in sight, but an unmarked car was parked several houses down from Lamb's. Rosie parked and walked over to the car.

"Morning. Lonnigan, 18th."

The driver nodded. "Perry and Walsh. You got the lead on this?"

"Yes, we'd like to question him. He's been ID'd by the housekeeper, but we have no evidence."

"Right. Less paperwork I have to do the better. How'd she die?"

"Stabbed. Chest and eye."

"Eye? Don't see that much. Any ideas?"

"Nope. Like I said, we've got nothing. We'll wait with you and see if he shows."

Rosie returned to her Ford and told Steele the plan. They put ten bucks on a show-up time. She took after noon and Steele before. It was 10:15.

While they waited, they got a call with priors on Charles Lamb. Two arrests for domestic abuse and one for battery at a bar. He had attacked a woman he accused of being a prostitute.

Chapter 65

Steele spotted the white Chevy a little before eleven-thirty coming slowly down the street from the north. A man matching Lamb's description was driving. The man turned into the driveway and stopped. Rosie radioed the station.

* * *

As Charles turned onto his street, he felt better because he didn't see any police cars. He turned into the driveway and pulled up to the garage. He thought he should put his car in the garage in case someone had seen him leaving Glenlake. But as he opened the garage door, he remembered he had spent the last week cleaning out the basement and moving boxes to the garage. Sarah had recently given him a long list of chores to do and was nagging him to get rid of the boxes so she could pull her car in. But he had put it off. He didn't care what Sarah wanted. It would take hours to move the boxes so he could pull his car in. But since he hadn't seen any police, he felt safe leaving his car in the driveway.

* * *

Rosie waited until he was almost to the front door before she and Steele left the Ford, followed by the detectives from Area South. Charles noticed them coming up the driveway and hurried to get the door open. They reached him before he did.

Rosie held up her badge, introduced herself, and asked if he was Charles Lamb.

Charles very nervously said he was and asked what they wanted.

She introduced the other detectives. "Do you know Amanda Brock?"

He looked quickly at the other detectives, who just stared at him. "Yes."

Rosie took a step closer. "Miss Brock has been murdered. We'd like to ask you some questions."

So it was true. Amanda was dead. Murdered. But why were they talking to him?

Charles fumbled with his keys and said, "Okay. I'll open the door and we can go inside."

"Okay," Rosie said firmly.

Charles dropped the keys. Perry picked them up and handed them to Charles.

"Why do you want to talk to me?" Charles asked.

"We're questioning everyone who knew Miss Brock."

Charles opened the door and they all walked into a sparsely furnished house. As they walked to the dining room table, Rosie pulled out a ten spot and handed it to Steele.

Chapter 66

Charles squirmed in his chair. No one was talking. The lady was staring at him.

"I thought you said you had some questions," Charles said nervously.

"We do," said Steele.

Charles looked confused. "Then why aren't you asking?"

Rosie waited another minute before starting.

"Did you know Miss Brock?"

"Yes, I worked for her."

"What work did you do?"

Charles had no idea why that would matter if Miss Brock was dead. "I was working on things around the house."

Rosie nodded. "That's what you do for a living?"

Charles hesitated. "Well, yes, but I've been out of work recently." He watched the lady make notes on a pad.

"How did she happen to hire you?"

Wondering whether he should make up something that sounded more reasonable, Charles said, "I met her in a gas station."

Rosie looked up from her pad. The detectives from Area South walked around the room, looking at everything.

"You're telling me Miss Brock hired someone she met in a gas station?"

Charles took a deep breath. He knew it didn't sound good. But it was the truth. He looked down at the table.

"Yes." He told them about the limo and the man with the gravelly voice.

"And how long have you been working for her?"

"A week. I started on Friday."

"I see," said Rosie. More notes on the pad.

Knowing the answer, Rosie asked, "And did Miss Brock always let you into the house?"

Charles again hesitated, wondering if he should be answering all these questions. "No, sometimes she wasn't home."

Rosie's eyebrows lifted. "So how did you get in?"

"Well, there was a cleaning lady."

"So, she let you in if Miss Brock wasn't home?"

"Yes." Charles looked down again. "But not always."

"So when the cleaning lady wasn't there how did you get in?"

"I had a key. Miss Brock gave it to me."

Steele stood up and sat on the table. "Are you trying to tell us that a woman you met at a gas station gave you a key to her house?"

"Yes," he said in a quiet voice.

"Does that make sense to you?"

Charles thought maybe it didn't, and his hands started to tremble.

He felt like a trapped animal as he looked from Rosie to Steele with wide eyes. "I don't know. You're trying to confuse me."

Rosie leaned back in her chair and crossed her legs. "No, we're not, Charles. We're just trying to get some information about Miss Brock so we can find who killed her. Will you help us?"

Charles nodded. "I want to help. I liked Miss Brock."

"I'm sure you did," said Rosie. "And I'm sure Miss Brock would appreciate you helping us find who killed her. Do you own a gun, Charles?"

He looked upset. "She was shot?"

"I asked if you own a gun."

He shook his head. "No." He wondered what that had to do with Amanda.

A sad look filled his eyes. He hadn't acted surprised by the gun question. He didn't seem too smart, and Rosie thought she could get him to mention a knife.

"So why do you think Miss Brock gave a stranger a key to her house?"

Charles straightened in his chair. "I needed to work. She said I was a nice man."

Rosie smiled. "You seem like a nice man. Thanks for helping us." And she believed that—he *did* seem like a nice man.

"Can you tell us where you were early Saturday morning from about three until seven?"

Charles looked down and said nothing.

"Mr. Lamb?"

He looked up at Rosie. "Why does that matter?"

"Because that's the time Miss Brock was killed."

A look of sadness filled Charles' face. He couldn't believe Miss Brock was dead.

Rosie leaned toward him. "Mr. Lamb, where were you?"

He shook his head and said, "At home, I guess."

With a furrowed brow, Rosie asked, "What do you mean, you guess?"

Charles took a deep breath. "I was at a bar Friday night. I don't remember anything about that night."

Rosie looked confused. "You don't remember when you got home?"

Charles shook his head.

Steele also shook his head.

Rosie continued. "What time did you leave the bar?"

"I don't know, but they close at two."

With disbelief, Rosie said, "So you are telling me you don't remember leaving the bar, driving home, or getting home."

Charles nodded slowly.

Rosie looked at Steele, who shrugged and tapped his temple.

"What *do* you remember?"

Charles thought and said, "I remember waking up."

"Good, what time was that?"

"About noon."

Rosie tried to hide her look of astonishment. "How much did you drink?"

Charles shrugged. "A lot."

Rosie made a mental note to check with the bartender. "What's the name of the bar?"

Charles hesitated, wondering if he should say. But then he realized it had been quite a while since he was in trouble there. "Lights Out."

"And where is that?"

"On Western, north of Diversey."

Rosie jotted that on her pad, "Okay, thanks Charles."

Charles looked confused and squirmed in his chair. "Why do you want to know where I was?"

"Because Margaret said you killed Miss Brock. So we have to ask."

Charles slammed his fist on the table. Steele stood up. "I didn't kill her! Why are you saying I killed her? I wouldn't kill her. She was the nicest lady I ever met!" He was breathing hard and trembling.

Rosie replied calmly. "I didn't say you killed her, Charles. We're just following up on what Margaret said. We'll listen to you just as much as we listened to her. We're just asking questions. Would you like some water?"

He shook his head no.

"Okay. I just have a few more questions." She picked up her pen. "How did Miss Brock pay you?"

Charles was nervous. He didn't want to tell anyone about the money. He didn't want Sarah to find out. But the lady knew he must have made money if he worked, so it was okay to tell her. "She paid me cash. Twenty dollars an hour."

Rosie smiled. "You must be very skilled to make twenty dollars an hour."

Charles would have worked for less but didn't want to say that.

Rosie did some figuring on her pad. "You said you started on Friday, so you worked there six days, right?"

Charles nodded.

"Eight hours a day?"

"Usually," he said cautiously. He wasn't sure why she was asking.

"So, at twenty dollars an hour, that comes to nine hundred sixty dollars. Is that right?"

Charles wasn't sure how to answer. He could not have done the math. "I suppose. But it's not all there."

"What do you mean?"

Looking from Rosie to Steele, Charles admitted he had spent some.

"Sure. How much did you spend?"

"I don't remember—some."

"What did you spend it on?"

Charles was silent and again looked from one to the other. He liked the lady—she called him Charles. He had spent a lot at the bar but had no recollection of Friday night, much less how much he spent.

"I'm waiting."

With hunched shoulders he admitted it was at the bar, but he didn't remember how much.

Rosie nodded. "Nothing wrong with that, Charles. Lots of people spend their money in bars."

Steele walked to the other side of the table and asked if Charles knew about the safe in the desk.

Charles responded, "Yes, that's where she kept the money to pay me." Charles stared at the pad where the lady was looking and wondered what she had written.

Rosie continued. "You said it's not all there. Where did you mean?"

"What?"

Rosie folded her hands on the table. "The money, where is it?"

He didn't answer. He didn't want anyone to know where his money was.

"It has to be somewhere, Charles. Did you put it in the bank?"

Charles was thinking as hard as he could. It wasn't against the law to hide money. He just didn't want Sarah to get it. "I don't have to tell you. It's my money."

Steele started to say something but Rosie stopped him. "You don't have to Charles. But I wonder what you're hiding. If you didn't do anything, there's no reason not to tell us."

"I—I don't want my wife to know. She would take it all."

Rosie nodded. "I understand that. Perfectly okay. And we have no reason to tell her. But you have to admit the situation is pretty strange—Miss Brock hiring someone she just met and giving him a key to her house. If she actually paid you, it would make more sense."

That made sense to Charles. "I hid it in the bushes."

Rosie smiled more broadly this time. "Great. Would you show us?"

As Rosie stood up she said, "Just to recap here, there should be nine hundred sixty dollars less whatever you spent at the bar."

Charles admitted that sounded right and led them outside, around the side of the garage.

* * *

Charles explained that he had put the money in an envelope in a plastic baggie and hidden it in the bushes. He pointed to where it was. They couldn't see it.

"Would you please get it, Charles?" asked Rosie.

Steele stood with his arms crossed, looking bored.

Charles stepped into the bushes, pushed apart the branches, and reached in and picked up the baggie. Steele put out his hand, but Charles handed it to Rosie, who had pulled on gloves, and they all walked back into the house.

Rosie opened the baggie and pulled a pile of cash out of the envelope. They didn't have to count it to see that there were several thousand dollars. Rosie started counting.

Charles stood still, wondering what was going on.

Steele stepped closer to him. "Mr. Lamb, you said there was less than a thousand dollars in that envelope. How much Rosie?"

"I need to count again to make sure, but I got three thousand, eight hundred twenty."

Steele whistled. "Can you explain that, Mr. Lamb?"

Charles had no idea. He shook his head. "Someone else must have put it in there."

Steele continued. "Who else knew the baggie was in the bushes?"

Charles shook his head. "No one." He didn't understand what was happening.

Rosie called Perry back into the room and asked him to stay with Charles. She and Steele walked to the kitchen and discussed the money in the envelope. They decided they had enough for probable cause and returned to the living room.

Steele stood behind Charles. Rosie came up on his left and said, "Mr. Lamb, you are under arrest for suspicion of the murder of Amanda Brock." She started to read him his rights.

Breathing in short gasps, Charles stammered, "Why are you telling me that? I didn't do anything wrong. They tell me that when I do something wrong!" His face was flushed and he was growing more agitated by the second.

"We're just trying to protect your rights, Charles."

"I don't need protection!" He was yelling. "I wouldn't hurt Miss Brock. Why does it matter that there's more money in the envelope?"

Rosie finished his rights and got out her cuffs. "Because her safe was robbed. Please put your hands behind your back."

With slumped shoulders he put his hands behind him and Rosie snapped on the cuffs.

Charles got into the back seat of the unmarked car and sat with his head bowed to his chest. Nothing was making any sense.

Steele asked Perry to get a search warrant and to call when they had it.

* * *

Jimmy saw the people with Mr. Lamb at the front door and had taken up his position in the tree house. They looked very important. He waited and watched as they came around the garage and Mr. Lamb showed them his hiding spot. They took the money. He wished he had taken it first.

Chapter 67

Steele processed Charles Lamb. Two hours later, Perry called and told Steele he had the search warrant. Rosie and Steele headed back to the Lamb house with Charles' keys.

The four detectives entered the house. Rosie and Steele headed upstairs and Perry and Walsh took the first floor. After ten minutes, Perry called upstairs.

"Hey, Detectives, you gotta see this."

Rosie followed Steele downstairs. Two varnished mahogany chests were open on the dining room table. One held a silverware dining set with knives, forks, spoons, and serving utensils. The other held a beautiful silver dagger with a snake wrapped around the handle. And next to the dagger was an empty spot that sure looked like it used to hold its twin.

Rosie and Steele took the chest with the dagger and headed back to the station.

Just as Perry and Walsh were walking out of the house, Sarah pulled into the driveway and got out of the car. She walked around the car with hands on her hips.

"Who the hell are you, and what are you doing in my house?" she yelled.

They introduced themselves and showed their badges.

"Are you Mrs. Lamb?" asked Perry.

"Who the hell else would I be! What are you doing here?"

Perry talked while Walsh stood to the side watching carefully. "Your husband has been arrested. He was taken to the 18th precinct."

"Arrested? Did he get in another fight? I told him if he ever..."

Perry stopped her. "No, ma'am. Suspicion of murder." While he explained the situation, Sarah fell back against the car and braced herself against the fender.

"Are you okay, ma'am?"

"Are you kidding?" She had lowered her voice, but was just as belligerent.

Perry told her he would get her the station address and phone number so she could find out when the bail hearing would be.

She gave Perry an angry look and said, "Unless it's under fifty dollars, it isn't going to matter."

* * *

Sarah walked into the house, slamming the door behind her and thought about bail. She hadn't had bail money for battery. She sure as hell wouldn't have it for murder. She could ask Charles' brother, but she really didn't want to. He would give her a lecture about psychology and how you can't change fate. Sarah had heard it all before.

As soon as Sarah entered the house she saw the chest of silverware and wondered what was going on. More importantly, she noticed the chest with the daggers was gone. Charles was lucky he wasn't in the room.

Chapter 68

Spencer had left early Monday morning and had spent the day in Milwaukee looking for an ex-husband who wasn't paying child support. He heard about the murder of Amanda Brock on the radio on his way home.

He stopped at the butcher shop before going home and picked up a ribeye. He also bought a late paper from the man at the corner shed.

As Spencer put the steak on the counter, he noticed the flashing light on his answering machine. There were three messages. The second was from Laura. She said she would call back.

As the steak cooked on the grill, Spencer read the article about the arrest of Charles Lamb that was accompanied by his picture. The article included the supposition that Amanda Brock was a lady of the evening and the hope that the Friday killings were over with the arrest of Mr. Lamb.

Spencer was doubtful. From what he read, Miss Brock was in a different league than the other victims. While it was certainly possible that the killer was the same, it didn't seem likely.

Chapter 69

Charles Lamb appeared in court about four p.m. for his initial appearance. The judge ruled there was sufficient probable cause. After hearing that Charles could not afford a lawyer, he declared that one would be appointed for him.

* * *

At 8:10 Monday evening, Benjamin Tucker arrived at the 18th precinct station and asked for Detective Lonnigan. She came out in a few minutes and handed Ben the file on Charles Lamb.

"Hello, Ben," said Rosie. She looked tired.

"Evening, Detective. You're keeping us busy."

"Wish I wasn't. Always thought I'd like to work in Mayberry."

Ben sighed. "Pretty idyllic. Just one day of Mayberry would be nice. Thanks." He found an empty interview room, sat down, and opened the file.

Charles Lamb. Forty-two years old. Married to Sarah for eight years. No kids. Six-foot three, two hundred thirty pounds. Been arrested three times, once for battery, two for domestic abuse.

Ben read through the arrest history and the events of the day, including the discovery of the money and the missing knife.

Several items seemed strange. Why would Brock hire someone she met in a gas station and then give him a key to her house? Why would he hide the money in the bushes? Ben rubbed the back of his neck as he read, trying to ease a slight headache.

The money discrepancy and the missing knife were certainly worrisome, even though there might be explanations for both. And why did the maid accuse Mr. Lamb? Also worrisome were the facts that there was no forced entry, Mr. Lamb had a key, and he had no alibi.

Ben let out a deep sigh. He would rather have been at home with a glass of wine. One of the things he liked about this job was fairly normal hours. That hadn't been true lately. The office was greatly over-worked. Wondering how this case would go, Ben leaned back in the chair and closed his eyes. He could easily have fallen asleep.

The sound of the door opening brought Ben back to reality. Rosie poked her head in and said, "Been looking for you. You can see your client. He's in visitation with his wife."

Chapter 70

Spencer's phone rang at a little before eight.

"Spencer?"

"Yes."

"Laura. Do you have a few minutes?"

He had as much time as she wanted.

"I do," he answered.

"I would like to meet with you to discuss your idea."

Trying to contain his excitement, Spencer agreed and asked when and where.

"Can you come to my apartment tomorrow at one?"

"I can."

"And this time try ringing the bell."

"Will do. Can I ask a question?" He thought he already knew the answer.

"Sure."

"This is a dangerous proposition. Why are you willing to do this?"

"I haven't said I would. And I don't want to talk about it on the phone. If I do decide to, I'll tell you tomorrow."

"Fair enough. See you then."

He hung up.

As he stared at the phone, Spencer realized he had lost his excitement. Even though Laura was amazingly well-protected, he was asking her to risk her life. He wasn't sure that *he* would agree to do it. But then it wasn't *his* sister.

Chapter 71

While Ben was reading the file, Sarah arrived at the station. She was told to wait a few minutes, then was led to the visitation room where Charles was waiting behind glass.

Charles lowered his head and sheepishly said, "Hello, Sarah."

She looked disgusted and just shook her head. After staring at him for a minute, she said, "I've supported you for years. I let you go off drinking and who knows what the hell else, and this is the thanks I get. Well, I've been taking care of you long enough. Now the taxpayers can."

As Charles started to reply, the door opened and Ben walked in. He stood behind and a little to the side of Sarah. Charles glanced at him warily and then looked back to Sarah.

"But I didn't do it. I wouldn't hurt Miss Brock. You need to hire a good lawyer," he pleaded.

"Perhaps you haven't noticed," she spat at him, "but one of us hasn't been working. Money is not something we have a lot of."

"Well, maybe money for bail," he said hopefully.

"What the hell is the matter with you? Didn't I just..."

"But Sarah," he pleaded. "I didn't kill Miss Brock."

Ben was shocked by what he saw from Mrs. Lamb. There was nothing but hatred in her reaction.

The small woman took a fighting stance, and with slow, measured words, said, "I don't care what you did or didn't do to Miss Brock." She set her jaw and squinted. In a staccato sentence, like a machine gun in slow motion, she asked, "Where - in - the - hell - are - my - daggers?"

Her controlled anger was equaled by his fear. She was two thirds his size but loomed over him as he cowered in his chair.

"I don't know what you're talking about."

Ben felt like he was watching a tiger preparing to pounce. He interrupted. "If I may."

"And who the hell are you?" barked Sarah.

"Benjamin Tucker. Public Defender's Office. I've been assigned to your husband's case."

"I suppose he needs a lawyer. But so much for the *good* part."

Ben had been through this before and kept his cool. "Public Defender doesn't mean not good."

"Then what *does* it mean?" Sarah asked belligerently.

"It means free, but my skills are just as good as a high-priced lawyer."

"And you expect me to believe that? If you had the skills, you'd *be* a high-priced lawyer."

On the outside, Ben didn't react. On the inside he needed something for the ulcer he was developing. This theme was getting old.

"Okay, Mr. Just-As-Good Lawyer, what about bail?"

"Well, there's a bond hearing in the morning."

She just laughed. "I can go as high as fifty bucks. Do you think it will be fifty bucks, Mr. Good Lawyer?" She glared at him.

After a deep breath, he politely said, "We'll have to wait and see."

"Right. You wait and see. I'll start making plans to visit him in prison." She glared at Ben. "Since I'm getting nothing from my genius husband, I'll ask you. Where are my daggers?"

She obviously cared more about her daggers than her husband. This was not going well.

With carefully chosen words, Ben replied, "The police have the case. They took it as evidence."

"Evidence? How could my daggers be evidence?"

Moving closer to the glass, Ben took a deep breath and let it out slowly, trying to stay calm. "Miss Brock was stabbed."

"And that has what to do with *my* daggers?"

"One of them is missing."

She stared at Ben as that sunk in and then slowly moved her stare to Charles. He immediately looked down.

Charles had seen that look before and knew it didn't mean anything good for him.

Her powerful stare continued. Charles continued to look down.

The tiger pounced. "You killed someone with my grandfather's dagger? You rotten bastard! I hope you rot in hell!"

Ben couldn't believe what he was hearing. "Mrs. Lamb, your husband is being held under suspicion of murder. He needs your support here. Can you tell me when he got home Saturday morning?"

She turned her angry stare back to Ben and left without saying another word.

Still standing, Ben said, "I'm sorry for this, this..." Ben waved his hand. "Usually we get a bit more support from family. She's just upset at the moment."

Charles shook his head. "No, she's upset all the time. What's going to happen?"

"There will be a bond hearing in the morning. We'll have to wait and see what the judge says. We'll talk more after I get a chance to look into this."

"Judges don't like me," Charles muttered. He looked up at Ben. His look was hopeless.

Ben requested that he be moved to an interview room. They talked for twenty minutes. Charles just kept saying he didn't kill Miss Brock.

Chapter 72

After a late night, Rosie went for a run and got to the station at ten Tuesday morning. The autopsy report was waiting on her desk, along with a lab report. They both got a quick response because of the prostitute angle. She let them lie and went for a cup of coffee. Steele's desk was across from hers. He wasn't there. They had a meeting at eleven with Andrews, Spanell, and the Lieutenant.

There was nothing in either report that surprised Rosie. All of it pointed to Charles Lamb. The only good prints on the baggie were his. There were also partial smudges. His prints and Miss Brock's were on the envelope. His, hers, and various others were on the money. The autopsy report stated that death was caused by the wound in Brock's chest from a weapon approximately three quarter inch wide and four inches long, matching the silver dagger with the missing twin. He had a key to her house and was there alone according to Margaret, and he had no alibi. Seemed open-and-shut. Rosie knew things weren't always as they seemed, but it was hard to see this any other way. The time of death was narrowed to between four and six.

Charles was also a person of interest in the Friday killings because of the knife and his arrest record for attacking a woman he accused of being a prostitute.

* * *

Benjamin met Charles in court at 10:30. Bond was set at $500,000. Charles was despondent. He spoke very few words and barely responded to Ben's comments except to say they didn't have any money, he couldn't live in prison, Sarah would be glad to get rid of him, and if he was going to die, the sooner the better.

Ben had learned not to get involved with emotions, but there was something about this big man that made Ben wonder. He seemed gentle and not very smart. He was the kind of man that things happened to while he stood still, not knowing enough to get out of the way. Ben told him he would talk to him on Wednesday. He watched the big man shuffle away with slumped shoulders and small steps, but didn't have time to think about him. Two more court appearances in the afternoon and tons of paperwork would keep him busy into the evening.

* * *

Everyone but Steele was in Stosh's office at eleven. Steele showed up at five after as Lieutenant Powolski was reviewing the facts and got a stern look from Stosh.

"Okay. We have a good suspect for the latest murder. What do you think about the others?"

"Well," said Andrews. "The m.o. is wrong. But Lamb's arrest record makes him look good for it."

Steele agreed and popped a piece of gum into his mouth. He rolled up the wrapper and shot it at the basket. He missed. It rolled under the desk.

"Nice shot," said Andrews.

With a lot of effort, Steele got down on his knees to get the wrapper. "You gotta admit, this looks pretty clean. Everything points to Lamb."

"Looks can be deceiving," said Stosh. "Give this a bit more thought before you fry the guy."

Steele re-rolled the wrapper. "I think better on a full stomach."

Andrews glanced at his stomach, but held his comment.

Steele shot the wrapper into the basket and glared at Andrews. "Two points, asshole."

"Are you two done?" asked Stosh. "Unless we get some more data that proves otherwise, let's treat this as two separate cases." Stosh turned to Lonnigan and Steele. "You two have some digging to do. There are other suspects. See if you can identify Brock's clients. We have phone numbers. One of you cross-check and get some names, and we'll chat about how to handle it from there. We don't want to ruin any loving marriages. One of you check the bar. Without forced entry, I think we can rule out home invasion. Had to be someone with a key. Look into the maid and find out who benefits from the will. I'll get somebody to check backgrounds on the maid and the victim."

"Margaret?" asked Rosie with a surprised look.

"Yup. She had a key. Not a likely suspect, but turn over all the rocks." He turned back to Andrews and Spanell. "We're checking records for someone with prostitutes in their past. You guys have anything new on our man *Friday*?"

"Not a thing," said Spanell. "We've been trying to tie the victims, but so far there's nothing there. I like Lamb. I hate to say it, but so far Spencer's name-suggestion theory is the only thing that ties them all together."

Stosh rolled his eyes. "Well, don't tell *him* that. Get outta my office."

Chapter 73

Spencer arrived at Laura's apartment right on time. He rang the bell and headed upstairs. He knocked on the door and she asked who it was.

She opened the door and let him in.

"The place look different with someone in it?" she asked with a slight smile.

Spencer grimaced. "I do apologize. Can't tell you how badly I feel."

Her smile broadened. "It's okay. Mostly kidding. But beware of the part that isn't."

"Noted."

"Don't mean to be inhospitable, but we're leaving."

There was no room for discussion. It was an order. Spencer was more than happy to follow and not ask questions. He certainly remembered what she was capable of.

Figuring that they were driving back to the empty building where he was held captive, Spencer was surprised when she walked across the street and entered the apartment building opposite hers. She held the door for him.

They climbed the stairs to the second floor where Laura knocked on 205.

One of the men Spencer had seen Saturday opened the door.

"You two remember each other. Spencer, meet Stretch. Stretch, meet Spencer."

They both nodded.

Spencer looked around the bare room. Four wood chairs, a small table, and a refrigerator were the only things in the room.

Laura invited them to sit.

Spencer walked to the window and looked out. "Nice view of your apartment."

"Yes, people pay big money for views like that."

Spencer turned and walked to a chair. "Well, not exactly like that."

She didn't laugh. "I guarantee you, I pay a hefty sum for this view."

"You have people watching your apartment?"

"Yes. Around the clock."

"Why?"

She took a deep breath. "We may get to that."

Stretch was watching and listening with interest. He hoped they would *get to that*.

"So, Spencer, your theory is that this fellow is copying Jack the Ripper and choosing his victim by their names?"

"Right."

She nodded and sat. "Tell me again how you think he finds their names."

"Not sure. But could be any of several ways, including following them home or just asking."

"So you think he is just walking up to girls and asking their names?"

"Well, probably a bit more conversation than just that. But yes."

Laura rubbed her temples. "And if the name isn't right?"

"Then he moves on and tries another."

"No sex?"

"My guess is, he's not after sex. He just wants to find the right girls and kill them."

With raised eyebrows, Laura asked, "And why is he doing this?"

Spencer shook his head. "I have no clue."

Laura nodded. "No, I didn't think you did."

Stretch just listened.

"Can I ask a question?" asked Spencer.

She nodded.

"Why are you interested in my theory?"

Lie detector tests start out with baseline questions that the technician already knows the answers to so he can set up a response guideline for other questions. Spencer already knew the answer to his question. He was interested to see how Laura answered. She got up, walked to the fridge, and offered soda or juice. Both men declined.

Laura sat and took a drink of ginger ale. A far away, sad look washed over her face. "I have a sister who disappeared a few years ago from our home down in Florida." She looked at Stretch and spoke directly to him. "I guess I could have told you before, but I am a control freak and didn't want anyone else in trouble if this didn't work."

Stretch just nodded.

"Stretch, I appreciate everything you have done. I obviously trust you with my life."

She turned to Spencer. "The police looked into it but got nowhere. After a few months, I started asking questions. One of her friends told me about the parties they would have. Sex and drugs and alcohol. It started with just friends from school, but other people started to show up. This friend told me one of the men, who was older than most in the group, was especially interested in my sister and she was pretty sure they met outside the parties. Then my sister didn't show up for school. And at the next party, neither one of them showed up."

Laura stood and walked to the window.

"I did some more digging and found enough to be pretty sure he had taken her away. Whether it was voluntary or against her will I had no way of knowing. But from the man's description, I found enough to think he had added her to some sort of sex ring and was moving her around. As Stretch knows, there have been several cities, Detroit just before here."

"You don't have a name?" Spencer asked.

She shook her head.

"So, you set yourself up as a prostitute to try and find this guy?"

"Yes."

"And that's what you're talking about with the girls on the street?"

"Yes."

Stretch chimed in. "And you're showing them your sister's picture?"

"Yes."

"Have you gotten anything?" asked Spencer.

She looked sad and empty. "No."

"I'm sorry," said Spencer.

"Me too," added Stretch.

She just looked at them with tired eyes.

Spencer broke the silence. "You haven't said why you're interested in my theory."

Looking straight at him, her eyes filled with tears, and she said, "Because my sister's name is Katherine."

* * *

Laura wiped her eyes on her sleeve and got back to being in control. "And how do you propose catching him, Spencer?"

"Set up a trap. Find a girl with the same name and see if he bites."

Laura's look was not encouraging. "First, other than my sister, good luck finding someone with the right name. Second, pretty dangerous."

"Agreed on both. The killer is probably having the same trouble with the names."

"I assume you've shared this with your police friends. What do they think?"

"They think it's interesting, but don't have the money or the personnel."

She nodded. "Of course. So, back to my question."

"We could talk to girls on the street and ask if anyone has been asking their names."

Stretch interrupted. "Don't know for sure, but I may have seen someone doing exactly that." Spencer and Laura turned to him. "There's this big fellow who has talked to several girls and not bought anything."

"Can you describe him?" asked Spencer, wondering if it might be Charles.

"Not very well. Just big. Pretty far away and dark."

"I have someone in mind. I'll bring a picture for you to look at."

"Has he talked to me?" asked Laura.

Stretch shook his head. "No. I've been watching him and wondering if he would."

Laura sighed. "Well, even if he does, my name isn't Katherine or Elizabeth. If Spencer's theory is correct, if he doesn't find a girl with the right name he won't do anything."

Spencer took a deep breath. "So, let's help him out." He explained his plan and they agreed to meet back in this room at seven before Laura again headed to Broadway.

Chapter 74

After lunch, Rosie and Steele started running down the clients of Amanda Brock. The ledger contained thirty-six obvious aliases, some with phone numbers that they cross-referenced, but they didn't recognize any of the names. Steele would look into the names they *could* identify for priors. Rosie decided to go and have a chat with Margaret.

Before she left, Rosie called Lights Out. The night bartender wouldn't be in until nine. Another long day.

* * *

Margaret's house was in a block of neat, well-maintained row houses on the near-north side of the city. Garages were in the back off the alley. Rosie parked on the street and rang the bell.

A tired-looking Margaret answered and invited Rosie into the kitchen. The inside of the house matched the outside. Simple, but clean and well-kept. Margaret offered tea.

As Margaret poured, she said, "I see you arrested Mr. Lamb. I am so glad."

"Yes, but I'm here to ask some questions."

Margaret looked at Rosie without emotion. Rosie was sure Margaret had nothing to do with the murder, but she had to ask.

"Margaret, we need to interview everyone who had a key to the house."

Still no emotion.

"One of those people was you."

Margaret's eyes welled up with tears.

"You think I would hurt Miss Brock?" she asked haltingly.

Rosie reached out and touched her arm. "I have to ask, Margaret." Sure that she already knew the answer, Rosie asked Margaret where she was Saturday morning between four and six.

Margaret looked surprised. "Why, here, asleep. I woke up a little before seven."

"Do you have anyone who can verify that?"

"What do you mean? How would anyone verify that?"

"Well, a husband or children who were here."

Margaret shook her head slowly. "No. No. My children are both grown and my husband died three years ago. Miss Brock was a savior for me. I did not know what to do for a job."

"How did you get the job with Miss Brock?"

"She was sent from heaven." She took a sip of tea.

Rosie smiled. "Could you be a bit more specific?"

"Well, I was applying for jobs at hotels as a maid. I applied at eight hotels downtown. They all put my name on a list. But I did not have any experience and they were not really interested. I was coming out of the Broadlee when someone running by grabbed my bag and ripped the strap. It spilled all over the sidewalk. Miss Brock was just getting out of a limousine at the curb. She rushed over and helped me pick up my things. I was very upset. She asked what I was doing there. I told her. She said she needed a housekeeper and asked if I could travel to the north side. She gave me her address and asked for me to start the next day. I couldn't believe what I was hearing. I told her I had no experience. I did not want to make her think something else. She said that was okay. She said she could tell I was a nice person. Then she asked how I was getting home. I told her I was taking a bus. She offered for me to take the limousine. I tried to say no, but she insisted. Then, when I went to work on the first day, Miss Brock gave me a key to her house because she was not home sometimes. That is how I worked for Miss Brock."

"She sounds like a wonderful person, Margaret."

Margaret nodded with tears in her eyes.

"What are you going to do now, Margaret?"

"I am not sure. I could try hotels again. I have experience now, but I have no one to recommend me."

Rosie sighed and finished her tea before asking, "Margaret, why do you think Mr. Lamb killed Miss Brock?" Rosie couldn't read what was on Margaret's face. She seemed scared and sad.

"I do not know," Margaret said softly. "It is just a feeling." She shrugged. "He was the only one with a key. I told Miss Brock that was not a good idea."

Still watching her carefully, Rosie continued. "So you have nothing specific. There was nothing that happened to make you think that?"

Margaret looked down and slowly shook her head.

"Okay, Margaret. Good luck and thanks for the tea."

* * *

Rosie drove back to the station feeling depressed. Acts of violence touch so many lives besides the victim's.

Chapter 75

Laura was on the street by eight after checking in with the hot dog man. Spencer stood near Stretch. This time he was part of the team. And this time he *did* have a gun. He had done the paperwork to transfer his dad's .357 Magnum but had also bought a new .38 Special.

The other difference was that Laura had agreed to implement Spencer's plan. Laura had changed her name to Katherine. Stretch had replaced the name tag in her apartment in case someone followed her home, but Spencer hadn't thought the guy would go to that much trouble.

They decided Laura could still talk to girls on the street about her sister, but just show her picture. Odds were her name had been changed anyway.

They watched for three hours. Laura talked with several girls and showed them Katherine's picture. One of them was more talkative than the others. She was older and perhaps wiser in her chosen occupation. She was also sympathetic.

"Listen, honey, I understand what you're trying to do, but this is no place for you. It's bad enough with just the nature of the job, but then you have this maniac killing girls."

Laura didn't tell her about her team.

"And I hear you had a chat with Ramon."

"I did?" Laura had no idea who Ramon was.

"Yes, the bastard who thinks he owns the girls on this street. He *is* pimping for a few of them, but this isn't a franchise deal. If he bothers you again, tell him to come and have a chat with Sunshine."

Laura smiled. "Sunshine?"

Sunshine smiled also. "Well, not my given name. But this is a pretty dark business. Thought I'd add a little ray of hope."

"I like it," said Laura.

Sunshine looked up and down the street. "Here's something else to think about, honey. Your sister could be private goods."

"What do you mean by that?"

"Not put on the street. Just kept for private occasions and personal pleasure."

Laura's stomach turned and she hoped she wouldn't throw up.

"Maybe this Ramon would know something."

Sunshine laughed. "Ramon doesn't know crap. Surprised he remembers his name."

"But he might recognize her picture," Laura said hopefully.

Sunshine shrugged. "Maybe. But probably not."

Laura described the guy who had taken Katherine. Didn't sound familiar to Sunshine. Maybe the lead that brought Laura to this part of Chicago was dead. She thanked Sunshine and wished her well.

"Watch your back, honey."

* * *

Just before ten, Stretch watched a drunk chatting with one of the other girls. He pointed him out to Spencer.

"The guy's a regular," said Stretch. "Seems to be some sort of prostitute evangelist. I've wandered over when he has approached Laura. Wants to save them from the evil sinning of their ways."

Spencer watched the show. "Everybody needs a hobby."

The girl the drunk was talking to just walked away and he teetered up the sidewalk toward Laura. Stretch told Spencer to stay and keep his eyes open and started across the street. Laura had told him she could handle the guy but he wanted to be close just in case. He noticed the other man on the team wasn't far away.

The man leaned against a street light near Laura and said, "The heathen yield to the temptation of Satan."

Laura just ignored him.

"I can see into your soul and I know you are not a sinner. I can help you change your sinful ways." He moved away from the pole and almost tipped over as he moved toward Laura. "Come with me and you will be saved."

He reached out and grabbed her top. As he pulled her toward him, he fell down, pulling Laura down on top of him. He rolled over, pinning her on the bottom.

Stretch was there in seconds and pulled the drunk off of Laura. She stood up and straightened her clothes.

"You okay?" Stretch asked.

She nodded. "I could have handled him. He's just drunk."

"Maybe. But I'm not taking a chance. There's a guy out here with a knife. Let's call it a night."

They left the drunk lying on the sidewalk.

The man Stretch was looking for hadn't showed. Maybe the guy was just in the wrong place at the wrong time and had nothing to do with the killings. They all met back at the surveillance apartment and decided to try again on Wednesday.

Chapter 76

Wednesday morning Ben met with Charles in the interview room of the station house.

Charles was sitting with his head bowed, slumped in the chair. He was scheduled to be transferred to County in the afternoon. Ben hated to think what affect that would have on Charles if he was already so depressed.

"Good morning, Charles. I hope you got some sleep."

Charles just stared.

Ben set his briefcase on the table and pulled out a pad with a list of notes and questions.

"I want to help you, Charles. To do that, I need to go over the evidence and ask you some questions. Is that okay?"

"Sure, I guess," said a very dejected Charles. "I didn't kill Miss Brock."

Ben had never had a client who admitted he was guilty. "Good," he said with little energy. "I have to find a way of proving that, and I need your help."

Charles nodded.

Ben picked up his pencil.

"Okay, let's start with how she hired you. Please tell me exactly how that happened."

Charles told the same story that was in the file. When Charles was finished, Ben tried to restrain his skepticism. "I'm not questioning you, but do you see the problem here? Does it make sense to you that someone would hire you at a chance meeting and then give you a key to her house?"

Charles looked confused. "I don't understand."

"Don't understand what?"

"That it doesn't make sense. It's the truth."

"But it's not normal behavior. A jury or a judge is going to think something else happened."

"But something else *didn't* happen. It's the truth."

This was not going to be easy. Charles didn't think like your average human being, much less a jury.

Ben took a deep breath and let it out slowly. "Okay. I'm going to ask you some more questions."

No response.

"What kind of work were you doing?"

Charles shrugged. "You know, just normal house repairs."

Ben wished he didn't have to drag everything out of him. "Like what?"

"You know, new baseboard, painting, new cabinets, fixing holes. Things like that. And I finished some work that wasn't done."

That caught Ben's attention. "What do you mean?"

"Things weren't finished. Baseboard, trim around windows. She was angry at me about it."

"Angry at you? Did you do a bad job?"

He shook his head and was upset. "I do good work!"

"I'm sure you do. So why was she angry?"

"Because I asked her if the work was started by the man who used to own the house. She got angry and just said no."

"And you didn't ask any more?"

He shook his head. "I didn't want her to be angry."

"I can understand that. You said she gave you a key. Were you ever alone in the house?"

"Sometimes."

"Did you ever see anyone else there?"

"The maid."

Ben tried not to act as exasperated as he felt. "I know about the maid. Was there anyone besides her?"

Charles shook his head and then his face brightened. Excitedly, he said, "There was the bum!"

"What bum?" Ben wished Charles would start making sense.

"The bum out by the rocks. I would go early to sit on the rocks and watch the waves. There was a bum asleep by the rocks. He had a bag."

"Okay, but I mean someone else *in* the house."

The excited reaction disappeared and Charles looked down. "No."

"Did you know about the safe in Miss Brock's desk?"

"Yes, it was open many times. That's where she got the money to pay me."

"And she paid you in cash?"

"Yes."

"Did she pay you every day?"

"Yes."

"How much cash was in the safe?"

"I don't know."

"But there was more than what she paid you?"

"Yes, a lot more."

"Did you ever think of taking that money?"

"I would never take Miss Brock's money."

But Ben noticed that Charles *did* hesitate.

"What did you do with the money she gave you?"

Charles looked worried and rubbed his hands together. "I put it in the bushes."

"Weren't you worried it would get wet if it rained?"

Charles sat up in the chair and looked almost proud. "I thought of that!" he said with excitement. "I put it in an envelope and put that in a plastic baggie."

Ben was getting insights into Charles that worried him. He wasn't very smart—seemed simple-minded. Thinking of the baggie was a big accomplishment.

"That was smart. Where did you get the baggie and the envelope?"

The excitement disappeared and Charles again lowered his head.

"Charles? Where did you get them?"

"I got the envelope from Miss Brock."

"Good. How about the baggie?"

Silence.

"Charles. That's a simple question."

Staring down at the table, Charles said, "I took it from the kitchen."

"Okay. Why was that so hard?"

He didn't look up. "Because—I didn't ask. I just took it."

Ben started to think about a psychological evaluation. This guy, who was accused of stealing thousands of dollars and committing murder, seemed remorseful about taking a baggie.

"That's okay, Charles. I'm sure Miss Brock wouldn't have minded. People take things like that every day."

Charles looked a bit relieved.

"Let's talk about the time Miss Brock was killed," said Ben. "It was Saturday morning between four and six." Assuming Charles would say he was home in bed, Ben asked, "Would you tell me what you were doing then?"

Charles shrugged. "I don't know."

Ben was confused. "How do you not know?"

"I was out drinking at a bar. I don't remember."

"Well, what time did you leave the bar?"

"I don't remember."

"What time did you get home?"

He just shook his head.

Ben looked amazed. "Are you telling me you have no memory of Friday night and Saturday morning?"

"Yes."

"What time did you leave your house Friday night?"

"About nine, like usual."

"And what is the next thing you remember?"

"Waking up at home."

"And what time was that?"

"Around noon."

Ben stood up and walked to the door and turned around. "You have no memory of what happened between nine and noon?"

Charles nodded. "Not after I started drinking."

"Does this happen often?"

"It happens sometimes."

"For how long?"

"A long time."

Ben walked back to the table. "How long? Weeks? Months?"

Another shrug. "Years."

Ben needed to talk with the bartender. "What's the name of the bar?"

"Lights Out."

"Do you know the address?"

"Not exactly. It's on Western north of Diversey."

Ben made a note.

"Why do you want to know?" asked Charles.

"I'm trying to help you by finding out where you were, and when. Is your wife home on Friday nights?"

Charles immediately tensed. "Why do you want to know about *her*?"

"You need an alibi. If she said you got home at two and were asleep the rest of the night, that would help a lot."

Charles didn't look happy. "I don't know if she was home or not. I don't wake up till noon."

Ben's forehead crinkled. "Let me get this straight. You don't remember leaving the bar, or driving home, or getting into bed?"

"No."

"What did you drink?"

"Beer and tequila."

"How much?"

"A lot."

That was the first thing that made any sense.

Charles squirmed and asked, "Can I go to the bathroom?"

"Sure." Ben called the guard. Two male officers escorted Charles to the bathroom.

Ben sat down with his head in his hands, staring at a pad full of notes and several large question marks.

* * *

There were three more questions on Ben's pad. He wanted to give Charles all the time it took, but needed to be in court at one. Might be another no-lunch day.

Charles was led back into the room. He looked like a beaten man.

"Charles, you said you couldn't remember if your wife was home. But if she *was* home, she would verify what time you got home, wouldn't she?"

He shrugged.

"What does that mean?"

"She doesn't like me. She's glad I'm in jail."

Ben certainly remembered Mrs. Lamb's anger, but thought that she would have calmed down by now. "I'll have a chat with her."

"Why do you need to talk to her?"

This was very frustrating. "Because you need an alibi."

Charles just repeated that his wife didn't like him.

"You said Margaret pointed at you and said you killed Miss Brock, correct?"

He nodded.

"Why do you think she would do that?"

He shook his head. "I don't know."

"Did you do anything to her to make her angry?"

"No, I just worked. I didn't talk to her."

This made no sense to Ben.

"Two more questions." Ben took a deep breath as he turned to a new page. "Miss Brock was killed with a knife or a dagger. The police have a chest from your home. There are spots in the chest for two daggers. One is missing. Can you explain that?"

Charles shook his head. "I don't know why it's missing."

"When was the last time you saw it?"

Charles hesitated. "I polished the silver last week. Sarah makes me polish it twice a year."

"The daggers, too?"

"Yes."

"And what did you do with the daggers after you polished them?"

He tried to think. Stammering, he said "I, I—just put them back."

"And you didn't take them out again?"

A very quiet "no" followed ten seconds of silence.

Charles' answers were not convincing to Ben. He knew they wouldn't be convincing to a jury either. There was no way he would put Charles on the stand.

"Last question, Charles. Do you know what Miss Brock did for a living?"

"She made a lot of money."

"Yes, but what did she do?"

"I don't know. I tried to think about it, but I don't know."

"What did you think about?"

Fidgeting in the chair, Charles replied, "The book I saw."

"What book was that?"

He squinted, like he was trying to see it.

"There was a green book on her desk with funny words and dates."

Ben knew that was Miss Brock's client list.

"But you don't know what she did? She never said anything?"

He shook his head and then looked thoughtful. "The man at the gas station called her a whore, but I thought he was just angry."

"Could she have been a prostitute, Charles?"

He became very animated and angry. "No! Miss Brock was a nice lady. She thought I was a nice man."

"Okay, I'm sure she was. I'll talk to you again in a few days."

Ben called the guard. Still time for lunch. Remembering the transfer, he turned back to Charles.

"They're transferring you to Cook County this afternoon. I'll see you..."

Before Ben could finish the sentence, Charles had flipped over the table and a look of utter terror filled his face. He had instantly turned from a lamb into a raging lion.

The guard yelled for help. Within seconds, two more officers were in the room. They all just watched as Charles ranted. He was shaking violently. All three officers had their hands on their weapons. Slowly, Charles calmed down. He had backed himself into a corner and two officers turned the table back on its feet. Ben asked Charles to sit down and he did.

"Charles, what's the matter?" As he asked it, he knew how stupid it must have sounded, to a normal person anyway. This guy was in jail for something he said he didn't do and was going to be transferred to a worse place, and Ben was asking him what was wrong.

Charles violently shook his head. "I can't go there. I'll hang myself. I can't go there."

"Why not, Charles? It's just like here." He knew that wasn't exactly true. It wasn't at all true.

"I just can't, that's all—I just can't," Charles said with a shaky voice and fear in his eyes.

"I'll see what I can do," said Ben.

He left the room wondering what had just happened, and asked one of the officers if Detective Lonnigan was in. He said he would check.

* * *

Rosie met Ben in the lounge. He explained what happened and told her he was going to request a psych eval. He asked if they could keep Charles here until the eval was done. He was going to try and have that done before the preliminary hearing on Friday. She said the inn was not full and she would check.

* * *

When Ben got home, he called Spencer and asked if Spencer could come to his condo at eight.

"Is it important? I'm working surveillance on Laura."

"Come up with anything?"

"Yup."

"Care to share?"

"I don't think so, other than she's okay and definitely looking for her sister."

"Nothing wrong with that," said Ben.

"No. But how she's doing it is a little out of the box."

"Are you involved?"

"I am now."

"Remember what happened the last time you were involved with her?"

"Don't worry. Never forget that. But this time I'm on her side."

"Okay. But we really need to talk. I need your help with the Brock murder. I'm defending Mr. Lamb."

"Do you think it's tied to the other killings?"

"Probably not. But pretty strange nonetheless."

Ben gave Spencer some of the background.

"Okay, I'll be there at eight."

"Thanks, Spencer."

Spencer called Stretch and told him he couldn't make the evening walk, but to beep him if the big man showed up.

Chapter 77

Spencer was ten minutes early, but Ben was waiting for him.

"Thanks for coming, Spencer. Grab a beer while I get my notes."

Spencer took his beer to the window. The view out over the lake from the twenty-sixth floor had always been something Spencer was jealous of. Floor-to-ceiling glass faced southeast, looking down on the lights of Navy Pier and the harbor light.

"Unit for sale on the floor below me," said Ben.

"This is beautiful. I'd have to retire cuz I'd never leave. What's up?"

"I'm sure you read about the arrest."

Spencer nodded. "Didn't buy that this guy is *Friday*."

"No, me either at first. But open your mind for a minute. One of my clerks did some digging into Charles Lamb. When he was ten his father was arrested and charged with the murder of a prostitute. He hung himself in Cook County before he came to trial."

Spencer's eyes widened and he stopped the beer in mid-drink. "Doesn't sound like a happy childhood."

Ben glanced down at his notes. "It continues. His mother was an alcoholic who disappeared after that happened. He was brought up by an aunt and uncle and his older brother, Steven."

"Geez. Remind me to shut up when I complain about my life. Can't be happy about being in jail."

"No, but it's gonna get worse. I told him they'd be transferring him to

County and he went crazy. Flipped over the table. Said he couldn't go to County—he'd hang himself."

Spencer whistled. "Poor guy. I can't imagine. You think he killed her?"

Ben gave Spencer a *what the hell is the matter with you* look. "Come on, Spence. You know it's not what I think that matters."

Crossing his legs, Spencer said, "Not in the long run. But in the short run, what do you think?"

Ben shook his head and told Spencer about Charles' arrest record. "But I'd like to think he didn't. Seems like a nice guy. Not too bright, but there's a little kid quality that's likeable."

Spencer emptied the bottle. "And then there's the flip-over-the-table guy— the guy who attacked the woman outside the bar." He stared out the window. "Maybe *that* guy could kill someone."

"Maybe."

"What do you want me to do?"

"Find something that proves he didn't."

Spencer laughed. "Sure. No problem. I'll get right on it." He told Ben about the man on the street.

"Interesting. Well, Charles is in jail, so let's see if your man shows."

Spencer nodded. "How did Brock die? Anything I didn't read in the paper?"

Ben related everything he knew over the second beers. Spencer took notes.

When Ben finished, Spencer got up and walked to the window. "Beautiful city till you look behind the doors. I have some questions you probably don't have answers to."

"So do I. What are yours?"

Spencer returned to the table and sat. "Where was he Friday night, and when?"

Ben sighed. "That's the million-dollar question. Spent Friday night drinking away his problems. He's a regular at Lights Out. Doesn't remember a thing from after he arrived at the bar till when he woke up at home around noon Saturday."

Spencer yawned and rubbed his eyes. "So there should be a bartender who remembers him, and his wife should be able to tell us when he got home."

Ben agreed. "You can check out the bar. It's on Western north of Diversey. But the wife isn't exactly your loving spouse. She's more concerned about her daggers than her husband. Might be good to find out why. I asked her what time he came home." Ben frowned. "She walked out without saying a word."

Spencer shook his head. "Nice. I'll have a chat with the lady."

"Don't turn your back."

Spencer laughed. "I've been through worse than what she'll have to offer. But maybe there's a good reason she isn't giving him an alibi. Maybe she *does* know when he got home and it wasn't in time to *give* him an alibi. And why did the maid finger him? She doesn't point him out, and he's still walking around, right?"

"Right." Ben tapped his pencil on the glass top of the desk. "That's one of the things I'd like to know also. Of course, the evidence is what put him in jail. They wouldn't arrest him just on her accusation. But that led them to the money and the missing dagger. Still, without her they don't find the evidence."

"Doesn't sound like enough to get a conviction."

"Maybe not. The knife will tell the story. Hopefully that'll prove him innocent."

"Sure, if he's still alive." Spencer got up and paced. "So, what we have to do is show suspicion somewhere else."

"Agreed. I'd start with the maid. See if you can get her to say why she accused Charles."

Spencer nodded. "Then there's the guy in the limo, but that's a pretty big longshot."

"If you can even find him."

"I can try—gas station may have records if he charged it. I need the date and time."

Ben made a note on the pad.

"There's also the problem that it seems only two people had keys. She was locked up for the night and getting ready to go to bed. There were no signs of forced entry so either she let someone in or someone had a key."

Spencer returned to his chair. "Perhaps she had another customer at home and she let him in."

Ben shook his head. "Not likely. Everything points to her doing business elsewhere."

"You never know. And maybe Lamb *did* kill her. Maybe he's a gentle lamb until he fills up with alcohol and then turns into a prostitute-hating Mr. Hyde. Sure would be nice to put someone else in that house. Next time you see Charles, ask him if there was anyone else who was there—even a delivery person."

"I *did* ask. He said the maid. He just doesn't think very well. And he mentioned a bum he saw out by the rocks the morning before he started work." Ben shook his head. "Things like that make this so hard. My client has no logical thought processes."

Ben raised his arms, palms up. "See what you can find out. Start with the bar and Margaret. See if you can get an answer to why she accused him." Ben read off her address.

"Okay, I'll see Margaret tomorrow. You have anything on her?"

Ben flipped through his notes. "Husband died three years ago. Twenty-one-year-old son lives with her, going to college."

"Great, thanks."

"And one more thing." Ben had started to close the folder and then remembered the partially finished work. He thumbed through his notes. "This is just a little strange. When Brock was showing Charles around, he noticed some work that wasn't finished. She got angry when he asked about it."

"Angry at what?"

"Well, that's a good question. He thought she was angry at *him* so he didn't ask any more."

Spencer took a deep breath. "Maybe none of these things mean anything, but there's enough strange things to make you wonder."

Ben closed the folder. "Yup. But there is one thing for sure—there was someone else working in that house. Maybe Margaret knows who."

"Worth asking."

They spent the next half hour talking about strategy. Spencer said he would stop by the bar on the way home, see Margaret in the morning, and Mrs. Lamb Thursday night.

Ben had to be in court for the hearing Friday morning at nine. He had received a message that the psych eval had been approved, but wouldn't be done until Charles was transferred. Another message was from Rosie, telling him they could only keep Charles until the hearing. If he was held over for trial, he would have to go to County.

Chapter 78

Spencer had to park on a side street three blocks away from Lights Out, and she was lucky to get that as someone pulled out. Parking in the city was never any fun. There was nothing different about Lights Out from any other bar. The music was loud, the crowd was louder, and a haze of cigarette smoke hung in the air. Booths lined the wall to the left and tables for two filled most of the linoleum-covered floor. The bar stretched along the right wall to a hallway at the back with *He* and *She* signs on the wall above the doorway. In back of the bar, the wall was lined with the customary mirrors and shelves of liquor.

Spencer looked for the bartender and found two. A woman with a white towel over her shoulder was filling beer glasses at the near end and a man with a bushy moustache was mixing drinks in the middle. Three waitresses were waiting with empty trays.

The booths were full, as were the tables, so Spencer took the only stool open at the bar. The place was packed on a Wednesday night. Spencer had noticed the *Twenty-Five Cent Draft Wednesday* sign in the front window. Nothing like cheap beer to pull in a crowd.

* * *

Spencer waited till the man came his way and ordered a draft Pabst. When the bartender set the glass down, Spencer said, "Thanks. I wonder if we could chat for a minute."

"Mister, this is a bar, not a coffee house."

Ignoring that, Spencer continued. "I have some questions about one of your customers."

"And I have a bar full of customers waiting for drinks."

"Fine. A subpoena will work too."

Giving Spencer a disgusted look, he looked up to the ceiling and said, "Not my night. Who are you?"

Spencer showed his license.

"Private dick, huh. Okay, if you want to wait until the crowd clears, we can talk."

"When's that?"

"Usually around eleven."

"That's two hours."

Spencer got a tough-guy look. The bartender pulled a bottle of Jack Daniels off the shelf and walked away.

Spencer watched the crowd while he waited.

* * *

Shortly before eleven, the bartender joined Spencer at a table, saying he could spare two minutes.

After introductions—his name was Mike—Spencer gave him the quick story of what he was looking for.

Mike looked surprised. "So you're working for Charlie? The cops were in here a few nights ago."

"Yes, I'm working with the Public Defender."

"Well that's different. Sweet guy, Charlie."

"So you know him?"

Mike laughed. "Everybody here knows him, especially after he started buying rounds. I don't know if he came into money or what, but a couple weeks ago he became the life of the party. Can't believe he was arrested for that murder. Did he really do it?"

"That's what we're trying to figure out. I'm hoping not, but there's not much to go on yet. Has he been coming here for a while?"

"Yup, years. Almost every Friday night. And a lot of Saturdays. And sometimes during the week. But during the week he just comes for an after-dinner drink. Weekends, he's here all night."

"Were you here last Friday night?"

"I'm here almost every night."

"Do you remember last Friday? Was Charlie here?"

"He sure was. Bought several rounds."

"And he drinks a lot?"

"He likes his beer and tequila. I will say that he seems to hold it well; maybe because he's so big. Most guys would be under the table."

"Do you remember what time he left?"

"That's not hard. I always have to kick him out. We close at two. But you know, sometimes he leaves early and then comes back."

"Did you tell the cops that?"

"Nope. Didn't think of it."

"Did Charles say anything unusual, like if he was going somewhere besides home?"

Mike scrunched his face, looked again up at the ceiling, and shook his head. "Nope. Nothing that stands out."

"He was arrested here a few years back. Do you remember anything about that?"

"I do. He hit a woman outside the bar. He was yelling something about a whore and had her pinned against the wall. Took four of us to pull him off. Sent her to the hospital and him to jail."

"Any other trouble?"

"Nope, always a gentleman. That thing was a real surprise."

Spencer put a ten on the table. "Add that to the tips. Thanks for your time, Mike."

"Sure. Help any?"

"Not much. Gives him an alibi until two. We could use later than that."

Mike nodded. "Wish I could do more. I like Charlie. Good luck."

Spencer got up and they shook hands. "Thanks."

* * *

Driving home, Spencer thought about Charlie. Seemed like a pretty lonely guy. Buying rounds bought you friends for a night, but the next time you walked in the door you had to buy them back again. He also sounded like a nice guy, and Spencer hoped he would find something that would help. He would go see the maid in the morning and Mrs. Lamb Thursday night. A light drizzle started as he drove. From what Ben had said, he was not looking forward to interviewing Mrs. Lamb, but he had several interesting questions. He figured her answers would be just as interesting. Most of all, he wondered why she would stay married to someone she didn't like as much as her daggers.

He hadn't heard from Stretch.

Chapter 79

Roll call Thursday morning. The usual pep talk about keeping the streets safe for humanity and a pat on the back to two teams who had done exactly that. Rosie and Steele were asked to see Lt. Powolski before leaving.

Stosh was on the phone when they walked in. He waved them to chairs and finished his conversation. Jan Brent from the D.A.'s office was sitting on the far side of the desk.

Stosh hung up. "I've asked Miss Brent to join us to let us know where this might go. The floor is yours, ma'am."

Jan Brent turned to Rosie. "Based on your interview, Detective, Mrs. Rivera has no good reason for accusing Mr. Lamb, just a feeling. She says she knows he did it. That's not worth much in court. We have the cash in a baggie with only his prints on it, the fact that only he and Margaret had keys to the house, the missing dagger, and he has no alibi. With those and his arrest record we have enough for suspicion. But if any are explained away, we're not left with much. We need a murder weapon. I assume you're looking, so I won't ask."

"Any questions?" asked Stosh of his detectives. There were none.

"Then I have some background on Mr. Lamb." He opened a folder and handed each of them a data sheet. "Not a pretty family picture. Charles' father, Samuel, was charged with the murder of a prostitute. He was sent to Cook County where he hung himself before the trial. Charles was ten at the time. Mother was an alcoholic—disappeared after the father died. Charles was raised by an aunt and uncle and his older brother, Steven, now a successful businessman. Owns his own metals company."

Rosie sat back in her chair and let out a long exhale. "Well, that explains it."

Stosh just raised his eyebrows.

Rosie explained. "When Ben told Charles he was going to be transferred to County, Charles went nuts—flipped over a table. Said he couldn't go there and would hang himself. Ben asked if we could keep him here for a few days while he got a psych eval. The preliminary is on Friday."

Stosh closed the folder. "This job never gets any easier. I agree. It would be good to keep him here a bit, but he has to be transferred at some point—we're talking murder here. Definitely has to be transferred after his hearing. And I'm going to have a chat with Andrews and Spanell. Despite the change in m.o., this makes him look good for the *Friday* murders. The battery arrest was for accusing a woman of being a prostitute and attacking her. I also got a report on neighborhood crime. Nothing matches. Anybody get to the bar?"

Rosie answered. "Yeah. Bartender confirms he's always there on Friday nights and many Saturdays. Drinks a lot. They close at two and he has to kick Charles out. So no alibi there."

Stosh nodded. "What's on your plate for the day?"

Rosie set the sheet on the desk. "Paperwork and then more paperwork."

Stosh nodded. "Steele, you awake?"

"Father killed a prostitute, took a stretch, alchy mother took a powder, suspect following in dad's footsteps. Got it."

"Get him outta here, Rosie."

Steele was a pain in the ass, but had been at this a long time and was a good detective. Several cases had been closed due to his diligence. But Stosh felt sorry for Rosie. When she transferred in, the other detectives were thrilled to see her. The newbie got Steele.

Chapter 80

Spencer was awakened at about six by the steady drumming of rain on the roof, a sound he found very comforting—even *more* comforting, knowing he could go back to sleep. A lifestyle that didn't involve an alarm clock was wonderful. He had set a goal of letting as little as possible interfere with that lifestyle. He did remember that he was going to see the maid, but there was no timetable.

When Spencer swung his legs out of bed and headed for a shower, the rain had stopped, but the sky was overcast and the forecast promised off-and-on rain all day. He stopped at Sunnyside Up for breakfast. Pancakes and two eggs over easy with bacon. Good food, but not nearly as homey as Beef's. As he ate, he thought about his first case and the happiness that had come out of great sadness.

* * *

The '65 Mustang was out of place in Mrs. Rivera's neighborhood. The streets were lined with more conventional cars. But the neighborhood was clean and neat. Lawns were mown and flower beds were weeded. Most of the houses were basically the same, with small personal touches. Mrs. Rivera's was painted pale yellow with green trim. Spencer parked, walked up the sidewalk in the light drizzle, and rang the bell.

A neat, conservatively dressed, middle-aged woman answered the door.

"Mrs. Rivera?"

"Yes," she said hesitantly.

"My name is Spencer Manning." He briefly flashed his license. "I'm a detective and have a few questions about Miss Brock if you have a few minutes."

Still hesitating, she responded, "I already talked to one of your detectives."

Spencer smiled and said, "Yes, Detective Lonnigan. I just have a few more questions. You know, sometimes something new needs to be followed up on."

"There is something new? I thought you had the man who did it."

He smiled bigger. "Would you mind if I come in? It's raining."

"Oh, I am sorry. Okay. May I take your jacket?"

He took off the wet jacket and she hung it on a hook inside a closet.

"Please, come into the kitchen." She led the way through a very neat house. Not a thing out of place. Very tidy, but not very homey. "I am having some tea, would you like some?"

"That would be nice, thank you."

While she got out cups, Spencer looked around the room. One thing caught his eye. There was a knife block on the counter next to a wooden cutting board. There were places for six knives. One place was empty.

Mrs. Rivera set a cup of steaming tea in front of Spencer and explained that it was a special blend from Mexico. He thanked her.

She sat, quietly sipping her tea.

Spencer took a sip. "Delicious."

She smiled. "I am glad you like it."

He put the cup back in the saucer. "You have a very nice house. It must take a lot of work to keep a house clean with a family."

She frowned. "My husband died three years ago and my son who lived with me has moved out to his own place."

"I'm sorry. Is your son nearby?"

She acted a bit flustered. "What questions do you have, Mr. Manning?"

"Can you give me any more information on why you think Mr. Lamb killed Miss Brock?"

She again acted flustered and picked up her cup. It shook.

"Mrs. Rivera?"

"Yes, I know. I really have nothing to tell you. It is just a feeling. He is such a big man and he did have a key to the house." She was breathing quickly in short breaths. "And he was a complete stranger." Her eyes welled up with tears. "I told her not to let a stranger into her house." She wiped her eyes with a napkin.

"Did he treat you badly?"

"How do you mean, badly?"

"Was he rude or mean to you?"

She looked down. "No, no he wasn't."

Everything about her reactions led Spencer to think there was something that she was not telling. "Mrs. Rivera, if Mr. Lamb killed Miss Brock, he belongs in jail, but we want to make sure. It would be horrible to send an innocent man to jail. Don't you agree?"

She nodded, looking away from Spencer.

After finishing his tea, Spencer said, "I just have one other question. May I ask?"

Another nod.

"Mr. Lamb was doing work on the house, right?"

"Yes." She again was making eye contact and her hand had stopped shaking.

"Mr. Lamb says some work was started but not finished. Do you know who else was working there?"

Now she completely lost her composure. She stood up, turned her back to Spencer, and carried her cup to the sink and rinsed it out. She shut the water off and said, "I would like to talk again to the lady detective."

"Detective Lonnigan?"

"Yes."

She was standing with both hands on the edge of the counter, staring out the window. Spencer knew she was done talking.

"Okay, I'll have her call you. I'll let myself out."

She just kept staring.

Chapter 81

Spencer found a pay phone and made two calls. The first was to Ben's office.

"Give me some good news," said Ben.

Spencer told Ben about Margaret's nervous reaction when he asked both questions.

"Hmm. Strange. Something's going on there. But that doesn't solve any problems."

"Well, then there's the missing knife," Spencer explained.

That got a better reaction from Ben. "You know, an empty slot doesn't mean there was a knife there. Did you ask her about it?"

"No."

"Seems that would have been the thing to do, Mr. P.I."

Spencer sighed. "Well, yes, seems so. But I thought it better to tell Rosie and let her ask."

"What? You all of a sudden shy?"

"No, I'm all of a sudden sorta leading Mrs. Rivera to believe I was with the police."

Silence. Spencer could see the reaction.

"Please tell me I didn't hear you right because of a bad connection."

"Can't tell you that, but I *can* tell you I didn't lie—just let her reach a conclusion that wasn't necessarily true."

"And you didn't bother to correct that conclusion?"

"Obviously not. But I showed her my license and she didn't ask to see a badge. I would have told her if she had asked."

"Good, that helps a lot."

"We in trouble here? Cuz I got something Rosie missed, and there *is* something she isn't talking about yet but *is* willing to talk about to Rosie."

"Hopefully I won't have to deal with a formal complaint. But you're going to catch hell from a certain Lieutenant."

"Yup. Won't be the first time."

"Good, that makes me feel better. Listen, I haven't turned in any expense sheets yet. Are you willing to work for nothing?"

"What you pay is pretty close to that. Why?"

"Because your looking into some things on your own is different than if you're hired by the P.D. office."

"Will that make it easier on me?"

"No idea. But maybe I won't lose *my* job."

Spencer laughed. "Sure. Where does this get us with Charles?"

"It gets us suspicion in another direction—someone with a key to the house who may have a missing knife. You talk to Rosie. I'll go see the D.A. Maybe we can get this dismissed, or at least get the bond lowered."

"Would you wait on that? I'd like Rosie to discover the missing knife."

"Okay, but make it quick. Hearing is tomorrow morning."

Spencer hesitated. "Hey, Ben. Remember the table-flip guy? It's possible we're trying to get a murderer out of jail."

"Can't help you there, Spencer. We're looking for the truth and my crystal ball is broken. Until we get more, I do my job and that is to defend Mr. Lamb."

They hung up and Spencer made his second call—to Rosie. He asked her if she wanted to get some lunch. She accepted.

Chapter 82

Rosie was waiting in a booth at a diner a block from the station. She pushed out the opposite chair with her foot and folded her arms across her chest.

Spencer gave her his best hurt look. "Don't give me that—I come bearing gifts." He sat.

She didn't laugh. "I too have gifts. First is a warrant—for impersonating a police officer."

Spencer's mouth opened and then closed.

Rosie uncrossed her arms. "I was hoping for a bit more than that."

"And I was hoping to break it to you gently."

She looked skeptical. "Or not at all?"

He squirmed. "Well, that would have been preferable. I assume you talked to Margaret?"

"No wonder you make all the big bucks. Yes, called her with a question and she tells me one of our detectives was just there. Who, I ask? Manning, she replies. Said you were going to tell me to call her."

"Yup, that's on the agenda. So, she doesn't know?"

"No. But we need to have a chat with Stosh."

Spencer grimaced. "If she doesn't know—"

"She figures it out and he finds out I know, it won't be pretty for Yours Truly."

"What about *this* Yours Truly?"

"You mean the one who impersonated a police officer?"

"Well, not exactly," he said. "And I *do* have gifts."

She sighed. "Okay, let's hear it."

The waitress arrived. Spencer ordered a burger, Rosie a turkey club.

"First, there's a knife block in the kitchen. A knife is missing. Second..."

Her right hand went up. "Back up to first. Are you saying I missed that?"

"Or it appeared, or disappeared, after you were there."

"Did you ask her about it?"

"Nope, figured you might want to do that."

"Well, thanks for that. Have you told anyone else?"

"Just Ben."

"You know, an empty slot doesn't mean there's a missing knife."

"Right. But should be asked."

"Agreed. What's second?"

Spencer told her about how strange Margaret acted when he asked her about accusing Charles, and how nervous she was when he asked her about the partial work.

"She knows something she isn't telling us, Rosie."

"Isn't telling *you*. Said she wants to talk to me. And what's with this *us* crap? You join the force recently?"

"No, but we're both on the same team."

The food arrived and she took a bite. "What team would that be? Seems to me we're on opposite sides here."

"Justice. We both want to get the guy who did it."

She nodded. "Okay, I'll buy that. But from now on, how 'bout you clear up that little P.I. ID thing."

"Does the knife buy me anything with Stosh?"

She shrugged her shoulders. "Can't predict anything there. You're on your own. But I'll beat around the bush as much as I can."

"Thanks."

Rosie was fidgeting with her spoon. "Can we chat about Saturday night?"

"Sure, what about it?"

She looked up at Spencer. "I had hoped that was the start of something more than friends. And I haven't heard from you since." She shrugged.

Spencer didn't know how to respond. He had thought about her a lot. She was indeed a wonderful woman, and a part of him also wanted more. But he cherished her friendship, and a bigger part of him felt safe and comfortable with that.

"That *was* a wonderful night, Rosie. And you are wonderful." He looked away. "I'm just not sure what I want. I don't want to lose a friend."

She wanted to reach out and take his hand, but didn't. With a forlorn look, she said, "I don't either. But it's possible to have both."

He sighed. "I'm not so sure."

Rosie felt sad, like she had just lost something, but at least it was out on the table.

"And you're right. We *are* on different sides. I've wondered if that would happen. We've always worked so well together."

She nodded. "Yes, we have."

"Still friends?"

"Sure." But she wasn't entirely sure.

Taking the last bite of his burger, Spencer said, "So, what's the other gift?"

Rosie wiped her mouth and sipped her Coke. "Like you deserve another gift?"

"Well, I wasn't too thrilled about the warrant."

She laughed. "Guess who is sole beneficiary."

"That's not too hard. Unless there's family we don't know about, Margaret is the only person she was close to. How much?"

"Around a half mil."

"Nice. Margaret know yet?"

"Not from me."

"You think she knew?"

Rosie shrugged. "Don't know."

"That takes more heat off Charles if she did. Gives her a motive, and she obviously has a key and a missing knife. And as far as I'm concerned, Charles doesn't have a motive."

"Sure he does—money."

He looked at her with wonder. "Come on, Rosie. He could have taken that money anytime; he was alone in the house. He didn't have to kill her for it. He could have worked two more weeks and made that much. The guy had a gravy train—why ruin it?"

"Yeah, doesn't make sense, but not everything does. Maybe he got tired of working for it. But the hooker/father angle could be a motive."

"Sure. But a stretch."

She shrugged. "I've seen bigger."

Rosie finished her drink and said, "Here's something interesting." She then told Spencer about how Miss Brock had met and hired Margaret.

"Anything new on Laura?" asked Rosie.

"Well, our relationship has changed a bit."

Rosie's eyebrows went up. "You have a relationship? Would you like to explain that?"

"Not really. But she's definitely looking for her sister. And she definitely is not a prostitute."

Spencer told her about Laura's team and the large man Stretch had seen on the street. "And this is interesting. Since Charles has been in jail, the man hasn't appeared."

Rosie set down her glass. "It is. So is Laura and her team. Don't think I like you involved in that, for several reasons."

Spencer shrugged. "Just standing on the street watching the crowd."

"Right. How's the bump on your head?"

Spencer smiled. "I've switched sides."

"Uh huh. Well, make sure your new side doesn't get you thrown in jail."

"Nothing illegal about standing on the street."

Rosie nodded, skeptically. "Be careful, Spencer."

"I will."

"And call if something happens. Don't go charging in on your white horse."

"Definitely."

Rosie wasn't entirely convinced.

They paid on the way out. On the way to Rosie's car, Spencer asked if they were going for their usual Saturday morning run.

"I'd better take a rain check. I'm working Friday night and it might be late."

"Okay. Maybe we can do something over the weekend. Give me a call."

He waved and walked away before she could reply.

Chapter 83

Rosie picked up Steele and they headed for Margaret's. The rain had stopped and breaks in the clouds were letting in a little sunshine. A slight wind had picked up out of the west. On the way, Rosie warned Steele about the Spencer situation and asked him not to mention it.

His reaction was not expected. "Hey, I like the guy. I'm all about private enterprise, and you gotta admire creativity."

Rosie liked the guy, too, but lately she had been wondering. They had had one great night, and it looked like that didn't mean anything more to Spencer.

Steele rang the doorbell. Margaret answered, looking worried and nervous. Certainly not the calm, collected person she had been on the last visit. She led them into the kitchen. This time she did not offer tea.

On walking into the kitchen, Rosie looked for the knife block. There was indeed an empty slot. She'd save it for last.

"What is it you want to talk about, Margaret?"

With a worried glance at Steele, Margaret said, "I thought it would be just you."

"Steele, you mind..." He was gone before she could finish.

Margaret took a deep breath and folded her hands on the table. "Detective Manning asked why I accused Mr. Lamb."

Rosie cringed inwardly at the *detective*.

"I really do not have a good reason, and I do not want the wrong man to be in jail. I told Miss Brock that it was not a good idea to give a key to someone you do not know. She just laughed and said she was a good judge of character. I do not want Mr. Lamb to be in jail if he did not do it."

"That's good, Margaret. We don't either. But there is other evidence besides your statement. And that's why we have juries. They decide if someone is guilty after a trial."

Margaret locked eyes with Rosie. "That's not really why I asked you to come."

Rosie waited.

"He also asked who did the other work in the house that was not finished. I said I did not know, but I do." Her face suddenly filled with sadness, and she started to sob.

"It was my son—Joseph."

"That's okay, Margaret. Why are you upset?"

"Because Miss Brock told him not to come back."

Rosie felt an immediate rush of emotions—mostly sadness. Margaret seemed overwhelmed, but Rosie wasn't sure why. Margaret seemed to be trying to control herself but her lower jaw was shaking and her face had lost all color. Rosie had seen that look in people's eyes before, but didn't understand why it was happening now. She felt like she was interfering with something very private. Most of her wanted to leave, but the detective needed to know why.

"I'm so sorry, Margaret. Can you tell me why that happened?"

Margaret got up to get a napkin to wipe the tears flowing down her cheeks. After a few minutes she had recovered some composure.

"I told Miss Brock about my son. He was in college and needed a job. His father taught him how to fix things. I wanted him to have a job instead of being always with his friends."

Rosie told her that was a good idea and waited.

"Miss Brock said she needed work done at the house and would pay him. She was such a wonderful person. But my son would not be home sometimes when we had to catch the bus. I told him many times. I made up excuses for him."

Trying to make this easier for Margaret, Rosie said, "So Miss Brock let him go because she couldn't depend on him?"

Margaret shook her head and looked totally defeated. Staring at a spot on the table, she corrected Rosie. "No, she told him to leave because he took money—from her safe." Her eyes didn't leave the spot.

Rosie had developed a trust for this woman. She was sure Margaret was exactly as she seemed—trusting and kind and honest. She could not imagine how that had affected a mother.

"I told her I would pay her back, but she would not let me. I told her I would get my coat and leave, but she would not let me. I told her I could not come back and face her, but she said that would be even worse for her, because she needed me and was my friend. She was sorry. But she was not sorry that she lost money—she was sorry for *me*." The tears started again.

"I'm sorry for you too, Margaret. That must have been very hard. Did you talk to your son?"

Margaret looked up and met Rosie's eyes. "I couldn't. When I got home he was gone. He took his things." She looked away.

"Do you know where he is?"

She just shook her head, trying desperately to control the sadness.

Rosie didn't want to be there, and she certainly didn't want to ask the next question. Trying to find an easy way, she decided just to ask.

"Margaret, there is one more thing I need to ask."

Margaret nodded.

"We are looking for the knife that killed Miss Brock."

Looking up at the ceiling and silently mouthing something, Margaret looked totally defeated, but said nothing.

Rosie ignored the feelings that were filling her with sadness. "There's an empty slot in your knife block. Do you know anything about that?"

It took a minute, but she finally said very quietly, "I know it is gone."

"When did you notice it was gone?"

"I noticed a few days after Joseph left when I needed to use a knife. But it may have been gone before that. I do not know."

Rosie didn't need to ask—she knew Margaret had put two and two together. Her knife was missing and Miss Brock had been killed with a knife.

Rosie had no idea how to deal with someone who was totally deflated. She just needed to do her job. "Margaret do you have a picture of Joseph?"

Margaret was very matter-of-fact. "I will get you one." She left the room and returned a minute later. She handed the picture to Rosie and said, "It is my fault that Miss Brock is dead."

"No, Margaret, it isn't. We can't be responsible for other people's actions. You were trying to do something nice. And we don't know anything for sure yet. We need to find Joseph. Are there friends he might be with?"

"I do not know. He had friends that I did not know."

"Could he have taken your key to Miss Brock's house?"

"I do not know. I always left it on the table by my bed."

"Did you ever notice it was missing?"

She shook her head.

"Do you still have it?"

"Yes, it is on my table in the bedroom."

"Let's go look."

The key was still on the table. Rosie told Margaret she needed to take it and got Steele to put it in an evidence envelope.

On her way out, Rosie said, "If you hear from Joseph, please call me."

Margaret nodded without emotion. "Is he going to be arrested?"

"No, we just need to talk to him." Rosie didn't want to tell her that it certainly didn't look good for Joseph. He had better motives than Mr. Lamb—anger, revenge, and money. "Try not to worry Margaret. I'll call you if we hear anything."

Margaret sat down with another nod.

Rosie filled Steele in on the way back to the station. She needed to call the D.A.

Chapter 84

Hello Jan, Detective Lonnigan."

"Afternoon, Detective. What have you got?"

"For starters, maybe the wrong man. I paid another visit to Mrs. Rivera this afternoon. Her son worked at the Brock house and was fired for stealing money. By the time Mrs. Rivera got home, the kid had cleared out and she hasn't heard from him."

"Nothing's ever easy, is it?"

"It gets worse. There's a knife missing from Mrs. Rivera's kitchen."

"So, another suspect."

Rosie gave a short laugh. "Well, maybe two. Mrs. Rivera is the sole beneficiary in a half million dollar will."

"Wow. Any more?"

"That's not enough? What do you think about Lamb?"

"I think a judge would laugh at us. I'll call Tucker and tell him we'll drop the charges. I think I can get that done today. I assume you're looking for the son?"

"Yes, and we'll keep an eye on the house."

"Okay. Good luck."

"Thanks."

Rosie thought about Spencer and knew he would get the latest from Ben. She also thought about calling him and telling him she could make the Saturday morning run. But she needed to do some thinking and put that on hold.

* * *

Ben answered his phone at three, Thursday afternoon.

"Hi Ben, it's Jan."

"Hi Jan, I was expecting to hear from you."

"You were? How does that happen?"

"Too complicated. Something new?"

"That you don't already know?" Jan asked sarcastically.

"Gotta hear it from you, Miss Brent."

Jan sighed. "Someday, tell me how you know things before I tell you."

"Someday."

"Okay. We have a new suspect." She told him about the knife and the son. "There's enough to release Mr. Lamb. Can you be in court at 4:30?"

Ben was elated. "Sure. He'll be thrilled he's getting out and won't be transferred."

"I'm not saying he's not still a person of interest. Some strange things there."

"Agreed. Thanks, Jan."

"Sure."

As Ben was picking up the phone to call Spencer, it rang.

"Hey Ben, you got anything yet?" asked Spencer.

"Yeah, just got off the phone with the D.A." He told Spencer about Joseph. "She'll drop the charges later today and release Charles."

"Great! Let's hope they find the son."

"Probably not hard. Just a kid."

"But a kid with a damned good motive and access to the key and the knife."

"The key?" asked Ben.

"Sure. He worked with Mom and knew Mom had a key. Would have been simple to have made a copy. And now we know why she fingered Charles. She was afraid her son did it, and Charles was the perfect one to blame."

"Nasty. But it makes sense."

"And there's something else. Your people can find out if they look, but Mrs. Rivera is the sole beneficiary of a half mil."

Ben whistled. "I wonder if she knew about the will."

"She could have. Brock may have told her, but from her behavior I'd guess not. You still want me to see Mrs. Lamb?"

"If you don't mind. Maybe you can find out why she behaved that way."

"I don't mind. I'd like to talk with her without Charles there. What time is court?"

"He should be out by five, but my guess is he'll make a bar stop before heading home. But try and get there as early as possible."

Spencer decided he could see Mrs. Lamb and still get back to meet Stretch at 7:30 for another night on Broadway.

"How about the limo guy at the gas station?" asked Spencer.

"Doesn't look like we need it."

"Nope. Talk to you later."

"Hang on, Spence. We got background on the loving wife. She used to work for Charles' brother, Steven."

"That mean anything?"

"No idea. Just file it somewhere."

"Hmm. Maybe I'll ask her about that."

"Don't be too concerned. Looks like we're done with this."

"Yes, but I like things to make sense and not much about this does. See ya, Ben."

"Yup."

Spencer made some file notes before heading south. He had expected to hear from Stosh. But since he hadn't, he reasoned that Stosh was waiting for their Saturday afternoon get-together. He could call and cancel, but figured he'd have to face the music sometime. Might as well get it over with.

Chapter 85

Spencer was waiting at the Lamb house when Sarah pulled in the drive at 5:30. He had immediately noticed the disrepair and wondered about Charles working as a handyman. He certainly didn't take care of his own house.

As Spencer got out of the car, he thought he noticed movement in the tree next door. Nestled in the limbs of a mature oak tree was a nice tree house. When Spencer was a kid, he and his dad had built a tree house in the wooded area behind their house. He had spent many fun hours in that tree house. Spencer watched but didn't see anything. Must have been a bird lost in the shadows. Given what he heard about Mrs. Lamb, he wished he could be in the tree house.

Mrs. Lamb answered the door a minute after Spencer rang the bell. At about five-foot four, she didn't look too tough to Spencer.

"Yes?" she said in a pleasant voice.

"Mrs. Lamb?"

"Yes."

"My name is Spencer Manning. I'm working with the Public Defender on your husband's case. Do you have a few minutes?" Spencer expected very little and that's what he got.

"For what?" The pleasant voice was gone.

"I just have a few questions."

Mrs. Lamb looked defiant. "Unless you have my daggers, I've got nothing to say to you."

With as much diplomacy as he could muster, Spencer said, "I obviously don't, but getting your husband released would get your dagger back."

After asking for ID, she sighed and reluctantly invited Spencer in. They sat at the dining table. This wasn't going to be easy. She obviously didn't want to answer questions over a cup of tea.

"Is it all right if I ask you some questions?"

"You got in didn't you?" Her face said she wasn't going to be giving many answers.

"We're trying to account for his whereabouts early Saturday morning." No reaction. "Bartender says he left the bar at two. I'm wondering what time he got home." Still no reaction. "Were you home after two on Saturday morning?"

"Where the hell else would I be?"

"Well, if you were home, do you know what time Charles got home?"

With arms folded and her face as cold as a block of ice, she methodically said, "I have no idea."

This wasn't going well. "Please pardon my confusion, but if you were home how could you not know when he got home?"

"I'm a very sound sleeper. And after years of my husband coming home at all hours of the night, I've learned to sleep through it."

Spencer shifted in the chair. "Was he there when you woke up?"

"Yup," she said with a frown. "Always is."

Progress. "And what time would that be?"

"A little after 7:30."

Great. Charles had alibis for all but the time Brock was killed.

"Now I have a question for *you*," she said.

Spencer waited, not really wanting to hear it.

"How is this going to get my daggers back?"

Spencer held his strained temper. "If we can show your husband didn't do it, they'll release the evidence."

"And if you can't show that?"

"Then they hold it till the trial."

"Jesus. Well, then I'm sorry I can't help."

Spencer needed to find something to talk about. The daggers seemed to be the only possibility. "The daggers have been in your family?"

"Yes. The daggers were my grandfather's, and the silverware goes back further than that. I take good care of it."

"I can see why. It must have a lot of sentimental value. I can understand that you were upset that one was missing."

Her face turned to a scowl. "That's not all that's missing."

"What do you mean?"

"There's silverware missing, also."

Spencer was confused. "But the police didn't take that."

She unfolded her arms and grabbed the edge of the table. "No, but I'd bet my worthless husband did. Probably sold it for gambling money."

Spencer shook his head with compassionate support. "He was out of work, I hear."

"Yes. I support this family. Have for the last couple of years."

"But he was working for Miss Brock, wasn't he?"

She looked disgusted. "So he says."

"You don't think he was?"

"Be serious."

"Well, where do you think he got the money?"

"Gambling. He got lucky and made a few bucks. He has a sickness. Usually he just *lost* my money, but you have to get lucky once in a while."

"That's a shame. I know that can be hard on a family."

She nodded her head vehemently. "That's for sure."

"I'm told he hid the money in the bushes. Does that seem strange to you?"

"Everything he did was strange."

"Did you know about the money in the bushes?"

She gave Spencer a disgusted look. "Now that's a pretty dumb question. If I knew about it, it would have been in the bank, not the damned bushes. Bushes don't pay interest."

"Do you have any idea why he would hide it in the bushes?"

She shrugged. "Not a clue. But like I said, nothing he did made any sense."

"Please pardon my wondering, Mrs. Lamb, but you seem like a dependable person. Why would you put up with someone like Charles?"

"That's a good question. And call me Sarah." She folded her hands in her lap. "I guess I didn't want to admit I was wrong. Would you like something to drink?"

He didn't, but asked for some water to keep the rapport he seemed to be building.

Sarah got the water. "Here you go."

After a drink, Spencer thanked her.

"What do you mean about being wrong, Sarah?"

"I like challenges. I'm afraid Charles was one. I worked for his brother, Steven, who constantly was having to get him out of trouble. One day he said what Charles needed was a good woman to straighten him out."

Spencer's surprise wasn't pretended. "And you volunteered?"

A twisted smile changed her face. "Well, I had some incentive. Steven offered a wedding present of $50,000. And Charles wasn't all bad. He had some good qualities that have long since been wiped away by alcohol."

"So Charles was the black sheep of the family and Steven was the success?"

"Yup."

"Sounds like you should have married Steven," Spencer said with a smile.

Sarah also smiled. "I would have, but he wasn't my type."

"Are you sorry you did it, Sarah?"

"Hell yes! Didn't take him long to spend the money—and not on anything worthwhile. This house needs a lot of work. That's why I don't believe he was working. He couldn't even fix his own house."

"Do you work?"

"Yes, I'm an accountant."

"Steven's company?"

"No. He shut down most of his company a few years ago when he got sick."

"I should probably contact Steven. Do you have his number?"

"I have a number for the company, but he won't be there."

"I'll give that a try." She gave him the number.

Spencer finished the water. "I'm sorry you've had to go through all this. I can see why you were so angry at the jail."

"What do you mean?"

"Mr. Tucker said you were pretty upset about the daggers."

"Yes, I get emotional. That's about the only thing that he hasn't lost or sold. We used to have a lot more nice things. I wasn't very nice to Mr. Tucker. Give him my apologies. I hope he finds something to help."

Deciding to tell her about the release, Spencer said, "Well he already did. Charles was released this afternoon."

She just nodded. Spencer couldn't tell if that was good or bad news. She seemed lost in thought and was staring at something beyond Spencer.

Looking back at Spencer, she asked, "Have they found my other dagger yet?"

"No, not that I know of."

"I assume they're looking."

"Of course."

She looked confused. "I would've thought they'd have found it by now."

Spencer shrugged. "It may never show up. Could be anywhere. Sometimes they just have to get lucky."

Now she started to look angry. "You mean they might never find it?"

"It's a possibility."

"Not one I would like."

"Well, cross your fingers. It wouldn't be for lack of effort. Thanks for your time, Sarah. I appreciate your talking with me."

"Would you like something else? I could make some iced tea." She didn't want him to leave.

"No thanks. It's been a long day. Good luck."

She showed him to the door.

As he got into the Mustang, Spencer glanced again at the neighbor's yard. Where there's a tree house, there has to be a kid. Spencer wondered how old this kid was. And he remembered that when he was a kid he had spent most of the time in *his* tree house watching the neighborhood.

He drove home thinking there were two sides to every story, and you never know what makes a person do what they do. He thought about Laura as he drove.

Chapter 86

Spencer parked and met Stretch as he was coming out of the apartment building. Laura had just crossed the street into the next block. Stretch explained that two men were already on Broadway. He said he usually followed Laura but would leave her in Spencer's hands and go ahead and check out the street and alert the hot dog man. Before Stretch left, Spencer showed him the picture of Charles he cut out of the paper.

Stretch shook his head. "Sorry, I just can't tell. Could be, but could not."

"Okay. Keep it in case you see the guy again."

Stretch put it in his pocket and walked ahead. As he passed Laura he told her Spencer had her back.

The street was busy. Laura checked in at the hot dog joint and strolled down the east side of Broadway. Spencer found Stretch and they followed on the west. Spencer tried to pick out the other two men but couldn't find them. Two police cars drove by in the first half hour.

Other than Laura talking to a few girls, nothing important happened.

A little after ten, Spencer noticed a large man on the same side of the street as him and Stretch and pointed him out. Not the guy. But the man seemed to be watching with more intent than usual. Ten minutes later he crossed the street, walked south past Laura, and entered a bookstore. Spencer watched the store.

The man came out after a few minutes and turned south. He stopped and talked to one of the girls Laura had talked to. He and the girl walked a few doors south and entered the doorway of a second-floor walkup apartment.

Spencer's first instinct was to follow, but remembered that business went on as usual despite the killings. And the killings had happened on Friday nights.

He mentioned it to Stretch who said he had Laura covered if Spencer wanted to go. He decided to stay but kept an eye on the door.

About a half hour later the man came out alone. He walked north, and as he passed Laura he said something to her. She nodded.

Spencer kept watching the door to the apartment and became more concerned as time went by. He was about to head over to the apartment when the girl came out. He sighed with relief and told Stretch to check out the apartment.

Stretch nodded. "Makin' a living."

* * *

Friday had walked out with more than his money's worth. For twenty bucks he now knew that the name of the other girl he had been watching was Katherine. The girl he paid had wondered why all he wanted to do was talk, but if she got twenty bucks for just talking, she wasn't going to complain.

* * *

Spencer and Stretch followed Laura back to the apartment where they discussed the night's activity. There wasn't much to discuss. Spencer brought up the man who had walked past her near the end and asked what he said.

Laura shrugged and raised her eyebrows. "Not much. Just 'have a nice night'. Why do you ask?"

"He had been watching for a while and then went upstairs with one of the girls you were talking to. Seemed a little strange."

"Don't think so," said Laura. "Guys will watch for a bit to get the lay of the land before approaching a girl. It *is* illegal, you know."

"Yeah, so I've heard."

Laura announced she was going to bed and would see them all Friday night.

Spencer thought she should be more concerned that tomorrow night was Friday.

Chapter 87

At two a.m. Friday, patrol officers spotted a person matching the description of Joseph Rivera coming out of a convenience store on North Avenue. When they stopped and got out of the car, he ran. The officers lost him in an alley. Four units responded and he was found an hour later hiding in a stairwell. He had no ID. He was taken into custody for questioning and charged with fleeing a police officer.

He was held at the 11th precinct station and transferred to the 18th a little before noon where Steele questioned him. The kid said he had been living with a friend since leaving his mother's. He gave the friend's address. It was not one of the best neighborhoods. He admitted taking the knife. He said he knew his friend lived in a bad neighborhood and he might need it for protection. When asked where the knife was, he said someone had taken it, probably his friend. When asked why he had left his mother's, he said he was afraid he would be arrested for stealing the money. He gave the same answer about running from the police. When asked if he knew anything about Miss Brock's murder, the kid said he didn't even know she was dead. When asked if he knew about the key, he answered, "What key?"

The only prints on the key Rosie had taken from Margaret's bedroom were Margaret's.

The kid was held on the flight charge. He called his mother, who called an attorney. He would soon be out on bail.

Steele knew they had nothing if they couldn't find the knife. Two suspects, two missing knives. Great.

Chapter 88

By mid-morning Laura had enough of sitting in her room. It was a beautiful morning. A light breeze rustled the shades and the bird songs made her wish she was outside enjoying the day.

At a little after ten, she left her apartment, made her way to the basement, and left the building by the rear door that led to the alley. It was the first time she had ever left without letting Stretch know. She felt free for the first time in over a year.

She walked to the end of the alley, turned right, and headed across Wilson. The thought of walking down the street without being watched was exhilarating.

* * *

Friday saw her before she crossed Wilson. He was amazed at the daytime transformation. But despite the clothes and the pulled-back hair he knew it was Katherine. He had watched her Thursday night until she left Broadway. He also watched two men who appeared to be following her and he followed behind them. One of them walked past her but the other stayed behind and followed as she turned onto Wilson. *Friday* wasn't sure what was going on so decided to come back and watch during the day.

But he didn't want to get too close to her apartment in case the men were watching her for some reason. So he parked on the cross street and patiently waited. At 10:20, his patience was rewarded.

Friday felt strangely protective. Part of him wanted to warn her that there were men following her; but it wasn't because he was worried about her—he wanted her all to himself.

Chapter 89

That night, Laura decided to leave her jacket behind and left her building at about ten. Spencer and Stretch followed. They had decided to pull the man out of the alley so there would be two men with Laura, one on each side of her on the east side of Broadway.

The street was as crowded as usual for a Friday night. Happy people laughed and jostled as they made their way to their favorite nightspot on Broadway.

Laura got the okay from the hot dog man and strolled the east side of the street. She nodded to two girls she had come to know well enough to nod to. They nodded back. She didn't see Sunshine. And she had not seen Ramon again. A patrol car drove by, slowly heading south.

After the patrol car disappeared, a young man, who looked to be in his thirties, walked up to her.

"Care for a cigarette?"

"No. Thanks."

He lit his own, blew a small cloud of smoke in her direction, and took it out of his mouth with his left hand.

Laura wasn't impressed and started to walk away.

"Hey, how about I buy you a drink?"

"No thanks. I prefer the fresh air."

He moved closer. So did her two men on the east side of the street. Stretch and Spencer watched from the west side.

"Well then, let's take a walk."

"I like the fresh air right here," Laura replied with no interest as people moved between her and the man.

The man moved to within touching distance. "I assume you're not out here for decoration. I'd like to make a deal here but you're not helping. Maybe if we were better friends. My name's Max, what's yours?"

"The only friends I need are presidents."

He nodded. "Okay, that's better. Any presidents in particular?"

"Yeah, Ben Franklin."

The man looked confused. "Are you messing with me?"

Laura raised her eyebrows. "Meaning?"

"Meaning, Ben Franklin wasn't a president."

Laura smiled. "Very good, I'm impressed. But he is the one on the bill I like."

Max whistled. "Pricey." He looked her over. "But, maybe worth it. I could come up with a Ben Franklin." He reached into his pocket.

Laura's smile was replaced by a smirk. "That's nice, but can you come up with five?"

Max looked shocked.

Without looking away from Laura, Stretch said to Spencer, "I'm guessing she just told him the price."

Spencer laughed.

Taking his hand out of his pocket, Max said, "I can't imagine what would be so special to make me spend that much."

Laura agreed. "No, I bet you can't."

"Go to hell, bitch." He turned and walked north.

"And so it goes," said Stretch. "That's why she doesn't have to worry about the alley."

The two men flanking Laura walked by each other and took up positions on the opposite side from where they had been. Laura never acknowledged their presence but was glad they were there.

Standing in a stairwell just north of Stretch and Spencer, *Friday* took it all in. The conditions had to be just right. Sometimes he watched his target for more than a week. Everyone would eventually have a last night on earth. He wondered if this would be Katherine's.

Another man had a chat with Laura twenty minutes later with the same result. Both of the other girls had disappeared. Busy night.

About eleven thirty, Stretch poked Spencer. "Check out the guy coming up from the south. Big. Green shirt."

"Yup."

"That's the guy I've been talking about who's been watching the street. He your man?"

"Nope. Same size but different guy."

As Spencer watched the man, he noticed the evangelist drunk and pointed him out to Stretch.

"Yup. Thanks. The guy never quits. What a way to spend a Friday night."

The big man approached Laura. As he neared her, her two guards were switching positions again and passed each other, both to the south of Laura, walking through a crowd of people.

Stretch saw the big man start to talk to Laura. When he did, the evangelist came over and started to rant about sin. When the big man pushed him out of the way, the drunk bowled into him with all of his pent-up righteous strength and knocked him into Laura. All three went down as Stretch ran across Broadway between cars.

Someone in the crowd yelled, "Fight!" and people started to gather. Stretch reached the pile and started to pull people apart. Spencer had been stopped by traffic and waited for an opening.

Stretch got the two men off of Laura and she moved away from the crowd to the north, unknowingly separated from her two guards by the crowd. As he started to get up, Stretch was knocked down by the drunk who had been belted by the big man and fallen into Stretch. The big man jumped on both of them and they were surrounded by the crowd.

* * *

Having seen exactly what he was waiting for, *Friday* made his way across the street between cars and came up to Laura who was standing apart from the crowd and the fight that was still going on.

He didn't bother with small talk. "How much?"

She gave him a blank look. "Five hundred."

Friday didn't even blink and started to reach into his pocket.

"Not here, you idiot!"

She turned, walked ten feet to the alley, and turned in, not at all aware that her entire team had lost track of her. *Friday* followed.

* * *

To Spencer, it seemed like things were moving in slow motion. It took only twenty seconds or so for the traffic to clear but it seemed like forever. He was the only one who saw Laura being propositioned and, amazingly, walking off with a man who was just as big as Charles and the guy in the pile.

Spencer reached the alley and looked in but couldn't see anything in the darkness. He pulled his gun out of the shoulder holster and walked slowly into the alley as his eyes adapted a bit.

As he passed the second dumpster, Spencer heard a scream and started to run. He turned left at the T and saw the large man holding Laura against the wall about fifty feet ahead. His left hand was around her neck.

Spencer yelled. *Friday* looked in his direction and then put both hands around Laura's neck.

Spencer raised his gun and fired two shots at the man's legs. At least one of them hit. The man let go of Laura and she collapsed to the concrete with her hands on her throat. The man went down on one knee as Spencer ran up to him.

As *Friday* reached into his pocket, Spencer aimed at his chest and said, "Both hands where I can see them and lie down on your stomach with your arms straight out to the side."

Friday hesitated.

"Right now, or the next bullet is into your chest."

He did as told.

Spencer had glanced at Laura and knew she was struggling, but still alive. "You okay, Laura?"

She tried to talk but all that came out was a gurgle. She raised her hand.

Less than a minute later, Stretch breathlessly joined the group, followed by one of the team.

"Laura, are you okay?" he asked with concern.

She again raised her hand and nodded. Spencer explained what had happened and asked that someone call the police.

Laura had regained enough speech to barely whisper, "Let's not." She pointed up the alley. "We have plans."

"And those are?" asked Spencer.

Looking questioningly toward Laura, Stretch answered, "I think you'd rather not know. But he'll get what he deserves."

Spencer looked from Stretch to Laura. "I have no doubt about that. I've seen your basement. But I just shot this guy. This is over right here."

Stretch looked at Laura. Laura looked at Spencer and, after a pause, nodded. Spencer thought he saw relief in her look.

Glad that she had made that decision, Stretch turned to Michael and asked him to make the call. "Tell them the alley behind 612 Raleigh."

Keeping his gun aimed at *Friday*, Spencer took a deep breath and took over the scene in the alley. He told *Friday* to turn over on his back, keeping his arms out to the side.

"Stretch, I'm guessing he has a knife on him. See if it's under his jacket."

Stretch pulled open *Friday's* jacket and exposed a leather sheath that held a knife. Stretch unbuckled the sheath and laid it by the wall.

"I hit him in the leg. Would you check it, Stretch?"

Friday's left pants leg was torn and blood stained. Stretch pulled up the pant leg.

"Just a flesh wound. No big deal."

Spencer nodded and told *Friday* to turn back over on his stomach.

Five minutes later, two squad cars pulled into the alley, one from each end.

Chapter 90

The first two officers got out of their car with guns drawn and told Spencer to put down his gun. As Spencer laid the gun on the concrete, he identified himself as a private investigator. The second car stopped and Jamie got out of the passenger side, also with his gun drawn.

When Jamie saw Spencer, he asked, "What've we got, Spencer?"

As Spencer explained, Jamie told the man on the ground to put his hands together and he snapped on handcuffs. He asked who was hurt. Spencer told him the guy on the ground had been shot in the leg and the lady by the wall had been strangled and couldn't talk. Jamie asked the other officers to call for two ambulances. He bent and picked up Spencer's gun.

"This registered?" Jamie looked worried.

"Yup."

"Good. This guy have ID?"

"Don't know."

Jamie took a wallet out of the man's back pocket. Martin Worley. *Friday* had a name.

Two more squad cars arrived along with an ambulance. The alley was lit up like a Christmas tree.

Stosh pulled into the alley fifteen minutes later, followed by Spanell and Andrews.

A medic confirmed Stretch's diagnosis of *Friday's* flesh wound. He would be taken to a hospital for treatment. Spanell would ride with him in the ambulance.

A second medic checked Laura and confirmed bruising but nothing seemed broken. A second ambulance pulled into the alley.

The officers got everyone's names and contact information and took brief statements. Laura would press charges for battery and attempted murder as witnessed by Spencer.

Stosh asked Spencer how many shots he had fired and asked officers to look for the bullets.

He turned back to Spencer. "Do I want to know how all this went down?"

"Don't see why not. But it could have easily happened differently."

"Yeah, everything can. Those split-second decisions are what defines you. Give your statement. You still up to getting together this afternoon at my place?"

"Sure."

"Good. Get some sleep."

"Will do."

"We have things to chat about, but thanks."

Spencer nodded.

Spencer walked over as Laura was being helped into the ambulance. She started to say something, but Spencer put his finger to her lips and told her not to talk.

Laura looked at him with tears in her eyes and kissed him on the cheek.

"You are welcome," Spencer said with a smile.

* * *

Spencer and Stretch talked about what had happened as they walked back to the apartment.

"You saved her life, Spencer." He shook his head. "All of our careful planning and everything fell apart."

"Best laid plans. Sometimes you just have to improvise and hope you get lucky."

"You think he'll be convicted?"

Spencer shrugged. "I sure hope so. But if he's not, it won't be because of us. We did what we could. Now it's up to the courts." For the first time Spencer understood what his dad and Stosh had always told him.

"Pretty frustrating."

"Sometimes. But most of the time the system works."

They climbed the stairs to the second floor apartment where Stretch gave the man on watch a hundred dollar bonus and told him his services were no longer needed.

Spencer shook hands with Stretch. "We did good, my friend."

"Yeah, I'm glad it ended the way it did. I've sometimes wondered about some of the things Laura did and the risks she took. But she was the boss. I didn't like what she had planned for Friday if we caught him. I might have quit. Thanks, Spencer."

"Sure."

* * *

On his way home, Spencer thought about the decision he had made. He knew it was the right one but there was a big part of him that wanted to let Laura and Stretch have their way with the guy. He also wondered about Laura. He did save her life but he was also fully aware he had put her in that position in the first place. That wasn't a pleasant thought.

Chapter 91

Saturday morning arrived with a beautiful sunrise. Stosh woke up at seven, thankful for a night's sleep without having to worry about the phone ringing.

He checked the fridge for beer and the cabinet for chips. He was set for Spencer's Saturday visit. He wasn't going to let Spencer get away without a chance to get some of his gin rummy money back. He needed to have a chat about the interview with Margaret that Rosie had told him about. It wasn't that big a deal, but he hoped Spencer was sweating a little. Bottom line was, Spencer got results because he was able to bend the rules a little. Stosh just needed to remind him there was a line that, if crossed, would lose him his license. Or worse. And worse was pretty close in that alley. That would take some chatting, also.

* * *

Spencer didn't get much sleep. He made breakfast and ate out on the deck. A light breeze and sunny morning promised a nice day.

He had a few errands to do before heading to Stosh's. He knew he would have to sit through a lecture, but wasn't worried. Bottom line was always results, and he had discovered that Margaret had a missing knife and started the chain that led to another suspect. He figured the arrest of *Friday* would get him off whatever hook he was on for the Margaret issue.

Before heading out, Spencer made a call to Florida and left a message for Tim to call him.

* * *

Spencer brought a six-pack of Schlitz and two bags of chips to Stosh's.
        "You can't buy me with snacks, P.I."

"Wouldn't think of it."

Stosh took two beers and put the rest in the fridge. The cards and coasters were already on the table.

"I see you have the afternoon planned."

"You've got my money in your pocket. I want it back."

Spencer sat at the table. "Give it your best."

Stosh handed a bottle to Spencer. "Okay, let's get this out of the way. Technically what you did with Rivera was not illegal. Misleading someone is not a crime. I just want to remind you that there's a line, and if you cross it you'll be sitting in my jail."

"Very aware of that. I have no desire to visit Chez Stosh."

Stosh rolled his eyes. "As usual, you manage to turn up important things as you wander through your job description, so I'm not as angry as Rosie thought I'd be. And speaking of Rosie, she is correct about being on different sides. There's a line there also."

"Speaking of lines," Stosh continued, "anything more I need to know about what happened last night?"

"Need?" Spencer took a drink of Schlitz. "No. All's good. But I've been thinking about it."

Stosh took a drink and waited.

"Laura wanted *Friday* to herself. I think she wanted to use him to get even for her sister. They had plans for him and I don't think it would have been pretty."

Stosh crunched a chip. "I'm glad you called us."

"Me too. But I thought about letting them have him. The guy deserves the worst."

Stosh sighed. "He does deserve it, but there are those things we in the business call laws."

"Yeah, I've heard."

"What made you decide to call?"

Spencer set down the bottle and looked at Stosh. "I knew that's what Dad would have done."

Stosh raised his bottle. "Proud of you, Spencer."

Spencer wiped moisture off his bottle. "Is the evidence going to hold up?"

"Looks good. His right index fingerprint matches the one we took off the coin. We've got the knife, and there were two more sets of coins in his apartment along with a lot of newspaper articles. I don't see him on the streets ever again."

Spencer nodded.

"Deal the cards, Spencer."

As Spencer shuffled, Stosh said he had one more point to make.

"I know," said Spencer as he dealt.

"You know what?"

Spencer set the deck down. "I know I put her life in danger."

Stosh picked up his cards. "Well, she had some say in that, but if you had asked me, I would have told you it was a bad idea. As I recall, I had already done that."

"Well, technically Rosie told me."

Stosh raised his eyebrows as he filled a straight and went out. "Gin."

"But the plan worked."

"And your friend came how close to being killed?"

"Understood."

"You got lucky, Spencer. The idea is to control situations so you don't need luck."

While they played, Spencer asked Stosh if the police could help look for Laura's sister, Katherine.

Stosh shook his head. "Sometimes I hate this job. Kids caught up in this damned world."

"Is there anything we can do?" Spencer laid down his cards. "Gin." He was ahead eight bucks.

"We can be a little nicer to the host."

Spencer laughed. "I meant about Katherine."

Stosh shuffled the cards. "I know what you meant. And I assume by *we* you mean me. Not a thing unless something happens."

"But something *did* happen. She was abducted."

"Perhaps. Perhaps not. And if she *was*, it wasn't from here. Aside from her sister being in town, there's no reason to believe she's in Chicago."

As Spencer started to talk, Stosh held up his hand. "I know, I know. We owe something to Miss Justine. But unless I have some cause or get a request from Florida, there's nothing I can do officially."

"But unofficially?"

"I'll see what I can do."

Stosh went out after three picks with a big smile. "My luck is changing."

"For one hand. Speaking of luck, I assume you haven't found the Brock knife."

"Nope. But not for lack of effort. We've had divers out in the water twice as far as you'd be able to throw a knife and south to the breakwall."

"How about the rocks?"

"Still looking. Lots of cracks. Those rocks stretch for a hundred yards. And before you ask, we searched the neighborhood too. If it's somewhere else it'll just have to turn up. Sometimes this job is just about luck."

"Well, let's hope it's *good* luck."

By five, Stosh's losses were under three bucks but some of his money was still in Spencer's pocket.

* * *

When Spencer got home, he called Ben and gave him the first-hand report.

"What an amazing story. Nice job, Spencer."

"Thanks, Ben. Bill's in the mail."

"So is the check!"

They agreed to meet for breakfast as soon as they could find some time. Spencer wanted a few days off.

Chapter 92

After roll call Monday morning, the Brock team again met in Stosh's office. The crowd was down to Stosh and the two detectives.

"Just so we're all on the same page, Joseph Rivera was arrested on a flight charge. He didn't have the knife. It wasn't at the friend's apartment. And no prints on the key. The kid's mom posted bail and he's free. Steele, you get anything from the interview?"

Steele shook his head. "I bought his story about being scared about stealing the money. I don't think he had anything to do with the murder."

Rosie gave a big sigh. "I sure hope not, for Margaret's sake. Bad enough the kid stole the money. If he was involved in the murder, she'd be devastated."

Steele started to say something, but Stosh stopped him. Steele was not big on sentiment.

Stosh opened the file on his desk. "So, back to square one. We have two persons of interest with very weak evidence. We also have the clients and the limo guy."

"Gotta come down to who had access to the key, and we've run out of possibilities," said Steele. "I think she let someone in for an early-morning rendezvous. Whoever it was saw the money in the safe and killed her for it."

Rosie stretched. "Conjecture. We still have Lamb and Rivera, each of whom had a key or access to one, and a knife. Joseph certainly could have wiped the key. All we need is the knife."

"Thanks for the news bulletin," said Stosh. "Till we find it, Rosie, why don't you hit the gas station and see if you can find the limo." He gave her the location and date and time. "Steele, you come up with anything on the client list?"

"I have names. I'll check for priors today."

"Let's do this again tomorrow morning unless you come up with something earlier."

They both nodded.

* * *

Spencer woke up Monday morning with nothing to do. The Cubs were on the west coast for a late-night game. There was more he wanted to know about the Lamb family, but it was now irrelevant. He wanted to call Rosie and see if things were back to normal. He didn't like being on the other side. After an hour of trying to decide, he picked up the phone and called the station. She was just leaving for the gas station.

"Morning, Rosie."

"Morning, Spencer. What can I do for you?"

"For starters, you can have dinner with me."

"That depends. What do you have planned *after* 'starters'?"

"Not a thing. Just starters. Get some food and chat."

She accepted. "Not much going on. Should be a normal day. How about I meet you at Logan's at six?"

"Great." He wasn't sure where he wanted this to go personally, but certainly wanted to see.

Chapter 93

Spencer was waiting when Rosie arrived. Logan's was a high-end burger joint. They both ordered cheeseburgers and beer.

They chatted about *Friday* while waiting for the food. Rosie told Spencer she was proud of him. When the burgers arrived, Spencer took a bite and asked if he was back on the team.

Rosie's eyebrows rose. "You were never *on* the team. You need a badge for that." She had a slight smile. Toying with Spencer had always been one of her favorite hobbies.

He looked hurt.

"More like an honorary mascot." Her smile broadened.

"Well, if that's all I can get."

"Again, there's that badge thing."

"Right. So you have two missing knives and two possible killers and not enough to hold either one. What's your feeling on the two?"

Rosie had wondered if she would talk shop with Spencer. They always had, up to a certain point, and they had been through a life-or-death situation together, but after the last week she wasn't sure. She looked in his eyes and saw her old friend. Whatever else, they had always been friends. Maybe he was right—maybe they should leave it at that. And she did enjoy talking with him. He was good at heading down the right path.

"I don't think the kid is involved. But I'm not sure about Lamb. Given the battery arrest and the father history, there sure is something going on there."

"Agreed," said Spencer. "What did you think of him when you arrested him?"

Rosie finished a bite of burger. "My gut instinct? Likable. I felt sorry for him. He truly had no idea why we were arresting him. Seemed timid and shy. But I've seen people like that go nuts with the right trigger."

Spencer nodded. "Like mentioning County."

"Yup, like that. Something snaps and someone flips a table over. Pretty abnormal behavior."

"Ben says the same thing. He was shocked when the guy flipped the table. There's a real fear of County there."

"I'd be surprised if there wasn't. Can't imagine going through that at ten years old. I wonder if he ever visited his father there."

Spencer salted his fries. "Yeah, that'd make a lasting impression. But maybe that's all there is to it, Rosie."

"What do you mean?"

"Maybe all these things are just a reaction of a ten year old kid. Maybe the timid, shy guy is the real Charles. Maybe you should go with your gut instinct."

"Gotta go with the reality, Spencer. No matter what my gut says, there's a lot of anger and violence there."

Squirting more ketchup on his burger, Spencer said, "He obviously can be violent when provoked. Just spontaneously goes nuts. And the prostitute angle seems to provoke him. So, where do you go from here?"

Rosie finished her burger and said, "I checked the gas station this afternoon for the limo. They weren't too thrilled about checking and had no charge records during that time period."

"How hard did they look?"

"I don't know. Took a coupla minutes."

"Hmm."

"What do you mean, *hmm*?"

"Just hmm. Are you still looking for the knife?"

"No, that stopped Saturday. Kinda like looking for a needle in a haystack with all those rocks. And if it was thrown into the lake it could be buried in sand or washed down the lake by now."

"Or someone could have picked it up."

Her brow furrowed. "Like who?"

Spencer shrugged. "No one in particular."

They paid and Spencer walked Rosie to her car.

"Thanks for meeting me, Rosie. I had a nice time."

"So did I, Spencer. I don't have a better friend." She kissed him on the cheek.

"Me either."

Spencer watched her drive away and waved. When he got to his car, he pulled out his notebook and flipped to the page with the address of the gas station. He turned around and headed south.

Chapter 94

Stosh was sick on Tuesday so the meeting was postponed until Wednesday. Steele walked into Stosh's office Wednesday morning in a brown suit that looked like he had slept in it.

Stosh filled Rosie and Steele in on some details about *Friday* that weren't covered at roll call. After a few questions, he said, "Let's get back to Miss Brock."

Rosie had nothing from the gas station. Steele had three clients who were in the system. Unfortunately, one was dead, one was in jail, and the third had moved to Tennessee two years ago.

Stosh rubbed the back of his neck. "Didn't think there was anything there, but we gotta try. Steele, make sure the guy still *is* in Tennessee. Both of you help follow up on calls from the public. We might be doing okay, but check with Williams and see if he needs help." So far, nothing had come of public tips.

As Rosie pushed her chair back, the phone rang. It was a resident north of Miss Brock's house asking for Lt. Powolski, relaying a message from Spencer. He wanted someone to come out to the rocks. He had found something.

* * *

Spencer arrived at the Brock house a little after eight. The sky was clear and a light breeze was blowing off the lake. He parked in the drive, walked out onto the beach, sat on one of the rocks, and looked up the shoreline. After about ten minutes, he saw movement about a hundred feet away. As he watched, a head appeared, and then two arms reached up and a person climbed onto the rocks. Spencer didn't know if it was the same person Charles had seen, but long hair, a beard, and ragged clothes put the man into the bum category.

Spencer considered asking him if he ever found anything, but decided to just watch for the moment. The man carried a plastic bag that did have something in it, but it wasn't the shape of a knife. Spencer thought the man might take off if approached, so he just watched.

The man continued to climb over the rocks. Ten minutes later he stopped, put down his bag, and got down on hands and knees. He stuck his arm down between two slabs of rock, but came out empty. He picked up his bag and continued north on the rocks.

Spencer let him move off a ways and then climbed to the rocks where the bum was. He didn't see anything other than rock. And then, as he moved his head to a certain angle, he saw the glint of something shiny between the rocks. He lost it when he moved and had to get the correct angle of the sun before he saw it again. There was definitely something down there, but too far down to reach.

He sat on the rock, took off a shoe and a sock and pushed the sock down into the crack so he could find the rock again. After putting his shoe back on, Spencer went back to Miss Brock's street and rang the doorbell of the house opposite hers. A lady answered. She wasn't sure what to make of Spencer's request. But since all he was asking was for her to call the police, she agreed.

* * *

Rosie and Steele and a patrol car arrived twenty minutes later. Spencer led them to the rock with his sock in it. They saw nothing. He told them they had to move their head until they caught the angle of the sun that would reflect off the object. He guaranteed there was something down in that crack. Steele saw it first.

"I got it. Holy crap, how did you find that?"

Spencer told them about the bum Charles had seen on the rocks.

It took Rosie another minute, but she found it also. "Looks like it's down six feet. How do we get it out? We're not going to move these rocks." The rock ledge was a good thirty feet wide and the object was about in the middle.

"Well, if we *had* to, we could move the rocks," answered Spencer. "But there has to be a better way."

"Like what?" asked Steele.

Spencer took a deep breath. "Did you ever try that game at a carnival where you had to lower a string loop down and catch a prize?"

"Never been to a carnival," said Steele.

"Geez, Steele," said Rosie. "What did you do when you were a kid?"

"Smoked cigars."

She sighed. "I know what you mean Spencer, but with those you could see the prize. We're not even sure what we're looking at."

"Worth a try."

"I agree. Be right back." Rosie went back to the Ford and returned with a flashlight.

She got down on her knees and shined the light into the crack. "Looks like a knife to me."

"What about the handle?" asked Spencer.

"Can't tell. Let's give it a shot. There's a hardware store a couple blocks west. Steele, you want to stay with the site?"

"Sure." He immediately pulled out a cigar.

Rosie briefed the two officers and asked them to keep people off the rocks.

* * *

Spencer and Rosie returned with a ball of thick string, two thin metal rods, and a roll of tape.

Spencer taped a length of string to the ends of the rods and made a loop in the loose end.

"You gotta be kidding," said Steele as Spencer lowered the string into the crack.

"I'm taking better ideas."

Steele blew out a cloud of smoke. "What's the other rod for?"

"If I get lucky, I can loop the string around the blade and it'll catch on the handle and I can pull it out. If I don't get lucky, we may need two loops working at the same time with one around each end of the knife."

"Not possible. How long before you get tired of doing that and give up?"

"I think it *is* possible, so I'll keep trying until someone comes up with a better idea."

There were none.

"Rosie, would you hold the flashlight?"

Spencer managed to get the loop around the blade, but it took ten minutes. As he pulled up, the knife tilted blade up and he saw the loop was going to slide off. He pulled the loop off the knife and tried again. This time it took twice as long to hook it. He jostled the knife a bit, hoping to tilt it the other way. No luck.

"Okay, this is going to take two loops. Step up, put down your quarter, and try to win a Kewpie doll."

Steele gave Spencer a blank stare that said *are you nuts*?

Rosie picked up the second rod.

"You want to try and loop the handle, or hold this one?"

"I'll give it a shot. I won a stuffed monkey once."

"Lucky you," said Steele.

Steele took the flashlight from Rosie. She hooked it within a minute.

"Okay, pull a little, Rosie."

When she did, the knife tipped up with the handle up.

"Good," Spencer said with excitement. "Now pull your end up slowly."

As she pulled, Spencer's string started to slide up the blade towards the handle.

"My loop is coming off the handle," she said.

"Okay, stop. Hang on while I pull my end up." When he pulled, the blade end came up, leveling the knife. "Okay, if we both pull at the same rate it should come up. Go very slowly."

A few minutes later the knife was close enough to see. It was covered with what looked like dried blood. And it wasn't a knife—it was a dagger, with a fancy snake body for a handle.

Steele put on gloves and carefully grabbed the dagger when it came to the surface. "I'll be damned."

Rosie was beaming. "Nice job, Spencer!"

Steele dropped the dagger into an evidence bag and they headed for the lab.

Spencer stayed on the rocks, wondering what the lab would find.

Chapter 95

Spencer's phone rang at eight a.m. Thursday morning.

"Spencer?"

"Ummm, yeah."

"Wake up," said a broken voice Spencer didn't recognize.

Not a polite, are you awake? Or did I wake you?

"Who is this?"

"Laura. Are you awake?"

"I'm awake. Are you okay?"

"Yes, thanks to you. Just wanted to say thanks."

"You already did."

"Well, not with words."

Spencer smiled. "I liked the other way better."

She laughed.

He asked what her plans were.

"I'm going to do whatever I need to do here, and then I think it's time for me to go home."

Spencer was relieved. "I think so, too." He paused to collect his thoughts. "Not sure exactly how to put this." Another pause. "You lost your sister. But ever since you started this, you've been losing you."

"I know. I realized that as I was riding to the hospital. I was relieved that it was over."

"But I do have a lot of respect for what you have done for Katherine, Laura.

Not many sisters would do the same. I'll keep my fingers crossed and my eyes open. And by the way, so will my friends."

"Thanks, Spencer. I just wish the results had been better with her. And I'd like to do something for the women I've met on the streets. I feel so badly for them."

"You already have. *Friday* is in jail."

"I mean something tangible."

"Like what?"

"Don't know. Some kind of fund to help them start a new life."

"Good for you, Laura. I'm sure you'll figure that out."

"Do you have a pencil?"

"Yup."

She gave him her number in Naples. "Thanks again, Spencer. You're the best."

"So are you, Laura. Proud to know you."

Spencer scrambled some eggs with bacon and ate out on the sunny deck.

Chapter 96

Spencer's phone rang at 3:35 Thursday afternoon. He was just getting ready to head for the lake to run along the path.

"Hey, Spencer."

"Good afternoon, Ben."

"That definitely depends on your point of view."

"Meaning?"

"Meaning lab report on the dagger. Blood is Miss Brock's."

"Sure. Nothing point of viewy about that."

"Nope. But prints all over the dagger belong to Charles Lamb. No others."

Silence.

"Spencer?"

Spencer sat and breathed deeply. "Yeah. Got it. So, I get the guy out of jail and then put him back in."

"Don't beat yourself up. The truth will come out. And if it points to Charles, so be it."

"Are you defending him?"

"Yup. Only makes sense. I already know the case."

"Am I still helping?"

"Not officially. You found the evidence that implicates him. Officially, I shouldn't even be talking to you. The prosecutor would have a field day with this."

"So I'm done?"

"Officially, yes, you're done."

"What are you saying?"

"I just said it. Adios mi amigo."

Spencer hung up and stared at the phone. He had never been fired before. Great. And he wasn't even getting paid.

* * *

Charles was arrested at 1:50 Thursday afternoon and charged with first-degree murder. He was transferred to County and put on suicide watch.

* * *

Jimmy watched the police cars pull into the driveway. He noted the time in his book. Eight minutes later, Mr. Lamb walked out in handcuffs with a policeman on both sides of him.

* * *

Spencer called Ben at 10:15. "How's he doing, Ben?"

"Not good. He only says two things—he didn't kill Miss Brock, and he wants to kill himself. Bond hearing in the morning. The preliminary hearing will probably be on Monday. But with fingerprints on the murder weapon..."

"Yup, pretty damning." Spencer paused. "I've been thinking, Ben. There are several things about this that we have thought were strange."

"Yes? Like?"

"Like the way he was hired. We thought he was lying about something. But Brock hired Margaret the same way."

"What do you mean, the same way?"

"I mean on the spur of the moment. Brock met Margaret by chance and wanted to help her. Told her to show up for work the next day. Gave her a key to the house."

"How do you know that?"

"A friend."

"So? We're not questioning Margaret."

"No, but we *are* questioning whether Brock hired Charles that way. And if she did that with Margaret, she could have done it with Charles. And if he isn't lying about that, maybe he's not lying about anything else either."

Ben leaned back in his chair and rested his elbow on the arm. "Okay, but his fingerprints are on the knife."

"He polished the silver a few weeks ago. Of course his prints are on the knife."

"But *only* his."

"Someone could have worn gloves."

"And have access to the knife?"

"Well, I'm not saying I've got all the answers. What's your plan?"

"I'm going to re-order the psych eval and hopefully save him from the electric chair."

"How about we try and get him off. His only chance is if we assume he's innocent and look somewhere else for the answers."

"What answers?"

"Ben, if he didn't do it, someone else had to have a key and someone else had to have access to the knife."

"Spencer, you could say *someone else* for every crime. The most obvious is usually the answer."

"Maybe he did it. But we'd be able to say we tried our best. I'd like you to ask him a question."

"Sure, what?"

"Why did he put the money in the baggie in the bushes?"

"Okay. I'm seeing him early morning. I'll call you. You going to be home?"

"Don't know. If not, page me."

"Will do. Get some sleep."

"You too."

Spencer knew he would be lying awake most of the night.

* * *

Thursday evening Sarah got a call from an attorney representing Steven Lamb, who had died the week before. He apologized for calling her so late, but he had been busy. The reading of the will was going to be in the morning. He asked if Charles could attend. She said he was indisposed and asked if she could come in his place. He said she could. Sarah went to bed with a smile on her face. Steven was worth millions, and Charles was his only relative.

Chapter 97

Sarah arrived at the law offices of Sparks and Reynolds five minutes early Friday morning. The secretary asked her to wait a few minutes and offered coffee. Sarah was too nervous for coffee. She was shown into Mr. Reynolds' office a few minutes later.

"Good morning, Mrs. Lamb. We're waiting for one more person."

"Good morning." She wondered who that might be.

A minute later, Marcy Jenkins, Steven's secretary, walked into the room and took a seat next to Sarah. They did not say hello. Sarah looked at her with a hateful glance and knew that in a few minutes she would be looking at Marcy with a smile.

"I'm sure you both just want to get to the will contents, so let's begin. It's really very simple. There are only three bequests. Mr. Steven Lamb has left a sum of $100,000 to his secretary, Miss Jenkins."

Marcy was overwhelmed and started to cry. Mr. Reynolds offered a box of Kleenex.

He continued. "To Mr. Charles Lamb, he has left his stamp collection, which he says Charles helped him with when they were children."

Sarah was confused. "A stamp collection! What about all his money?"

"He has left the remainder of his estate to charity."

Sarah was incredulous. "All these years and I get a *stamp* collection? Are you *kidding*!"

"No, ma'am. That is how the will reads."

"But, that isn't fair! There must be *something* I can do."

"I'm sorry, ma'am, but the will is very specific and clear. You can of course hire an attorney, but I assure you he'll tell you the same thing." He turned to Marcy and told her his secretary would contact her about the bequest. Marcy left.

Sarah sat, still and dumbfounded.

"I'm sorry, ma'am, but I have another appointment in five minutes."

She walked out without saying another word.

* * *

Friday morning, Spencer called the number for Steven Lamb's company. He got an answering machine. A pleasant female voice said, "You have reached SL Metals. If you would like to leave a message we will call you back." Spencer left a message.

* * *

Spencer had errands to do, but decided to stay home and wait for phone calls. Ben called a few minutes after one.

"You find out about the bushes, Ben?"

"After some work. He said it didn't matter. He refused to answer any of my questions for a half hour."

"And?"

"He says the first day he worked, his wife went through his pockets and took his money."

"How did he know she took it?"

"He woke up late Saturday morning and wanted to take the money out of his pocket and put it where she wouldn't find it. But when he went through his pants, the only things there were his wallet and the key to Brock's house. The money was gone."

"But how did he know *she* took it?"

"She told him she found it and made it clear that any money he came home with was hers. So he decided to find a hiding place and settled on the bushes. He was happy she didn't find the key."

"Ben, how does he know she didn't find the key?"

"Well, I guess because she didn't take it."

"Yes, she didn't take it. But she may have *found* it. And she could have taken it anytime he was in a drunken stupor and made a copy to use later."

"Use for what? She didn't even know where Brock lived. What good would the key be?"

"Don't know. But it's possible she either knew about or had a copy of that key."

"Are you accusing her?"

"Just trying to put the pieces together, Ben."

"Well, if you get something more concrete let me know."

"Will do."

* * *

Twenty minutes later the phone rang again. This time it was Marcy Jenkins, Mr. Lamb's secretary.

"Thanks for calling back, Miss Jenkins. I'm a private detective in Chicago working on a case that involves Charles Lamb, and I want to let his brother Steven know what's going on."

"Well, you're a bit late, Mr. Manning. Mr. Lamb died last week."

"I'm so sorry, Miss Jenkins. Sarah Lamb did tell me he had been sick for a couple of years."

"A couple? He was diagnosed with cancer eight years ago—actually just before his brother got married. He was only supposed to live a year, and he made it eight."

"That's strange. I wonder why she would tell me a couple."

"Who knows why she would say most of the things that come out of her mouth."

"I take it the two of you didn't get along."

Marcy laughed. "That's an understatement. We couldn't stand each other. She's a lying bitch. She sucked everything she could out of Steven."

"And he let her?"

"She showed some interest in his brother Charles, and he wanted his brother taken care of after he died. He pretty much brought up his brother after a bad childhood. He tried to make life better for him, but Charles got into one bad thing after the other."

"So where does Sarah come in?"

Marcy cleared her throat. "Sarah was a good worker and smart enough to con Steven. He bribed her with a rather sizeable wedding check to marry Charles."

"I heard."

"It's nice to see that conniving bitch come up short."

"What do you mean?"

"I always figured she married Charles for the inheritance he would get. She couldn't have Steven, so Charles was her only hope at getting his money."

"Yes, she told me she didn't marry Steven because he wasn't her type."

Marcy laughed again. "He wasn't any woman's type—he was gay."

"Interesting. So, she married Charles to get the inheritance after Steven died?"

"I'd bet my house on it."

"Amazing. You said she came up short. What did you mean?"

"Ah, the icing on the cake. The will was read this morning. That's where I was when you called. Sarah was there too. Steven left me $100,000 and left Charles his stamp collection. The rest of his millions went to charity."

Spencer could imagine Sarah's reaction. "I bet she wasn't happy about that."

"She hit the ceiling. Made my day, even more than the money."

"Well, it worked out well for you. Thanks for returning my call."

"No problem. Goodbye, Mr. Manning."

Spencer sat down at the kitchen table and started a list of who had access to what and when.

Chapter 98

After a two-hot-dog lunch, Spencer stopped at the station. He asked for Rosie and was told she wasn't in, probably gone for the day. Same for Steele. He asked if Lt. Powolski was available. He was.

Spencer knocked on the door frame.

"Come on in, Spencer. Is this the most excitement you could find on a Friday afternoon?"

Spencer sat down on the corner chair. "Don't sell yourself short. People would pay good money for this show."

"Let me know who—might help with this budget I'm working on. What brings you here?"

"Actually wanted to see Rosie or Steele, but both are out so I'll settle for you."

"Lucky me."

Spencer pulled a note card out of his pocket and set it in front of Stosh. On it were three Illinois license plate numbers.

"And this is?"

"The plate numbers of the cars that paid for gas with a credit card at Lamb's gas station between eight and eight thirty on the night in question."

Stosh looked puzzled. "Lonnigan said she struck out on that."

"She did. I didn't."

"And your secret is?"

"A little help from my friend Andrew Jackson. People just become more accommodating when he's around."

Stosh shook his head. "Okay. We'll see if one was a limo. Thanks, Spencer."

"How's the Friday case look with the D.A.?"

"She says it looks good. He talked till he was hoarse. Good evidence. Should be a slam dunk."

"Great! Speaking of talking, is it okay with you if Rosie joins us tomorrow? I'd like to bounce some thoughts off of you guys."

"Fine with me."

"Okay. See you tomorrow."

"Right." Stosh watched Spencer walk away and let himself wonder for a minute about all the rules and regulations that protected the citizens and tied his hands. He was glad Spencer was on their side.

Chapter 99

Stosh and Rosie were watching *Flying Leathernecks* when Spencer walked in. He turned to Rosie. "Enjoying the entertainment?"

"What's not to enjoy?" asked Stosh. "It's John Wayne, ain't it?"

Rosie rolled her eyes.

Stosh shut off the TV. "So what's up, P.I.?"

"I would just like to see if we're all on the same page with the Lamb case."

Rosie sat up straight and started to talk, but Stosh stopped her. "I think we don't all *have* to be on the same page given that we're not all on the same side here."

Stosh also stopped *Spencer* from responding.

"Who you working for, Spencer?"

"I'm not working for anybody. Ben has chosen not to use my services."

Stosh looked surprised. "And why is that?"

With a look of chagrin, Spencer said, "He took offense at my methods. Something about getting him fired."

Stosh laughed. "Well, I'm glad we're not the only ones you drive nuts."

"Glad to be of service. So, I'm left in the lonely position of just wanting to find the truth, without the help of any jurisdictional agencies."

"Did you practice that speech?"

"No, but here's one I *have* practiced. I don't think he did it."

Rosie leaned forward and cocked her head. "If you have some good reason for that, I'd love to hear it. Not fond of sending innocent people to jail."

Spencer took a deep breath and let it out slowly. "Follow along and let me know if I'm wrong. Miss Brock was killed with a dagger. You have a dagger with her blood on it, and the size matches the wound. And Charles' prints were the only ones on the dagger. Someone stole money from her safe, and money with Charles' and her fingerprints on it was found in a baggie in the bushes at Charles' house. There was no forced entry, so whoever did it had to have a key. Right?"

"So far so good," said Stosh.

Rosie nodded.

"So, the murderer had to have a key, know where Miss Brock lived, have access to the knife, and know about the baggie in the bushes. Right?"

"Right," said Rosie. "Thanks for making our case."

Spencer held up his hand. "Hang on. *Who* had access to *what*?"

"The only one who fits all four is Charles," said Stosh. "We gonna play any gin?"

Spencer ignored him. "Yes, Charles was the only one who knew about the baggie, had held the knife, had a key, and knew where the house was. But Margaret and her son also had access to the key."

"Spencer. Where the hell are you going with this? You're just digging a hole for Lamb. Margaret and her son had nothing to do with the dagger, and they didn't know about the money in the bushes."

"I agree. But Joseph has a better motive than Charles."

"Which is?"

"He was angry about getting fired. And he already stole money. Maybe he wanted more. Maybe there's another explanation for the money in the baggie."

Rosie continued. "Okay, I'll grant you the motive, but there's no evidence. His knife is still missing, but it wasn't the murder weapon."

Spencer shook his head. "You don't know that. Maybe there were two knives used."

"That's crazy, Spencer. This all points to Charles."

"I agree, but it doesn't make sense. And I like things to make sense."

Stosh sat in his favorite chair with his eyes closed, but he was listening and letting Rosie handle the argument.

"What doesn't make sense?"

"He could have taken that money anytime he wanted. There was no need to kill her. And he put his pay in an envelope and then in a baggie so it wouldn't get wet."

"Yeah, so?"

"Brock *gave* him the envelope but he *took* the baggie." He stopped Rosie from responding. "And he felt bad about it. He was truly remorseful that he had taken that without asking. That's not someone who sticks a dagger in someone's eye."

"I agree, Spencer, but you have no idea what that person would do after drinking for four hours. He has no clue what his actions were that morning."

"I'll give you that. But I don't agree."

"Your privilege. And now, if you're done?"

"I'm not. I think the *key* is the key."

Stosh squinted. Rosie sighed.

"Would you both agree that whoever did it had to have a key?"

"Yes."

"And how many people are there?"

"Three. And only one of them had access to the dagger *and* the baggie."

Spencer got excited. "And therein lies the fallacy."

That aroused Stosh. "Like hell. Charles was the only one with access."

"Yes, of the three. But I think there were four."

"Rosie, wake me up after he's gone," Stosh said.

"No, hang on." Rosie looked thoughtful. Spencer could see wheels turning as her face got brighter and brighter. "Sarah?"

"Sarah."

"Lay it out, Spencer," said Stosh who was now sitting up and listening attentively.

"I asked Ben to find out why Charles hid the money in the bushes. The first night after he worked, Sarah had gone through his pockets and taken the money Brock paid him. He needed to find a hiding place she wouldn't know about. Hence the bushes."

"And how does that get her a key?" asked Stosh.

"He went through all his pockets and was relieved that she hadn't found the key that Brock had given him."

"So? That just shows she *didn't* have the key."

"Right, but it doesn't mean she didn't *know* about it. This is not a normal person. I guarantee you if she found the money in one pocket, she would have gone through all the rest. From what I've seen of her, I would call her conniving and sly, among other things. She'll do anything to win you over and then stab you in the back. I talked to the secretary of Charles' brother Steven, who just happens to have died last week. Sarah is no prize. The secretary is sure that Sarah married Charles because she knew Steven was dying and would leave his fortune to his only relative, Charles."

Rosie whistled softly. "I'd call that conniving."

"Sarah is really angry that Charles is so worthless and has sold or lost many of her valuables, including some of the silverware, to feed his gambling habit. But she had to stick with him because of the will. The problem is, Steven was only supposed to live a year or two, but he lasted eight."

"Oops. So the brother is dead," said Stosh. "How much?"

"Millions."

Stosh let out a long breath and widened his eyes. "Nice. That makes the wait worthwhile."

"You would think. But listen to this. He left Charles his *stamp* collection. One hundred grand went to the secretary, and the rest went to charity."

"Ouch. Bet she wasn't happy."

"Nope."

Rosie brought the conversation back to the murder. "So, she has access to the key. Could have made a copy. But there are some problems here, Spencer."

"I know." He looked disappointed. "Go ahead."

"You can have a key, but you have to know what lock to put it in. Do you have anything that points to her knowing where Brock lived?"

"No."

"Do you have anything that points to her knowing the money was in the bushes?"

"No. But I did ask her if she knew about it."

"And she said?"

"Said it was a dumb question. She's an accountant. Said if she knew about the money, she would have put it in the bank. She said bushes don't pay interest."

"Can't argue with that." Stosh raised the recliner. "Again, you're making our case."

Rosie was looking thoughtful again. "What if she wanted to set Charles up? She *did* make him polish the silver. I bet she knew his prints would be all over the daggers because he wouldn't wear gloves. What better way to get rid of him than to park him in prison? She would have all that money to herself. I like running with the conniving theme here."

Spencer wrapped it up. "So, if we accept the setup, how does that help Charles?"

"It doesn't," said Stosh. "Unless you can find evidence for the two holes in your theory, Charles is still going to prison, and maybe to the chair. You have to show she knew where Brock lived and about the money in the bushes. How are you going to do that?"

"I have no idea. Ben thinks..."

"Hey! I don't want to hear what Ben thinks."

"Sorry."

Stosh shrugged. "I agree that it makes sense. But we deal with evidence, not conjecture. Without those you got nuthin', Spencer."

"Yeah, I know. But I don't need both—I just need one or the other."

Stosh started to get up. "Still ain't gonna be easy. But you have some time to look. The preliminary hearing is Monday, and who knows when the trial will be."

"Yeah, but the problem is he may not live that long. Charles really believes he'll kill himself in County."

"He'll get a psych eval. Maybe the docs can help."

"Maybe."

Standing, Stosh asked, "You guys got anything else? I gotta hit the head."

"Nope."

"Then, why don't you take this lovely lady out to dinner and let me finish my movie."

"Rosie?"

"I'm game."

"Okay, let's go eat."

As they walked out, Stosh pointed out that it was nice to get a good night's sleep on a Friday.

Rosie and Spencer continued the discussion over pizza and beer. Stosh fell asleep before the end of *Flying Leathernecks*.

Chapter 100

Spencer met Ben for breakfast Sunday at Sunnyside Up. Spencer was on his second orange juice when Ben walked in and sat down.

"So, Spencer, you must feel like a man of leisure with no one to take up your evenings."

"I'm trying not to think about it," Spencer said with a smile. "But sitting down with a book is pretty nice."

Ben shook his head. "I'm still in shock over the *Friday* caper. I wish I could have a chat with Miss Justine."

Spencer laughed. "No, you don't. That's one scary woman. The next time you care about a client, please call someone else."

"I'll think about it, but I pride myself on giving my clients the best."

"And I pride myself on staying alive, something I'm going to spend a lot more time thinking about in the future."

"But she was lucky you were there."

"Well, there's another way of looking at that. If I hadn't come up with that plan, she wouldn't have been in the alley in the first place."

Their food arrived.

"And *Friday* would still be out there," Ben pointed out. "And who knows what else might have happened to Laura. Given the result, I don't think you should question how it happened."

"Yes, good result. But don't think I'd do it again."

"Okay, pal. You coming to court tomorrow?"

"Nope. What good would that do? I know what's going to happen there. Despite his very capable attorney, he's screwed. He'll be bound over for trial on first-degree murder charges. Maybe you can keep him out of the chair with an insanity defense, but maybe not. And maybe he'll succeed in hanging himself in County. Why would I want to watch that?"

"Okay, I'll pray for a miracle."

"You do that. Good luck, Ben."

"Thanks, Spencer."

They ate in relative silence with a few comments about the Cubs and the weather.

Chapter 101

Monday morning, Spencer was in a bad mood that even catching *Friday* couldn't change. His gut told him Charles didn't kill Brock. How frustrating not to be able to do anything about that. He thought about going to court. It might get his mind off of his frustration. The trial was downtown in Room 802 of the county courthouse.

He ate, then got in the car and started driving. But he soon found himself driving south. Forty minutes later he was parked in the driveway of Charles Lamb. He just sat in the car for a half hour, thinking and wondering.

* * *

Jimmy was actually watching a robin when the car pulled into the driveway next door. Jimmy couldn't see the driver, but no one got out. He kept watching after noting the time in his notebook. A half hour later, a man got out of the car, walked around to the side of the house, and looked at the bushes. Jimmy wrote that down too.

* * *

Spencer had the strangest feeling that he was being watched, but figured he was just reliving his childhood up in the tree house. He looked into the bushes and thought that wasn't a bad hiding place. He couldn't even see in a foot. How would Sarah ever have found the baggie? But she must have, if he was going to help Charles. Or he had to place her at Brock's house. And there was no evidence she knew where that was. Proving either seemed impossible.

He started to walk back to the car and then stopped. The strange feeling was still there, and he could plainly see the tree house he and his dad had built in the woods.

He looked up at the tree house. Where there's a tree house there must be a kid. "Hey kid."

Nothing. He said it again. This time he identified himself as a private detective. Still nothing. He turned and started to walk away.

"Hey, mister."

Spencer froze and caught his breath. He slowly turned around. Peeking over the edge of the fort was the shaggy head of a boy about twelve or thirteen.

"Mister, are you really a private detective?"

"Sure am. Spencer Manning."

"Can I see your badge?"

Spencer reached for his wallet. "We don't have badges, we have ID cards." He held it up.

"I can't see it from up here."

"Okay if I come up?"

"Sure."

Spencer relived the joy of climbing the ladder up to the tree house. What great memories that brought back. When he got to the top and climbed in, he handed the card to the boy, whose eyes were as big as saucers.

"Wow! This is great! Wait till the army sees this!"

"Pardon?"

"I'm going to be in Army Intelligence when I grow up. I have a notebook of very important things. See!" He held up his notebook.

Spencer admired the notebook. "That sounds like a great plan. I had a notebook like that when I was a kid."

"You did?"

"Sure. And a tree house just like yours. Did your dad make this for you?"

"Sure did, mister."

"You can call me Spencer. What's *your* name?"

"Jimmy."

"Okay, Jimmy, nice to meet you."

Jimmy set down the notebook. "What are you doing here?"

Wondering how much he should tell, Spencer decided it didn't matter. "Mr. Lamb was arrested for killing someone, and I'm trying to find evidence to prove he didn't."

Jimmy was enthralled. "Wow, this is the coolest thing that ever happened. Just imagine what the army will think of this!"

Spencer shook his head. "I'm afraid you can't write that, Jimmy. This is official police business."

"Oh yeah, I knew that. But what are you looking for?"

"Well, it's kind of complicated, but Mr. Lamb hid money in those bushes right down there, and that is very important in this case."

Jimmy was all of a sudden silent and withdrawn and looked frightened.

"What's the matter Jimmy? Did I scare you?"

He just stared at Spencer with a quivering lip.

"I'm sorry, Jimmy. We can talk about something else."

Jimmy decided that if he was going to be part of Army Intelligence, he should tell the truth. He was afraid because he had taken some of the money.

"No, I'm not scared. I'm twelve."

Spencer nodded. "Good, that's good."

"I know about the money. I took some of it."

Spencer was silent. He realized that if Jimmy spent as much time in the tree house as Spencer had, he probably saw Charles with the money.

"That's okay, Jimmy. We can talk about that later. What do you know about the money?"

"I saw the man hiding the baggie and putting in money."

"You did? Do you remember when?"

Jimmy perked up. "I don't have to remember. I wrote it all down."

Spencer couldn't believe what he was hearing.

"That's excellent work, Jimmy. It would really help me a lot if I knew when he put money in there."

"The lady too?"

That stopped Spencer dead in his tracks.

"What lady?"

"The lady who lives there."

"Are you saying Mrs. Lamb was taking money out of the baggie?"

Jimmy shook his head. "No. She was putting money *into* it."

"Into it? When was that? Do you have that written down?"

"Sure, is that important?"

"Very important."

Jimmy opened his book and flipped the page back. "Here it is. Two Saturdays ago at 10:15 in the morning."

The day of the Brock murder.

"May I look at it?" Spencer asked.

Jimmy handed him the book. There it was in beautiful blue ink. Date and time and *Lady gets out the baggie and puts money in.*

"You've done a fine job, Jimmy. Can I borrow your notebook? It's very important in Mr. Lamb's trial."

"Sure. As long as I can get it back. I'm going to show it to the army."

"Absolutely. It may be a few weeks, but I will definitely bring it back to you." Spencer gave Jimmy one of his cards, thanked him, and climbed out of the tree.

As he walked to the car, he wondered how Mrs. Lamb knew where Miss Brock lived. He had no idea. But she must have.

Spencer headed for the courthouse, driving as fast as he dared.

Chapter 102

The hearing had progressed as predicted. The state prosecutor presented irrefutable evidence showing that Charles Lamb had murdered Amanda Brock. Charles sat completely still with a look of utter despair. He was bound over for trial as predicted.

Ben told Charles he would visit him at County and explained the psych evaluation that would be done sometime this week. Charles said he didn't care. He would not be alive.

The court consisted of two sets of rooms on either side of a center hallway with floor-to-ceiling windows at the two ends. Three public elevators were in the center of that hallway. Behind the courtrooms were the judges' chambers and a set of secure elevators for the prisoners and judges. Normally, prisoners were led out the back of the courtroom and down a secure elevator. But the side of the floor behind room 802 was under construction and the elevators weren't working. So the deputies waited until the courtroom had cleared to take Charles across the hall into a secure elevator on the other side of the floor.

When the public had left, they asked Charles to stand, handcuffed him, and led him out of the courtroom into the hall.

* * *

Spencer pulled into the parking lot, hoping he was in time to give the notebook to Ben. He had no way of knowing the hearing had ended. He parked alongside the building and started to walk around to the front. He had made it halfway across the lot when he heard an explosion of shattering glass.

* * *

Charles became more agitated with every step he took. He didn't kill Miss Brock. He was not going to County. He had no idea why they were doing this to him. When he got to the door of the courtroom, he was shaking. The deputy holding his arm told Charles to calm down.

With wide eyes and a look of rage, Charles pulled his arm away from the deputy, ran down the hall as fast as he could, and crashed through the eighth floor window.

* * *

Spencer heard the explosion and looked up to see a body falling into the parking lot. It landed on the hood of a Buick. He ran over and was devastated when he remembered the picture in the paper and realized it was Charles. His body was twisted in ways bodies weren't meant to twist. His head dangled, almost twisted backwards.

Spencer looked up and saw people looking over the edge of the opening. One of them was Ben.

Feeling helpless, Spencer just thought to keep people away. He knew someone would call for help, but he also knew it would be too late for Charles. He didn't hang himself, but his neck had been broken just the same.

* * *

An ambulance arrived in about ten minutes. Ben made it down at the same time, along with Rosie and the prosecutor. The police had cordoned off the area. Ben didn't have to explain—Spencer knew what had happened in court.

Spencer was still holding the notebook.

"What's that?" Ben asked.

Unaware that he was holding it so tightly that his knuckles were white, Spencer looked down at it and said, "Nothing important. Is there anything I can do, Ben?"

"No. There's nothing anyone can do."

Spencer could feel the pain in his eyes. "How about I come over and we spend a quiet evening?"

"I think I need to be alone for a while, but thanks. I'll call you."

"Okay, buddy. Please do." Ben walked away.

There were tears in Rosie's eyes. Spencer put his arms around her and she sobbed on his shoulder.

"My God, Spencer. How do you get used to this?"

"You don't."

She wiped her eyes on her sleeve. "What's the notebook?"

"The notebook is the answer to Ben's prayer. Just a little late."

"Huh?"

"Let's find the D.A. and get some coffee."

Chapter 103

Three weeks later, Spencer made a plane reservation for Florida to visit Uncle John, where life was peaceful and sunny and all he would have to worry about was Arnie the alligator who lived in the pond in the middle of the golf course. He had also made a call to Naples and was invited for a walk on a sunny beach.

Sarah Lamb had been arrested and charged with first degree murder. The police had found the extra key in her jewelry box. She'd admitted killing Amanda Brock and figured Charles was not only gambling, but spending money on a hooker. It had seemed like the perfect crime—Charles would be blamed, and she could still collect the inheritance with him in jail. What a strange ending to her marriage plans.

Jimmy got a special certificate from the Chicago Police Department, presented to him by Lt. Powolski. He also gave back the money he had taken.

Ben didn't call. Spencer left messages that weren't returned. His secretary said he was taking some time off.

* * *

Spencer's plane took off on a sunny Wednesday morning at 11:10. Uncle John was thrilled he was coming down, and Spencer was thrilled he was going.

If you liked this book, please post a review at:
Amazon.com/dp/1939548071

To be notified of other Rick Polad books, go to
rickpolad.com and click on "Join Us".

To be notified of future Rick Polad books, "Like" my Facebook
page and post a comment:
Facebook.com/SpencerManningMysteries

CALUMET EDITIONS

PRESENTS

Spencer Manning Mystery #3
Dusty Roads

COMING SOON
Turn the page for a preview.

DUSTY ROADS

I turned off Highway 41 just south of the Wisconsin border onto a dirt road, as instructed, and wound down a ridge through small stands of Oak trees. The question had been raised if I should be going off to the middle of nowhere by myself. I had weighed that and decided it wasn't the dumbest thing I had ever done, and I had survived that.

A cloud of dust billowed up behind my baby-blue Mustang. Around a bend I saw deserted buildings left over from days when the area was a weekend getaway for those who couldn't afford the expensive real estate on the lake.

Single, small, dilapidated wood units with numbers one through six painted above the doors stood next to a slightly larger building with a faded sign that said Office. On the other side of the office were three bare concrete pads with pipes stubbed up two feet—expansion plans gone awry. Only one door was closed. Two were missing. Broken windows, missing shingles, and rotted wood left no memory of what must have been better times. A signboard precariously attached on the roof above the office advertised the Wayside Motel in faded red letters. The landscaping was dry, sandy soil and weeds—lots of weeds.

I stopped thirty feet from the office and got out of the car. The air was hot and dry, so hot and dry that my lungs hurt with every breath. The only sound was muffled tires whining on the concrete highway the other side of the ridge. No one was in sight and there was no evidence that anyone had been there in quite a while. But the caller had specifically said that what we were looking for would be here.

I got out of the car, walked around the buildings and into every unit. Nothing. The cabins were empty. Every piece of furniture was gone. The walls were bare except for a crooked picture of a sad clown hanging in unit 3. I guess nobody wanted a sad clown. The remains of a nest in the cubbyhole of a bare counter in the office was the only sign of life. It was the right spot and I was exactly on time. The place was deserted.

After waiting an hour, I left and drove back to the highway. I stopped at the first gas station and called Stosh who answered with a hopeful hello.

"Nothing, Stosh. The place is deserted. Not even a cockroach."

Stosh let out a worried sigh. "Spencer, I'm sure you will recall the many discussions we have had about the line that you better not cross or you'd have to deal with me."

"How could I forget with all your reminders?"

There was a long silence.

"Spencer, the line is gone—find her."